Testing the Prisoner

Phil Giunta

FB

Firebringer Press
Elkridge, Maryland

TESTING THE PRISONER

Published by
Firebringer Press
6101 Hunt Club Road
Elkridge, MD 21075

ISBN: 978-0-9773851-1-9

March, 2010

Printed in the United States of America

Cover design by Lynn Murphy

DEDICATION

To Evon. The bonds of love conquer all. Patience helps, too. XOXOXO!

To Steve Wilson, friend and mentor, for opening the doors of opportunity when I came knocking.

To Lynn, Amanda, Gayle, Vicki, Eli and Sandy. Thank you for taking the time to proofread, edit, suggest, and most of all *support* this story.

And to friends, neighbors, and co-workers who indulged me as I babbled about this book for two years. Now, I'll stop talking while you read.

Prologue

The Scars from Other People's Wars

1976

The five-year-old boy in the passenger seat of the speeding blue hatchback fixed his gaze on the raindrops as they spattered the windshield and were quickly erased by the wipers only to reappear and be erased again.

As the car passed beneath a streetlight, the boy noticed that the drops fell diagonally to the right. Though the radio's volume was low, the windshield wipers moved almost precisely in time to the steady beat of the music yet the rhythm did little to soothe the boy's distress. He turned his head slightly to the left, just enough to glance at the man behind the wheel.

Danny Masenda sensed his father's mounting anxiety, watched as the man nervously ran a chubby hand through his receding black hair, listened as he muttered under his breath, and shrank away as he pounded the edge of the steering wheel with his fist, apparently oblivious to Danny's terrified gaze.

With fear welling up somewhere in his stomach, Danny turned his attention back to the diagonal rain and wondered simply, *why*?

Earlier in the evening, Aunt Maureen had stopped by his father's apartment with a birthday gift for Danny. She was one of the few adults that he was always happy to see. It seemed that all of the others were always arguing with each other for reasons that he didn't understand.

No sooner had Danny opened his new toy, a police car almost as long as his arm, than his father told him to take it outside on the patio so he and Aunt Maureen could talk. A few minutes later, their discussion became heated and loud enough for Danny to overhear through the open screen door.

"You shouldn't have done it in the first place, Gary!" Aunt Maureen shouted. Danny froze. She had a loud voice even when she talked normally. He'd never heard her angry before and it scared him. "You don't use your kids as pawns to get—"

"Don't fuckin' lecture me! I don't want to hear it! Theresa is sick in the head, she can't be talked to and she can't be reasoned with. I'm glad she's scared now! Let her worry! The bitch has it coming.

"I'll be almost completely broke after this fuckin' divorce. Look at this place! After everything I worked for, all I can afford now is this one bedroom shithole. Between the alimony and child support, I'll barely scrape by! I made almost nothing from selling the damn house!"

"And none of that was Danny's fault, was it?" Maureen countered. "This is not his battle. Your son deserves better than this, for Christ's sake!"

Gary sighed. "You know what, Maureen? I didn't even want any damn kids. It was her idea, not mine."

"Oh, that's a great attitude, Gary. If dad were alive to hear that, he'd knock your head off."

"Yeah, well, he ain't around and I'm sick of arguing with you about this."

"*You're* sick of arguing?" Maureen repeated furiously. "You used us! You used mom, my daughter, and me. You lied to us when you said that Theresa let you take Danny for the entire month while she moved back to Baltimore. So, of course, we were all too happy to take turns watching him while you were at work.

"What if the damn cops showed up at one of our homes while Danny was there? We could've been charged with accessory to kidnapping! Did you bother to think about that? No, you never think about anyone but yourself. I know you better than you know yourself, little brother. Someday maybe you'll grow up and realize that your thoughtlessness can have severe consequences and not just for yourself, but for people close to you like your son!

"How do you think Danny's going to react someday when he learns that you didn't even want him or that you used him against his mother?"

There was a moment of silence that lasted for nearly a full minute. On the patio outside, Danny had begun to get a vague understanding of why his father and aunt were arguing. For some reason, he wasn't supposed to be here. His mom was looking for him—with the cops!

Danny looked down at the blue and white plastic police car. As he pushed it along the concrete, he envisioned himself in the back seat, being driven away from his dad. It didn't make sense. Mom and Dad lived together in a big house! Maybe Dad was just here on vacation like when he rented that cabin in Maine last summer and took Danny fishing.

Yet somehow this didn't feel the same, just the opposite in fact. That's when Danny started to get nervous. He abandoned the toy car and sat with his back against the wall beside the screen door, staying just out of sight from inside the apartment. There was a dull ache forming in the pit of his stomach. It was a familiar pain, one that happened almost every time he got scared.

No, this was nothing at all like last summer.

When Gary finally spoke again, his tone was resigned. "Okay, fine, I'm sorry. You're right, Maureen. The only thing on my mind was getting back at her and I think I'm starting to regret it now. I'll apologize to mom when this is all over."

"It ends tonight," his sister said emphatically. "That's what I came here to tell you. I talked with Theresa and she assured me that if you bring Danny home by ten o'clock tonight, she won't press charges and she won't tell her lawyer. It'll be like it never happened. She's giving you a chance, Gary. If I were you, I'd take it."

The repetitive clicking of a turn signal brought Danny's thoughts back to the present. The rain had stopped and now there were a lot more streetlights lining the road leading off of the highway. His father had stopped talking to himself and didn't seem so angry now. As such, Danny gathered up enough courage to speak, though his tone was timid.

"Where're we goin'?"

"I'm taking you home to your mother."

"But I want to stay with you..."

"You can't stay with me!" his father snapped. "Do you want your daddy to go to jail?!"

"But why?" Danny screamed back in panic as tears ran down his face.

With a sigh, his father lowered his voice and placed a hand on Danny's shoulder. "Just calm down, buddy, you're going to be okay. Nothing to worry about."

Staring up at the streetlights as they passed one by one brought Danny some comfort. Bright spots in the darkness allayed his fears, if only partially. His dad told him that he was going home.

Danny remembered their house, the long hallway leading from the living room to his bedroom where he used to run with his hobbyhorse and push his toy fire truck along a pretend street. The backyard that seemed as large as a football field, where he would kick his soccer ball and fly his red kite.

"Is Mane going to be there?" Danny asked quietly though he dreaded the likely answer.

"Uh, no," his dad replied distractedly. "Mane won't be there. Sorry."

Mane was the neighbor's collie that always stuck his snout through the chain link fence between their yards so that Danny could pet him. They named him Mane because the fur around his entire head resembled a lion's mane. Danny had seen a lion at the zoo once, and on TV. He liked the collie better. Danny remembered how soft his fur was.

Soft like his mother's hair when she would pick him up and he put his arms around her. Suddenly, Danny recalled sitting beside her on the floor of their empty living room. He had wondered why everything was gone but hadn't asked. The front door had been left wide open, letting in the afternoon sunlight. Danny had been playing with an airplane, Snoopy the Flying Ace. His mother had said that they were waiting for his daddy to pick him up for the weekend.

It seemed so long ago now. Fleetingly, he hoped that at least the cartoon beagle would be waiting for him at home even if the collie wouldn't. Somehow, he knew that he would never see that house again. Wherever his dad was taking him tonight, Danny decided that it was a place he did not want to go.

Filling the living room of a modest Baltimore row home, the family of Theresa Quinn-Masenda gathered in anticipation of her son's return. The men, including her father Vaughn and two brothers, Paul and Kurt, were more than eager for Gary's arrival. It took every ounce of dissuasive reasoning from Theresa and her mother, Carolyn, to keep them at bay.

"You should've had the bastard arrested," Paul snarled in his bass voice, repeatedly punching his open left palm with his right fist. Though his thin, lanky build gave him a meek and almost frail appearance, he had a reputation for a quick temper and surprising strength.

From the storm door that overlooked the front porch, Theresa turned to address her older brother, long brown hair framing her soft jaw line. "I want to handle this quietly. The divorce already put me through enough. Besides, I don't want Danny to have a father in jail."

"He was never a father to begin with!" Vaughn snapped. A few years ago, the elder man would have been the tallest among them. Though his white hair had thinned and his shoulders slouched with age, his ire remained as fierce as it had been in his youth. "Do you really think he did this to spend more time with his son?" He's just—"

"I *know* why he did this!" Theresa cut him off, her voice turning shrill. "I'm not stupid and I'm not a child so stop talking down to me. I've had enough of that from you over the years!" Taking a deep breath, she collected herself before continuing. "Now I'm asking you guys, please don't go near Gary when he shows up and *don't* threaten him. In fact, keep quiet unless he provokes you, which he won't. Last thing I want is to give the neighbors a show. When he gets here, I'll go out alone to get Danny. Are we clear?"

Reluctantly, all three men agreed.

"Fine," Kurt chimed in. "But he should lose his visitation rights for this."

Vaughn looked at his watch. "He's already forty minutes late. Do you really trust him to be here?"

"Why, are you in a hurry?" Carolyn gibed. She stood beside her daughter at the front door. If Theresa ever wondered what she would look like at the age of fifty-eight, she need look no further than her mother. The difference in their appearances was marked only by years. When Theresa was in her twenties, she and Carolyn were often mistaken for sisters.

"This is your grandson," she reminded her husband. "We wait."

The tone of her voice served to quiet any further complaints. "Besides, I think the answer to your question just pulled up across the street." She looked at Theresa. "It figures he'd make you walk across the road to get Danny out of the car."

"Of course! He knows we're all here! He's too scared to park in front of the house," Vaughn remarked.

Everyone moved to the windows as Theresa sighed and stepped out onto the porch, all composure a façade, and slowly made her way across the street to Gary's car. Without hesitation, she opened the passenger door and unbuckled Danny's seat belt. Exchanging no words with Gary, she pulled the boy from the car with a little more force than intended.

No longer upset, Danny shot one last mournful glance at Gary before looking around in a silent daze at the unfamiliar surroundings. Theresa had moved into the neighborhood during her son's absence. Thus, she knew that this was the first time he would see his new home. Clutching his hand, Theresa hurried him across the street and onto the porch where her mother greeted them and took Danny inside.

"Can you handle him?" Carolyn nodded toward Gary, who remained behind the wheel of his car.

"No problem," her daughter replied in a low voice.

Returning to the car, Theresa stepped around the front to the driver's side where the window was rolled down and the radio played softly. Refusing to look at his ex-wife, Gary spitefully fixed his gaze forward.

"What the hell were you thinking?" Theresa snarled. "What were you trying to accomplish other than pissing me off? Kidnapping is a federal crime, jackass. If you ever pull this again, I *will* put you in jail."

Gary muttered under his breath, something that sounded like *fuck you*, for which he was met with a slap across the face.

At that, he threw the car door open and leapt from the vehicle. "Bitch, I'll knock you—"

"There are three guys in the house just lined up to beat the shit out of you so please, do something stupid. Remember the last time you hit me? I slammed a vase across the side of your head. Exactly how many stitches did you need? Try it now and you'll be leaving in a box, you fat fuck."

Turning his head slowly, Gary risked a fleeting look toward the house just as Theresa's father and brothers stepped out onto the porch, glaring directly at him.

"They won't always be there for you," Gary said, just loud enough for them to hear.

"Don't threaten me, you little pussy," Theresa seethed. "You're good at beating women but piss yourself when you're up against a guy. You should be damn grateful that I didn't call the cops. I can still call my lawyer."

"So what do you want?"

"An increase in alimony and child support. It's very simple, Gary, you pay me and maybe this little kidnapping stunt of yours never happened."

Gary paused, shaking his head. "You're getting enough as it is." He climbed into the driver's seat and slammed the door.

"Then I'll see you back in court." Theresa growled as he started the ignition.

Ignoring her, Gary turned up the radio's volume to deter any further discussion.

Theresa backed away from the car as it screeched away, speeding through the stop sign at the end of the street and turning out of sight. With a sigh, she casually made her way back to her house. To her chagrin, she had not avoided the watchful gaze of a few neighbors. She greeted them with a forced smile and a brief wave, confident that they could not have possibly gathered much from the evening's events. The last thing Theresa needed was the entire block knowing her personal problems.

Danny wasn't entirely certain where he was. He had a vague idea that this was to be his new home but beyond that, he was far too nervous to think, let alone speak or move. He merely stood in the center of the living room as Theresa's family finally departed. Before they left, she had thanked them for their support despite their own recent quarrels. Danny had no idea what that meant so he simply dismissed it.

Alone finally, Theresa closed the door with a sigh and massaged her forehead for a moment before regarding her son. She shook her head with an expression of disgust. This served to heighten Danny's apprehension to which Theresa seemed oblivious.

"He didn't take care of you at all!"

Exasperated, she threw up her hands at the sight of Danny's stained clothing and disheveled hair, its typical sandy color darkened with sweat. He turned and caught a glimpse of himself in the glass of the china closet in the dining room. He looked as if he hadn't bathed in days.

"First order of business is to get you cleaned up." Taking his hand, Theresa started toward the steps leading to the bathroom. Abruptly, she halted. "Wait, stay right there."

She hurried toward an end table and opened the top drawer. After a minute of rifling through it, she removed a small vinyl carry case. Opening it, she checked to ensure that the camera was loaded with film and batteries.

"I'm going to take some pictures of you," she began. "But I don't want you to smile, okay? You're all dirty because your daddy didn't take care of you after he stole you from me and I need to show some people how you looked when he brought you home. So remember just look at me and don't smile, okay?

"My lawyer's gonna love this," she muttered, aiming the camera.

The ordeal lasted for all of three minutes, but may as well have been all night to Danny. As the flash erupted is his eyes, the very thought of smiling couldn't have been further from his mind.

1983

Home was not a place that Danny was terribly fond of. In fact, life there was nothing short of a nightmare.

Two years ago, on his tenth birthday, his dad had suddenly stopped coming around. He hadn't even sent a birthday card. Of course, this had fueled his mother's anger toward him, something that required no encouragement as it was. For himself, Danny had only been mildly disappointed, mostly because he wasn't surprised. For months, his father's new wife had made slow, deliberate efforts to drive a wedge between him and his family. During one of Danny's last visits to their house, he had overheard a conversation in which she urged Gary to leave his "old life" behind because there was no room in their future for his son.

Despite his dad's disappearance from Danny's life, the constant battles between Gary and Theresa had not diminished in the least. Gary had moved at least three times in the past seven years in an effort to evade alimony and child support payments. Recently, Danny had been told, the courts ruled to automatically deduct these from his father's paycheck.

Doubtlessly, this had served to inflame Gary's hatred toward his ex-wife. *And maybe me, too,* Danny wondered.

He understood the enormous stress that his mother was dealing with as a single parent, let alone what Gary was putting her through. Worse, Theresa had no more than a high school education and had been out of work for the first five years of Danny's life. As such, she was hard-pressed to find full time employment, forced to settle for part time jobs that paid barely above minimum wage.

Which is why Danny dreaded the moment he stepped through the front door. Hearing his mother in the kitchen, he swiftly made for the steps and nearly reached the safety of the second floor.

"Danny," Theresa called from the kitchen doorway. "I need you to go to the store."

Lifting his right arm to scratch his opposite shoulder, Danny slowly descended the stairs and stopped as Theresa approached.

"What's wrong with your shoulder?" she asked.

"Just a little itch," Danny replied dismissively.

"Here," Theresa thrust forward a grocery list along with coupons and cash.

Danny took them with his free hand and gracelessly shoved them into his pocket. Unfortunately, the motion tussled his shirt just enough to reveal a section of the stain that he was attempting to hide.

"What's that?" Theresa frowned.

When Danny remained silent, she forced his arm to his side to see a large mud stain. She closed her eyes and sighed. "Is it at all possible for you to keep just one item of clothing clean? Is that too much to ask? Half the clothes I bought for you are ruined!"

Theresa's voice grew louder and more shrill in direct proportion to her temper. "This shirt cost me ten dollars! God knows the cost of the other clothes you wrecked over the years. When you are going to learn to take care of things?"

Theresa's grip on Danny's wrist had tightened painfully but the boy was far too scared to protest. Long ago he had learned when to keep his mouth shut.

His mother took a deep breath before continuing. "My attorney called this morning to tell me that for the fourth time your...*father*...just quit his job and moved without telling anyone. So now we won't be getting any more money from him until we track him down *again*. Do you think I can afford to keep buying clothes for you because of your carelessness?"

"I'm sorry," Danny croaked. "We were playing—"

"I don't care!" Theresa barked. She dragged him toward the front door. After taking back the grocery money, she opened the storm door and shoved him onto the porch. Stumbling, he collided into the wrought iron rail shoulder first. "If you want to sleep in this house tonight, you owe me ten bucks."

"I don't have any money," Danny replied in a low voice.

"Well, until you do, I don't want to see you."

With that she slammed the door, leaving a panic-stricken Danny to figure out where he was going to find the money. He was accustomed to the fear and the physical wounds that his mother typically inflicted upon him, but this latest dilemma was new and seemingly insurmountable.

With a fleeting glance at the neighboring homes, he was thankful to see no one about. It was difficult to keep these incidents private in such close quarters and he didn't want to add embarrassment to his day.

As he left the porch, Danny winced and massaged his shoulder. Ironically, it was the same one that he had earlier pretended to scratch. He started up the street aimlessly and eventually found himself at the local playground a few blocks away. There, he recognized the familiar face of one of his schoolmates. Miranda Lorensen was a bright young girl with blonde hair and sky-blue eyes.

She was propelling herself on a swing while her mother, Karen, sat on a nearby bench engrossed in a book. Miranda waved as Danny approached and took an adjacent swing. The girl brought herself to a stop, digging her heels into the dirt and kicking up a dust cloud.

"Hey, Randy," Danny mumbled.

"Hi!" she greeted him cheerfully. "Are you okay?"

Miranda's blue eyes were piercing and seemed to have an uncanny ability to detect others' moods and emotions. Perhaps it was Danny's wan smile that tipped her off as well. Her question opened the door and Danny revealed what had transpired at home.

As soon as he finished, Miranda leapt from her swing and ran to her mother. Alarmed, Danny called after her. After a minute or two, Miranda waved him over as Karen tucked her book into her purse. Inviting him to sit beside her, she questioned him on the incident with his mother.

"Maybe we should all go to your house and I can talk to your mom."

Danny shook his head and started massaging his shoulder. "If my mom finds out I told you, she'd kill me. She doesn't like it when I tell people about our family problems."

"What happened to your shoulder?"

Danny stammered for a moment. "I…fell on our porch. I'm okay."

With a sidelong glance at her daughter, Karen produced a ten-dollar bill from her purse. "Tell her you found it in the park. You wouldn't exactly be lying."

Tentatively, Danny took the money with an expression of disbelief.

Karen smiled. "You can pay me back someday."

Thanking them both, Danny carefully folded the bill and slipped it into his back pocket before saying good-bye.

When Danny was well out of earshot, Miranda turned to her mother. "Thanks, mom. I'm really worried about him. I told you what his mom did to him the last time I was at their house."

"I know," Karen nodded. "That's why you're not allowed back there again."

"But we gotta help him!" Miranda pleaded.

"We just did," Karen glanced at her watch. "It's time for dinner. Let's go."

"You just happened to find this in the park."

Danny nodded, his expression innocent. "Not right away. I walked everywhere before I saw it…near the swings. I guess it fell out of someone's pocket."

Theresa glared at him, frowning in obvious suspicion. She pointed at him accusingly. "I might call some of your friends' parents and if I find out that you got this from one of them, I will beat you bloody. Now put those clothes in the laundry and go to bed. I want you out of my sight for a while. Christ, you cause me nothing but problems."

Her chastisement ended with the typical mumbling to herself, although the word 'bastard' was audible enough. Though Danny had become accustomed to the term, he still felt humiliated every time she said it.

With an internal sigh of relief, he trod up the stairs to his room. Incurring his mother's wrath had become a frequent activity. There were days that left him to wonder about those guardian angels they told him about in school. If he had one, then he or she must be working double-overtime to have kept him alive this long. Danny removed his shirt and reached into his dresser to retrieve his pajamas. He caught his reflection in the mirror and stared for a moment at the black and blue mark on his shoulder. Twisting slightly, he grimaced at similar bruises on his back.

He turned away from the sight. Painful reminders of a few days earlier when he had forgotten to turn off a light before leaving the room. He had been absent-minded and the lamp remained on for several hours. It had happened once before with the television. Punishment was delivered much more severely the second time. Such mistakes cost money. His mother was right, of course. Danny understood this; surely he had it coming.

Glancing up at the small wooden crucifix that hung above his door, he thanked the good Lord that his mother did not know Miranda's phone number. The girl had only visited his house twice. Most of the time, they saw one another at school.

Danny held up his shirt before him. The mud stain was more evident than he had realized. He took it into the bathroom. Soaping up a damp washcloth, he wiped it vigorously. To his relief, it faded to a light tan. He was confident that the washer would take care of the rest and he will have redeemed himself in his mother's eyes.

Wringing out the excess water, he balled up the shirt and tossed it into the hamper in the hallway. Turning off the light in his room, he climbed into bed and buried himself under the covers, careful to lie on his left side facing away from the door. In doing so, he felt more secure somehow, as if shutting out the fear and uneasiness of the day before slipping away into his only true escape.

Chapter One

Twenty-Five Years Later

Port Kirkland was a small town nestled in Virginia's Eastern Shore along that small peninsula between the Chesapeake Bay and the Atlantic Ocean. On this unseasonably warm afternoon in mid-March, a crowd had gathered to celebrate the opening of a new facility. On the dais before them, nationally renowned philanthropist Gayle Shartle rose from her seat amidst a standing ovation and took to the podium.

"Ladies and gentlemen, thank you for attending the third annual charity outdoor banquet benefiting ESCAPe. As you know, ESCAPe stands for The Eastern Shore Child Advocacy Program. We began five years ago with only one youth center converted from an old warehouse in Richmond. Through the generous donations from both the public and private sectors, we've since been able to open several more throughout the state of Virginia.

"Our centers provide a safe, healthy and creative environment for children and teens in trouble. Whether they're struggling with drug or alcohol addiction, coping with an abusive or unhealthy home life, or simply looking for a place to belong, our doors are always open and our staff dedicated to helping them. After all, the children are the future generation of our communities.

"Today, the founders of ESCAPe would like to honor someone whose unfailing support and overwhelming generosity have been unparalleled in our history. Thanks to him, we are proud to open our fourth youth center here in Port Kirkland. Please show your heartfelt appreciation to Mayor Daniel Masenda!"

As the mayor rose from his seat, the crowd did the same. He shook Shartle's hand gingerly, as she was upwards of seventy-years old, before addressing the citizens of his town.

"Thank you, Mrs. Shartle, and thank you all very much," Daniel began. "For occasions like this, I tend not to prepare a speech. Instead, I prefer to speak from the heart. Of course, sometimes this practice gets me in trouble, but nothing I haven't been able to talk my way out of."

Laughter erupted from scattered members of the gathering as Daniel continued. "When I arrived in Port Kirkland, I had no intention of sticking around. My finances, however, dictated otherwise. I left home right after college and never looked back. I bounced around the country for a while doing what I like to call 'exploring my options'. Finally, I landed here with no money to go any further. That was fourteen years ago. Not much of an explorer, I guess.

"Frankly, it was the best thing that ever…"

Something odd in the back of the crowd caught Daniel's attention but it did not register in his mind immediately.

"...happened to me..."

He was about to lead into how his experiences back then related to the reason for today's gathering when he noticed a young boy, perhaps six or seven years old, staring directly at him from behind the last row of seats. Daniel felt an inexplicable chill as he observed the boy's gray, nearly ashen, pallor. Their gazes met for only a moment before the child turned and casually walked toward a pair of police officers. If they noticed the boy, they didn't acknowledge him nor did they react as he stepped between them—and vanished.

The mayor realized that he was stammering and forced his attention back to the task at hand. Several heads in the audience turned in the direction where he had been staring, trying to find the reason for his distraction.

"To, uh, make a long story short," Daniel continued. "Just as I was made to feel welcome and safe in our small town back then, so we should continually strive to do the same for our children.

"This building behind me is not just a simple youth center where kids can stop by and play basketball or volleyball. This is a safehouse for children in need of guidance, protection and in some cases, nurturing that they might not receive anywhere else. If my time as mayor of this town leaves no other legacy, I would be proud because in my heart this ESCAPe center will probably be my most important contribution.

"Except maybe when I lowered boat storage fees down by the docks."

Again, laughter among the crowd was accompanied by mild clapping.

"In closing," the mayor said with a smile. "Thank you for joining us today in support of this beautiful moment in Port Kirkland's history."

As the audience cheered, Gayle Shartle moved beside Daniel and quietly asked him to remain at the podium with her. A young man stepped up to the dais carrying a triangular shaped object covered in a swatch of black satin. He was just one of the many teens who had benefited from ESCAPe's youth centers. He stopped just behind Shartle, cradling the base of the object with both hands.

Shartle leaned toward the microphone. "Before we close this event, it has become a tradition to show our appreciation to our most dedicated supporters."

The boy reached out and handed the mystery item to the elderly woman. She removed its satin veil to reveal a glass pyramid, approximately eight inches tall, centered on a black marble base.

Rotating it in her hands until she found the appropriate side, she read the inscription aloud.

"For unwavering support of the children of our community, this year's ESCAPe award is presented to Mayor Daniel Masenda."

Daniel accepted the award with a handshake and held it above the podium for all to see. Cameras flashed, clapping resumed, and cameramen from at least two television news stations moved in for a close-up.

None of this ceremony mattered to Daniel. It was all merely icing on a long awaited brick and mortar cake. The true reward was for the children.

The next forty-five minutes saw the mayor besieged by microphone-wielding reporters. Frank Parelli, the township's public relations director, was beaming at the sight of his mayor and his town being honored so. Daniel calmly handled the interviews with a graceful, modest aplomb.

He also had a throbbing headache.

He shot a glance at Parelli, who took his cue to intervene and began ushering the group toward Gayle Shartle who happened to be standing nearby. Casually, Daniel began scanning the area in search of the strange little boy that disturbed him earlier. Surely someone else must have noticed a child with gray skin and lifeless black eyes! He arched his back to peer around the throng of reporters but saw no sign of the youngster in question.

"What's up, Dan-o?"

With a start, Daniel spun to face his best friend and occasional deputy mayor, Bruce Hargrove. Bruce was a lifetime resident of Port Kirkland and the first real friend that Daniel had made almost a year after moving to the town. He also owned and operated two charter boats offering tours and fishing trips on the Chesapeake Bay. Though he was older than Daniel by only four months, the boat captain's tendency toward alcohol and cigarettes, in addition to his leathery tan skin, had aged his appearance beyond his years. When he spoke, it was with a casual, very slight, southern drawl.

With a heavy sigh, Daniel rolled his eyes. "Don't do that!"

"Do what?"

"Never mind."

"Jumpy today, are we?"

Bruce was dressed in his usual manner—untucked short-sleeved shirt, khaki cargo pants, and deck shoes with no socks.

"Nice shirt," Daniel commented. "What are those, yellow-fin tuna?"

The boat captain nodded. "Got it for Christmas. First time I wore it. All you said was 'at least wear a collared shirt, please'. So I did. Hope I didn't embarrass you *this* time."

"You? Impossible."

Bruce never failed to stand out in a crowd, much like the disappearing boy.

"So what happened up there? You seemed a bit shaken up at one point. Y'all right?"

Daniel closed his eyes for a moment and massaged the bridge of his nose. "Yeah, I'm fine. Did you see that creepy kid back there?" He pointed toward the last row of seats which were now empty.

Bruce turned to look. "Which one? They're all creepy to me. Besides this is a kid's center, they're everywhere. My God, run for your life!"

Daniel smiled and shook his head. "I forgot you don't like kids."

His friend shrugged. "Of course I like kids, I just can't eat one whole."

"You have an answer for everything, don't you?"

"Yes, but enough about me. You look like you're about to pass out."

"Is it that obvious?" the mayor replied.

"Only to anyone who's actually here today. I think it's safe to assume that if they're not here, they didn't notice."

Daniel looked deadpan for a moment before replying. "Ladies and gentlemen, you can catch Captain Bruce at Smart Ass Comedy Club during Happy Hour every night this month."

"Probably pays better than deputy mayor," Bruce quipped. "Maybe you should go home and crash. Duck out of here before one of these rich, stuffed shirts comes over here wantin' to give the town even more money. You've been pushin' yourself hard for the past few months."

Daniel nodded his agreement. "Good idea. I got a lot to do on Monday. Budget meeting first thing. Then we're doing the ribbon cutting for the re-opening of the Matson River Trail. The whole damn thing's finally paved. Then I'm doing lunch with Vicki."

"Oh yeah, where is she?" Bruce asked.

"Boston," Daniel replied flatly.

"It's a shame she missed this."

The mayor shrugged. "Well, she was just put in charge of the distribution and packaging division of her daddy's corporation, so she feels the need to impress him by working almost seven days a week."

Bruce nodded his understanding. "Well, maybe I'll show up for the ribbon cutting on Monday if I can roll out of bed."

The pair shook hands. "Just leave the beer keg home this time," Daniel said as he began walking away.

"What do you care? You don't drink."

"I suppose it would be a waste of breath to remind you about appearances."

Bruce folded his arms in mock indignation. "And what exactly's wrong with my appearance?"

Daniel shook his head and waved dismissively before making his way toward the parking lot in search of his car.

Although he appreciated the award, which became more cumbersome to carry as the hour wore on, Daniel had a reputation for shying away from publicity whenever possible. Today was no exception. Some blamed his youth for that, claiming that this tendency would fade as he became a more seasoned politician—a concept that unnerved him even more than all of this pomp and circumstance.

With one last look over his shoulder, he climbed into his car and pulled out of the parking space. For a moment, Daniel thought he saw the eerie figure of the boy in his rear view mirror. Upon second glance, however, he was gone. Had he not been so exhausted, he might have been convinced that what he saw was a ghost.

There were few advantages to growing up in a single parent home. If Daniel could point to any positive aspects at all, they would be discipline and responsibility — both of which had been learned at a very early age. Without a husband, his mother had come to rely on him to take on many domestic responsibilities.

Two decades separated him from those days, yet during quiet moments Daniel found himself reminiscing. Today, he owned a house of his own with a deck that provided a beautiful view of the Matson River. Five years ago, he was the youngest person ever to be elected mayor for two consecutive terms after serving as the township treasurer for seven years. What more could he possibly ask for? While his life had certainly improved financially since childhood, he still felt an unavoidable pang of guilt when he thought of his mother.

They had not spoken in fourteen years. Their relationship had never been truly loving and only deteriorated as Daniel grew into adulthood. Still, if nothing else, she had raised him to be independent and he was glad of it.

He tossed the last of his laundry into the basket and tried to expel any further thoughts of his past. As he carried the load up to his bedroom, he caught a glimpse of his mailbox through the window and remembered that he had yet to retrieve yesterday's mail.

Depositing the basket on the floor, he stepped outside and jogged down the concrete steps to the curb. A moment later, with a stack of envelopes and an issue of The Planetary Report in hand, he started back toward his house and was met with a stream of water that struck him directly between the eyes and continued halfway down his shirt. Fortunately, the magazine was sealed in plastic and was on top of the other mail, thereby sparing it all from the surprise soaking.

Daniel wiped his face with his sleeve and sighed. Peering up at the neighbor's front balcony, he smiled thinly at the giggling cherub with the Super Soaker that was nearly as large as he.

"Nice aim," Daniel shouted. In response, the aquatic assassin merely laughed louder at his bemused target, which became his undoing.

"Teddy! What are you doing?!"

The trigger-happy tot fell silent as his mother stomped out onto the balcony and surveyed the scene. Her shoulders slumped as she looked from Daniel to the weapon of mass nuisance—and the water gun clutched in his stubby fingers.

"I'm so sorry, sir," she said to Daniel. "It's a gift from my brother and he just won't put it down! He drenched the hamster two days ago."

Daniel waved dismissively. "No problem, the shirt's drip-dry." He had a fleeting urge to make a joke about a drip-dry hamster but nothing came to mind. "Have a good one!"

"You, too. Thanks."

Shaking his head, he bounded up the steps and back into his house as the woman began to admonish the boy. He didn't know them very well, only that she was a single parent. Every few weeks, Teddy's father arrived to pick him up. He seemed nice enough. Still, Daniel couldn't help but to harbor some sympathy toward the kid.

Again, he found his thoughts wandering back to his own past.

"Whatever."

Hanging up his shirts in the closet, he caught a glimpse of himself in the mirrored sliding door. His eyes betrayed fatigue earned from weeks of long hours and little rest. Tomorrow was Friday and he was never more grateful for it. He felt as if he could sleep for two days straight. Turning away from his reflection, he removed several empty hangers from the closet and tossed them into the laundry basket at his feet. He closed the door and stooped to pick up the basket when something odd in the mirror caught his attention.

What he saw sent him reeling backward. He slammed into his dresser with a startled yelp. The face that stared back at him was not his own. Speechless, his mind racing for an explanation, Daniel could only stare at the bruised and bloodied face of a young boy and his tear-streaked, wide-eyed look of absolute fear.

Daniel managed to collect himself enough to gaze beyond the apparition —for what else could it possibly be? In the background, a dingy white door and cracked blue plaster walls seemed oddly familiar yet too surreal to recall distinctively. He looked frantically around his own bedroom to reassure himself that reality hadn't completely abandoned him. The laundry basket was tipped over but still very much there; the dresser was firmly at his back and the bed to his right. Bright sunlight illuminated the room from the bay window. Daniel drew some small comfort from the latter. Everything was as it should be, except for the nightmare playing out in the mirror.

The boy was speaking now. His lips were moving but he uttered no sound. Daniel couldn't help but compare this vision to some silent horror movie. Nervously, the boy looked over his shoulder to the door behind him just as it was thrown open with a force that made Daniel's heart skip.

The silhouette of a tall, thin figure stood in the doorway. Somehow, Daniel sensed that it was evil though no features were discernible. A sickly yellow glow from somewhere behind it cast its long shadow over the boy. The child writhed as if suddenly wracked with pain. He extended a pleading hand toward Daniel who pressed himself back against his dresser as the boy's arm reached *through* the mirror to within inches of his legs.

While the silhouette remained still, its shadow began to twist and contort around the boy, pressing his arms to his sides, wrapping around his throat until it yanked him violently backward toward the doorway.

"No!" Daniel had seen enough. He didn't know what was happening but instinct told him that the child was in danger. A swell of rage stirred within him. He leapt to his feet and dashed toward the mirror.

"Leave him alone!" he roared, slamming his fist into the glass. It shattered instantly, black shards exploding all around him releasing a sound like the scream of a tormented soul.

In a cold sweat, Daniel sat bolt upright. Instinctively, he shot a glance at the alarm clock. It was nearly four-thirty in the morning, far too early for the buzzer to sound. He took a moment to calm his mind and realized that the persistent, electronic screeching was coming from just outside the room.

The smoke alarm!

Tossing the covers aside, he raced to the door and threw it open. Immediately, the alarm fell silent. Stepping out into the hallway, Daniel flipped on the light. When a cursory inspection revealed nothing out of the ordinary, he patrolled the entire floor to ensure that all was well before returning to the bedroom. He paused at the doorway and glared up at the smoke alarm on the ceiling. Its small green LED light calmly flashed every ten seconds or so as normal. Daniel considered replacing the battery but recalled that he had done that a week ago. Even if the unit required a new one, it typically indicated so with two short beeps every few minutes.

With slumped shoulders and a heavy sigh, he leaned against the doorjamb and closed his eyes. He practiced a breathing exercise to calm himself while attempting to make sense of the night's events. The timing of the alarm was an eerie and unnerving coincidence within the context of his dream. He shot a glance toward the closet doors.

At this angle, Daniel could see only the reflection of the dresser and the wall behind it. With a deep breath, he re-entered the room and stood before the mirror. After a moment, he smiled sheepishly at his naked reflection. Although he knew it was absurd, he suddenly felt uncomfortable in the nude and pulled on a t-shirt and shorts from the dresser.

Shaking his head in disbelief at what was probably the most vivid and disturbing dream he had ever experienced, Daniel treaded wearily into the bathroom and splashed his face with cold water. He closed his eyes, forcing his breathing into a steady rhythm, and remained hunched over the sink for almost a full minute before reaching for a towel. After drying off, he opened his eyes and peered into the mirror.

At once his breath caught in his throat and his heart sank into his stomach. The face that stared back was certainly his, but the bloody nose, split lip, and swollen eye were like something out of a nightmare.

Yet Daniel was wide awake this time.

Slowly, he raised his hand to the mirror and pressed his fingers against the glass. His reflection mimicked his movements precisely.

Why should I expect otherwise?

Daniel yanked his hand away and slowly made his way back into the bedroom. He stopped just short of the closet doors. He closed his eyes and took several deep breaths. His frantic thoughts ran together as he struggled to make sense of it all.

What the hell is going on? This is impossible. Am I possessed? I don't feel any different. There's no pain. My thoughts seem to be my own. I don't hear any voices. No, that can't be me. No way. No goddamn way. Someone's fuckin' with me.

Opening his eyes, he stepped forward and turned to face his full length reflection in the closet door. The face was still the same—the swollen discolored skin, the open wounds.

The blood.

Daniel's stomach turned.

He spent the rest of night huddled in the corner of his locked office down the hall. It was, after all, the only room on the second floor without a mirror.

The following day, the mayor was missing in action.

Vicki Harlan had known Daniel for several months before they began dating three years ago. During that time, he had never stood her up or ignored her phone calls. When both happened on the same day, the only conclusion was that something must be awry.

She tried unsuccessfully to reach him at his office before calling his assistant on her cell phone. Samantha explained that the mayor had left a voicemail stating only that he wasn't feeling well. She could offer no further details as she had taken the day off to visit family.

Vicki had then called Daniel's home and cell phones to no avail.

Her head snapped up at a knock on her office door. It was her father, Walter. Formerly a body builder, Mr. Harlan had maintained a healthy physique even at the age of sixty-eight. He was also the owner of the company for which she worked. This had its advantages and disadvantages.

"You jumping in on this conference call?" he asked, pointing a thumb toward the general direction of his office at the opposite end of the hall.

"Oh, uh," Vicki stammered. "Yeah, in a minute. I can't seem to get in touch with Dan."

Mr. Harlan sighed. "I'm sure Mayor Boy-Toy is fine. You can play with him later. This call is about your Singapore trip, remember?"

Casting a sneer in his direction, Vicki undocked her laptop computer and rose from her seat. "Thanks, dad," she muttered as she breezed past him. "Always so supportive."

"I gave you a job, didn't I?" he retorted as they walked beside one another down the hallway.

Vicki clenched her jaw. Moments like this proved to be a frustrating *dis*advantage.

Undeterred, she sent an email to Daniel during the meeting. She wasn't entirely surprised when he failed to reply.

Her concern having turned to worry, Vicki left her office immediately after the conference call and drove directly to Daniel's house. Upon arriving, it appeared that he wasn't even at home. All was in complete darkness, not one light shone from any window. The only evidence that suggested otherwise was his mini-SUV parked in the garage, visible only by the moonlight that reflected from its metallic blue hood.

Vicki jogged up the short flight of steps to the front door and rang the doorbell. Daniel had provided her with a key but she decided to give him the benefit of the doubt rather than simply barge in. After the third ring went unanswered, she let herself in.

Although a twin, the house was reminiscent of a bi-level. A short stairway led down to the garage while another longer one led up to the main floor. Vicki flipped the light switch just inside the door and high above her, the ceiling fan began to rotate as the lights came on.

Ascending the steps to the main floor brought her directly across from the kitchen where the combined lights from various appliances provided a meager glow. To her right was a bedroom typically used for guests while to her left a small dining area opened into the living room. The overhead lights illuminated the scene just enough to allow Vicki to make her way to the living room and turn on a floor lamp. As many times as she had been here both alone and with Daniel, she had never felt uncomfortable—until tonight. The additional lights served to abate her mounting apprehension but something was definitely amiss.

She parted the vertical blinds covering the sliding glass doors that led to the deck. In the distance, the rotating glow from a distant lighthouse rhythmically caressed the gentle currents of the Matson River.

Vicki tossed her purse on the sofa with a sigh. She paused for a moment wondering if she should inspect the rest of the house or just sit and wait for Daniel to appear. Hunger began vying for attention through her grumbling stomach.

Then a sound from the guest bedroom froze Vicki in her place. Someone was shuffling about in the room. She fought the urge to call Daniel's name, for if it was *not* him in there, then she wasn't about to announce herself. Swallowing hard, Vicki Harlan summoned all of the courage in her petite frame as she crept around the kitchen counter and nearly knocked over one of the stools. With a look that should have turned it to cinder, she steadied it quietly before reaching over the counter and producing a carving knife from one of the drawers.

Her evening was starting to resemble a scene from an average horror movie, a comparison that was not lost on her as she crept toward the room, her culinary weapon held high. The door was ajar, ominous darkness within. Light shined down the hallway from the ceiling fan and cast her long shadow ahead of her as she pushed the door open. Without hesitation, she reached for the light switch—

"I prefer it dark."

—and screamed. In a panic, Vicki flung the knife clumsily toward the source of the voice and heard it clatter against the far wall. Several expletives followed before she collected herself. In her professional world of exceedingly proper grammar, it was sometimes refreshing and downright funny to hear her lose it.

"What the hell are you doing sitting here in the dark? I damn near had a heart attack!"

The weak light from the hall was just enough to reveal the fact that Daniel was sitting on the floor on the opposite side of the bed.

He leaned over and retrieved the carving knife. "Sorry," he replied simply. "You know, you throw like a girl." His voice was barely above a whisper. He tossed the knife atop his dresser and hung his head once more.

"Shut up!" she snapped before forcing a softer tone. "I tried calling you everywhere when you didn't show up for lunch."

Daniel nodded. "I never left the house today. Called out sick."

"Funny, I never thought about a mayor calling out sick." Removing her coat, Vicki tossed it onto the bed. Now that she had regained her composure, she peeled off her high heels with an exhausted sigh and sat down beside Daniel.

He immediately turned his face away.

"Hey, what's wrong?" she asked, sliding her arm around his waist. "Are you mad at me?"

"No," he said ardently. "No, this has nothing to do with you. I...just don't feel well."

"Okay, well, can you at least look at me?"

"I don't think you want to see me right now. I'm not exactly looking my best."

Vicki chuckled. "I think we've been together long enough that we're past all that."

Daniel sighed. What would he have to lose? "Okay, fine, but just remember you asked for it." He rose to his feet, stepped around Vicki, and turned on the light. "This is why I've been hiding."

She frowned in confusion. "You stood me up for lunch because you're having a bad hair day?"

"What? No!" Daniel risked a glance into the full-length mirror and cringed at the disfigured face that stared back. He pointed to the mirror. "What do you see?"

"Two days growth? You *could* use a shave, Mister Mayor."

His shoulders slumped. Closing his eyes for a moment, he ran a hand through his sandy hair, merely rearranging already disheveled locks. A surfeit of emotions riddled his thoughts. He was both surprised and relieved that Vicki could not see the grotesque vision that appeared to be haunting only him. At the same time, he couldn't help but to be confused as to how and why.

During his entire day of solitude Daniel piled question upon question in his mind, all the while avoiding every mirror and reflective surface in the house. He felt no physical pain in his face; its shape and contours normal to the touch of his fingers. However, he dare not step foot outside until he could be assured that his unsightly appearance was invisible to others.

Daniel was convinced that he was not insane. His ability to reason was still very much intact. He didn't believe that one awoke in the morning with dementia as easily as a sore throat, although his current behavior with Vicki probably indicated otherwise. He made an effort to calm himself.

Earlier, he had arrived at the conclusion that what was happening to him was of a paranormal nature, merely indicating something beyond the norm. He wasn't ruling out the possibility of the supernatural but for some reason, that term sent a bolt of fear through his heart. He was more comfortable referring to it mentally as paranormal, albeit he wouldn't verbalize that to anyone yet. It simply wouldn't do to have the mayor removed from office for reasons of insanity. All he needed was to be assured that no one else would notice anything *different* about him. That should buy him time to unravel this mystery while proceeding with his normal routine as much as possible. In the interim, he would force himself to endure his altered reflection.

"Sorry, Vicki, guess I'm just a little burned out," he explained in a controlled, cogent tone. "You know I deal with bouts of depression from time to time and today I, uh, crashed…*hard*. I just needed some time to myself but I do feel bad about missing lunch."

Vicki picked herself up and shrugged. "Well, don't worry about it. I just thought maybe you had a date."

Daniel smiled in spite of himself.

"That's better." She kissed him and they held each other until the rumbling of Vicki's stomach sent them both laughing.

"I take it you're hungry?" Daniel asked. "The kitchen is stocked or… we can go out—"

At that moment, the telephone rang.

"I'm way too hungry to wait for food. How about if I find something to cook," she offered. "While you answer that."

With a sigh, he reached for the phone beside the bed as Vicki exited the room. His hand hovered over the cordless receiver for a moment before snatching it up.

"Hello?"

"Yeah, uh, hi, I'm looking for Dan Masenda."

The man's deep voice was unfamiliar, the words audibly slurred and if he were tired or intoxicated.

"Speaking," Daniel replied.

"OK, uh, this is, uh, gonna sound a little weird," the man stammered. "But just to confirm that I got the right guy, your mom's name was Theresa Quinn?"

Was? Daniel frowned, perplexed by this mysterious caller. As he replied, his tone was hesitant. "Yeah…who is this?"

"Aw, thank Christ," the man said in obvious relief. As he continued, his words ran together as they spilled out. "Dan, this is Paul, your Uncle Paul, you mom's older brother."

Slowly, Daniel lowered himself to the edge of the bed. In the center of his stomach, a knot began forming. "Yeah, Paul, I remember you. It's…been a long time. How are you?"

He had not been in contact with his uncle Paul in nearly fifteen years. To say that they were never close would be an understatement. Throughout Daniel's childhood, his mother's side of the family had constantly been beleaguered with petty infighting, the various causes of which were typically ludicrous and beyond his comprehension at the time. All he knew was that if his mother had a falling out with someone, Daniel was tacitly expected to cut ties with that person as well. The reasons were never relevant and any behavior to the contrary was typically met with severe punishment. The philosophy of "you hate everyone who I hate" was drilled into Daniel repeatedly.

Thus, the concept of family pride and togetherness had never become intrinsic in his life. Once he had moved out on his own, he cut ties with his family and practically wrote them off. He had decided that there would be no place in his life for other people's grudges.

The last time he saw Paul was at his grandfather's funeral and they had barely spoken other than to exchange condolences. Here and now, Daniel wondered where his uncle had obtained his phone number. It did not take long to find the answer as Paul quickly delved into the reason for the call.

Perhaps twenty minutes passed when Daniel finally hung up the phone and emerged from the guest bedroom. Any relaxation that he had felt earlier in Vicki's arms was entirely gone and he was once again on edge. This had been one of the worst days of his life and it left his nerves raw.

He dropped onto a stool in the kitchen, elbows on the counter, head in his hands.

"I'm making chicken stir-fry," Vicki announced as she opened and closed cabinet doors in search of a frying pan. "Or I will be."

She had changed clothes and was now wearing gray sweatpants and a black t-shirt. In the master bedroom upstairs, Daniel had set aside a small dresser for her in the event that she decided at the last minute to stay overnight.

He muttered incoherently before raising his head. She mentioned something about 'Singapore' and 'expansion' yet her words went unheard, as did the soft music from the stereo in the far corner of the living room. He didn't even react when a stack of pots and pans tumbled out of one of the cabinets and crashed to the floor.

"Found it!" Vicki picked out the appropriate pan from the pile and after a brief washing, placed it on the stove. She leaned down and began putting away the rest as she continued her one-sided conversation. "So, I just wanted to warn you in case I need to hop on a plane at the last minute. Knowing my dad, I'll be lucky to get a day's notice."

After a moment, Vicki stopped and faced Daniel. Tilting her head, she looked at him curiously. "Were you listening?"

Daniel's lips parted but it took a few seconds to find his voice. "What? Yeah, um, I'm sorry. You said you're taking a trip somewhere?"

"*Men,*" she sighed and held up a hand. "Never mind, we'll talk about it over dinner. So, who called?"

"That was my Uncle Paul," Daniel said simply.

"Everything okay?"

"Not really."

Vicki closed the cabinet door, and then opened it tentatively to make sure everything inside was secured. Satisfied, she closed the door again and went to the freezer. "Why, what happened?"

"My mother died last night."

As if on cue, the cabinet door burst open again, releasing a deluge of cookware.

Chapter Two

Salt In The Wounds

If Daniel thought that his nerves were raw over the weekend, Monday morning found him all but numb. He could barely mask the quiver in his voice when he left messages for Samantha and Bruce, announcing his need for an extended bereavement period.

Never before had he been more grateful for one of Vicki's impromptu visits. She had provided comfort when his troubled mind would not. At the same time, she hadn't pressed him for details about his mother's death and Daniel told her only what he knew.

Theresa had been battling breast cancer for nearly a year.

To his relief, Vicki hadn't questioned him as to why he had never mentioned such a dramatic family crisis. Perhaps her woman's intuition had told her that Daniel was in no state of mind to answer. In fact, he would have had to reveal that his own mother had ordered her family to keep her illness from him. According to his uncle Paul, she had not even wanted Daniel to be informed of her death.

Imparting this to Vicki would only have forced him to divulge a family history that he had strived to forget over the past twenty years. He had nearly succeeded until this living nightmare began two nights ago. Somehow, perhaps purely by instinct, Daniel knew that his dream and subsequent visions in the mirror were connected to Theresa's death. The timing was too perfect to be mere coincidence. He resolved to file away that line of thought for later exploration.

Of course, Daniel knew that he would eventually need to explain all of this to Vicki. It was too much to keep inside and he desperately wanted to confide in her but the time was not yet right.

All of this and more weighed heavily on Daniel during the three hour drive that brought him back to the familiar town of his childhood. He took note of the changes—some minor, others drastic—but most of all he marveled at how *small* the neighborhood truly was. The streets were narrower than he recalled, and shorter. He recognized the library, the church, and the playground along the main road. While almost all of the old shops contained new occupants, they had apparently worked to preserve the antiquity of the architecture.

In his mind's eye, Daniel saw himself twenty years younger on his way to his first job as a janitor at a local department store, now long out of business. Traversing further into his past, he recalled one winter's day when he and another boy had trudged home from school in knee-deep snow when the school bus service was canceled. In the playground where he and his middle school archenemy had brawled on more than one occasion for reasons only callow teens of the time would have deemed important.

Then there was Miranda, the little girl who had listened to Daniel when he had nowhere else to turn. They had grown into adulthood together, confiding in one another along the way, helping each other through life's tribulations, from the death of her pet rabbit Oliver when she was six years old, to the loss of her father to emphysema ten years later. For Daniel, she had become the only source of comfort when he moved to this town after his parents' divorce and the ordeals that he had suffered soon thereafter.

Sixteen years ago, their relationship had intensified and friends became lovers. Over a year later, he had nearly proposed to her, knowing that he wanted to be by her side forever.

Inexorably, the reality of his life had tapped him on the shoulder and he turned to face it, realizing that he would once again fail himself for the sake of someone else.

1977

"Why do things have to die?"

Danny looked at Miranda seated beside him on the antique wooden bench on her front porch. She and her father had just buried Oliver in the backyard earlier in the afternoon. Miranda had said that her parents bought him from a shelter two years ago, unsure of his age. He had apparently been much older, and sicker, than they thought.

"Everything dies," Danny said. "That's just the way things are. Old people die to make room in the world for babies, same with animals. Are you gonna get a new rabbit?"

Miranda shrugged. "I don't know. Maybe I don't want one. They don't last long."

"Maybe Oliver was old or sick," Danny suggested. "Did you ever take him to the vet?"

Miranda shook her head.

"My mom says that nothing lasts forever, so we should take care of things while we have them."

"That's what my dad said, too. He said we should be good to people because life is too short."

Danny didn't respond. He wondered if his mother would agree with Miranda's dad. If so, then maybe things would be better at home, maybe he wouldn't be so nervous all the time and could stop worrying about—

"What happened to your arm?" Miranda asked.

Danny tugged at the sleeve of his t-shirt to cover the black and blue marks on his upper arm. "I fell yesterday, trying to climb that stone wall in my backyard." He had become accustomed to thinking quickly when asked such things. As a result, he had also become a skilled, convincing liar.

"I'm sorry about Oliver," he said, deliberately changing the subject. "I'm sure your mom and dad will get you another bunny if you ask them."

"So if somebody dies, does that mean you just replace them?"

1987

"He was one of a kind, your dad."

As he entered the funeral home, Daniel heard conversation across the room and looked to see Miranda, her mother, and several other mourners standing before her father's casket. The assistant funeral director, a short, robust man with flat spiked hair, greeted Daniel and asked him to sign the register. After doing so, Daniel sighed sharply as he straightened his tie and made his way up the aisle, hoping that he was not wearing his nerves on his sleeve. Miranda turned as he approached.

"I'm so sorry, Randy," he said as they wrapped their arms around each other.

"Thanks, Danny." She kissed him on the cheek and he felt the warmth of a tear. "And thank God you're here."

"Danny."

He turned to face Miranda's mother. "Mrs. Lorensen. I'm very sorry for your loss."

With moist eyes and the tracks of dried tears on her face, Karen Lorensen choked out a thank you before turning away to face her late husband. His casket was surrounded by bouquets of roses, carnations and gerberas, most of which were orange yet none were as plentiful as the tiger lilies that lined the side of the coffin. Daniel suddenly remembered that orange had been Marc Lorensen's favorite color. To the far right, past the cluster of mourners, a giant poster rested on an easel and displayed a collage of photos from Mr. Lorensen's life. Curious, Daniel made his way over for a closer look. There were baby pictures, photos of Miranda's grandparents, Karen and Marc at their wedding, and several shots of Miranda from childhood to present day.

"He looks so peaceful, you know," an elderly woman said.

"They always do," another replied.

"They did a fantastic job, you know, on his skin and such a nice suit, too."

"Oh, my God, I gotta get outta here," Miranda whispered, taking Daniel by the hand and leading him outside. When they were alone, she leaned against the wall of the building and rubbed her face.

She seemed so tired, so fragile. He had never seen her this way. He didn't know what to do.

"I can't listen to the way they're talking about how peaceful he looks and what a great makeup job they did and how nice his fucking suit is! Jesus, he's dead. My dad is dead. How can they talk like that?"

Miranda broke down into tears and Daniel held her instantly. Her typically soft, airy voice strained under the weight of her grief. "He wasn't even fifty, dammit, dammit! Why did he have to die?"

Everything dies. That's just the way things are.

Silent minutes passed between them. Miranda rested her head against his chest. He listened to her sobbing, felt her body rise and fall with labored breathing.

"I don't know what we're gonna do now…" she muttered.

So if somebody dies, does that mean you just replace them?

"Whatever you need, I'm here."

He kissed her on top of her head and she looked up at him. He wiped the tears from her cheeks. Before he could think, he found his lips against hers. He pulled back, at once scared and embarrassed. She put her hand on the back of his neck, stopping him, and brought herself up to kiss him.

In pressing her close to him, he wanted to absorb her pain, take it away, replace it with his strength, his love. To make her know that the loss of her father's life did not mean the loss of hers. In reality, he knew that that would take time. She would grieve now and for a long while and he would be with her through it all as he had always been, as they had always been for each other.

1994

"You just graduated from college a year ago and now you want to get married?"

Theresa Quinn, having dropped her married name several years prior, cast a sour look at Daniel from her favorite recliner. "You haven't even begun to live your life. You don't know the first thing about the world and you want to run off and flush your future down the toilet?"

Daniel knew going in that this would be a tough sell. Thus, he tried to prepare himself for every angle his mother would take. During his high-school years, he had lost many good friends to his mother's interference and faultfinding. For most of them, it took only one or two visits to Daniel's house before they cut ties with him. Others, who were more understanding, or maybe just more sympathetic, requested that he meet them elsewhere. Then there was Miranda who stayed with him through it all. Daniel would be damned if he would let his mother destroy that.

"I'm not throwing anything away. I've known Miranda all my life and—"

"As children!" Theresa slammed her fist on the arm of her chair. "You're both children! You don't know what the hell you're doing!"

"You just don't want me to make the same mistake you did."

She was on her feet instantly. "You're damn right! Do you think I want you to have the same regrets that I do?"

"I suppose I'm one of those regrets," Daniel shot back.

Theresa sighed. "That's not what I meant."

"Whatever. Our lives aren't the same. Miranda and I are not you and Gary. Look, I know you're trying to protect me and I appreciate your concern but you had to know that someday I'd leave. Go off on my own."

"And where do you think you're gonna live?" Theresa asked, folding her arms over her chest.

Daniel shrugged. "I'd imagine that we'd start with an apartment like a lot of young couples."

Theresa stared at him for a moment before speaking again. When she did, her tone was calm and deliberate. "You know I can't afford the rent here on my own. Where am I supposed to live when you're gone? I bet you didn't think about that, did you?"

Daniel looked away for a moment, unsure of how to answer. Truth be told, he hadn't thought of that at all. It was like a punch in the stomach. There was no way in hell that he could continue to live with her and inviting her to live with Miranda and him was out of the question. She would ruin their lives within a week.

Theresa threw up her hands. "That's what I thought. You don't give a damn about your own mother. Your friends have always been more important to you than me!"

Daniel met her burning gaze, his own anger brimming. "That's not true. I know how much you sacrificed for me as a single parent and I'll always love you for that, but I've given up a lot for you. Look at everything I had to endure from you over the years, lost friends, invasion of privacy, verbal and physical abuse, loss of dignity. Do we need to recap all the shit you put me through?"

Theresa's eyes widened. "You watch your mouth when you talk to me, you disrespectful bastard! You're no better than your goddamn dago father! Drop the past! I told you that my nerves were shot back then, and I don't owe you an explanation for anything.

"I took care of you when your father turned his back on you! Would you rather have lived with him? He wouldn't have given a shit about you! He never wanted you. He hates kids! Now, I am sick and tired of you throwing the past back in my face!"

Daniel clenched his jaw, felt his teeth grind. He took a deep breath and held up a hand to signal his desire to end the argument. "I came here with what I thought would be good news. I knew you wouldn't approve but I'd hoped to reason with you. I should've known better, considering how you are, how you've always been."

"What the hell's that supposed to mean?"

"You can't be talked to like a normal person. *Don't interrupt me!* I'm tired of you running my life and manipulating me with your guilt trips. The way your life turned out was *not* my fault but you always took it out on me every time something went wrong.

"But you know what? You've convinced me. You win. There won't be a marriage but I sure as hell am *not* going to live my life wallowing in bitterness and resentment like you. I can see so clearly now what I need to do. Thank you, mom, for showing me my next course of action."

You won't see me again.

As it had been throughout his childhood, Daniel realized that he would once again crumble and sacrifice his chance for happiness, but this time it was not simply in acquiescence to his mother's demands.

Rather, he did it for the woman he loved.

For if he truly loved Miranda, how could he have felt justified bringing her into his embattled life? One that was mired in hatred and truculence where verbal abuse supplanted rational conversation between mother and son?

In escaping from that prison, however, he had abandoned Miranda and a life that could have been. For that, and that *alone,* he still felt a sincere pang of guilt. He had dreamt of a bright future filled with the spark of young romance, and knew that he would never once take it for granted. So why had he allowed it to slip from his grasp so easily? Why had he permitted himself to be bullied by a mother who begrudgingly, perhaps fearfully, watched her son grow into adulthood and hinder his reach for independence at every opportunity?

Later he had realized that his guilt had been that of a coward who, for only a few scattered moments in his life, had been able to be himself and had settled for that. All other times, he had been allowed to be himself on his mother's terms and had settled for that, too.

For the first few years since he had embarked on what he mentally referred to as his 'new beginning', his free time had been spent in self-imposed isolation. He had considered this necessary toward emotional healing, to regroup and find new direction.

Upon reaching Port Kirkland, Daniel had found a small apartment and took a job with the township, but formed no new friendships immediately. Rather, he had erected a wall around himself, a barrier against the world until such time as he felt comfortable, confident, and secure in himself.

It had been a liberating, yet foreign notion to have all decisions be solely his, second-guessed by no one. All goals, dreams, and ambitions had finally seemed within reach with no one to hold him back.

The time had come to be himself, on his own terms.

Edwards Funeral Home was easy enough to find. It had been in business as far back as Daniel could remember. The viewing would begin in thirty minutes, followed by the funeral at Saint Philip's Roman Catholic Church ten minutes away.

Daniel took a deep breath before stepping out of his car. As he entered the building and signed in, his thoughts were forced into a strange state of objective, almost clinical, detachment. His earlier nervousness was suddenly replaced by composure through no apparent effort on his part.

He shook hands with members of his extended family, some of whom he had never met before, yet all of them may just as well have been complete strangers. He felt no sense of family here, only a heartless obligation. As cruel as it may seem, the fourteen-year estrangement from his mother had left him with a peculiar apathy. Perhaps this was merely a temporary defense mechanism, another barrier, raised by his mind to protect him from the dismal reality of the situation.

If so, it was failing miserably.

Death itself was a barrier, permanent and most profound, that separated body from soul, thought from mind, energy from matter. In its unyielding grip, so much more is extinguished than the mere corporeal flame. So, too, are chances and opportunities. Daniel considered all of this in his weary, meandering thoughts. Fatigue threatened to undermine his composure and weaken his resolve with familiar pangs of guilt and shame. Yet, in another part of his mind, something disguised as righteous anger fought back. It was pride most certainly and as usual he felt that quickly evaporate where his mother was concerned.

Daniel thrust these embattled thoughts aside as he gazed upon her for the final time. He wondered if she had truly found peace now—and if he ever would. From somewhere beyond his attention, Paul and the funeral director exchanged soft words. Daniel realized then that they were looking at him.

It was time.

He nodded pensively and the lid of the casket was gently closed. In his mind, Daniel saw only an impenetrable wall thrust down between mother and son behind which, all hope was lost and over a decade of intransigence threatened to become an eternity of regret.

Vicki met him at the church, as she had been unable to attend the viewing due to pressing business matters. Few words were exchanged as Daniel, along with his two uncles and their sons, carried the casket into the church and gently placed it atop a skirted metal table in the center aisle.

Taking their seats for the funeral mass, Daniel chose a pew in the front row. Beside him, Vicki clasped his hand in hers.

Daniel's attention drifted and returned throughout the mass, though his gaze remained fixed on the massive crucifix that adorned the front wall high above the marble altar. It was at this same church where he had attended his grandfather's funeral sixteen years ago, and his grandmother's four years before that. He hoped that his mother was with them, and that all grudges and bitterness were cast away leaving only peace, something that Theresa never seemed destined to find in life.

At some point during his musings, Daniel's mind registered a change in atmosphere. It was an inexplicable feeling as if the temperature suddenly dropped ten degrees and a wave of cold air passed over him. An organ began playing and suddenly, the church was filled with the song of a joyful choir. The music was familiar, and utterly out of place. It was a Christmas song.

Abruptly, Daniel brought his focus back on the here and now. He tightened his grip on Vicki's hand only to find that it was no longer there —nor was she. Perplexed, Daniel slowly looked around.

The casket was gone!

He leapt from the pew to find that his family had also disappeared. Behind him, a throng of parishioners was slowly exiting the church. In was then that he noticed the Christmas decorations—wreaths hanging below each stained glass window, lighted pine trees flanking both the main doors and the altar, and poinsettias placed generously throughout the interior.

The music stopped and the church was nearly empty save for an elderly couple engaged in whispered conversation seated toward the end of the adjacent row. Leaving his pew, Daniel slowly made his way toward them. As he approached, they looked up in his direction.

"Oh my God..." Daniel blurted. It was all he could manage before his breath caught somewhere deep in his throat. Reflexively, he stepped backward, nearly stumbling into another pew.

As if oblivious to his reaction, his grandparents merely smiled and waved, appearing as he remembered them when he was no more than seven or eight years old.

Unable to speak, Daniel raised his hand to return the gesture before realizing that they were not looking at him, but seemingly *through* him, to someone across the church. He looked over his shoulder to see a young woman lighting a tall candle before a statue of Mary. Beside her, a young boy no more than six years old glanced at Daniel's grandparents and smiled sheepishly before being abruptly yanked by the arm and rushed down the aisle toward the door. The woman never acknowledged the elderly couple or Daniel as they exited the church.

"I feel sorry for him," Carolyn Quinn mumbled.

"Who?" Daniel managed to ask. His question went ignored.

Vaughn nodded in agreement. "He's gonna have a hard road."

"Who?"

Daniel was home again.

He stood before the ten year old artificial Christmas tree that was erected in a small open space between the living room and dining room in the house of his childhood. Antique glass ornaments adorned its branches, some dating back to his great grandparents.

He spun around, taking in his surroundings while his mind raced to make sense of what was happening. He recognized everything—the furniture, the lamps, even the color of the rotary phone. This was no dream. He had returned to the place from which he wanted nothing more than to escape during every minute of his youth.

Daniel was given little time to absorb any of this before the front door opened. He turned at the familiar sound of an angry female voice and knew immediately who it was. His disbelief and confusion began to transform into curiosity. Although somewhere in his thoughts, he knew that all of this was completely impossible, he wondered what his mother's reaction would be when she saw him.

Entering the home behind her, the target of Theresa Quinn's wrath merely looked at her in silent fear. Daniel's breath caught in his throat as realization struck him. While the face was unmarred by bruises, it was unmistakable nevertheless.

He was the boy in the mirror!

He was Daniel. Although at that age, everyone referred to him as Danny.

"You know that I'm not speaking to them!" Theresa shouted. "And you know why! They were never good parents to me, the way they treated me all of my life. The way they turned their backs on me after my divorce!

"And do you stand by me? Of course not! You smile and wave at them like we're all one happy family. You're no son to me, you traitor! You should be damn grateful that I don't treat you like my so-called parents treated me."

Theresa removed her coat and tossed it on the sofa. As he watched her pull off Danny's hat and gloves, Daniel, the adult, realized that he was at least ten years older than his mother was at the time of this incident.

"*Mom…*" he whispered as she turned her attention back to the boy.

"Now, I told you to ignore your grandparents if you saw them, didn't I?"

Danny nodded.

"And you didn't obey me, did you?"

"I'm sorry," he whispered. "I thought—"

Theresa spit in his face.

Daniel felt his right hand curl reflexively into a fist. This was a moment from his childhood that he had never forgotten. It had provided his first glimpse into his mother's true colors. Beyond frightened, he remembered feeling intimidated and, in a strange way, even violated.

"No, you didn't think, Danny! That's your problem! Instead, you ruined my Christmas, you little bastard! As punishment for your disobedience, I think I'll take all of your gifts back to the store. You get nothing this year."

Theresa grabbed the boy by his hair and flung him toward the stairs to the second floor. "Now get out of my sight."

Danny began to weep as he climbed the steps. Making his way into the bathroom, he washed his face and hands and tried to calm himself. He took a few deep breaths before crossing the narrow hall to his bedroom. There, he sat atop his bed, back against the scratched, worn headboard. It was a used bed, old and rickety, donated by one of his elderly aunts or uncles. After a few minutes, he slid under the covers, all the while staring at the small wooden crucifix that hung over his bedroom door. Even at his age, it had become a symbol of hope and protection through every one of life's crises.

And for his age, he had already been through far too many of those.

"Dan."

Hearing nothing, his gaze remained fixed on the iron crucifix as the limousine passed the tall gates of Holy Trinity Cemetery.

"I was right there with them," he muttered. "My grandparents, my mother, but they didn't see me."

"Dan?"

With a start, Daniel turned his head away from the window to face Vicki. Eyes wide, he reached down and grasped her hand as he fought through a cloud of disorientation and brought himself back to the present.

Vicki frowned. She had never seen him this way. "Are you all right?"

He paused, speaking slowly. "I…don't…know."

"Sorry, guess that *was* a stupid question."

Daniel sighed. "No, I…I just wish I had a better answer."

A short time later, after the last of the mourners walked off to gather in clusters near their cars, Daniel was left alone beside his mother's casket. Around the perimeter of the lid was a carving of flowers on a twisting vine. Daniel absentmindedly ran his fingers over a section of it as he glanced up at the headstones surrounding him, the trees that lined the edges of the cemetery and the overcast sky above.

"I really was sorry," he whispered.

Following the funeral, Paul and his wife, Emily, hosted a brunch at their home several miles outside the city. Daniel had never been there before. In fact, it had been so long since he was in contact with his family that he had never met Paul's youngest two children until today. 'Children' was hardly the word to describe them, as none of Daniel's cousins were under twenty-one.

During the first hour of the gathering, Daniel found himself fielding a barrage of questions regarding his travels after college, his position as mayor, and life in general. Though he prefaced his response by acknowledging Port Kirkland's ranking as the third most impoverished town along Virginia's eastern shore, he was nevertheless proud of his role in reducing that standing from first place. He went onto explain that much of the credit for that achievement was due to the opening of Harlan Industries' packaging and distribution center, managed by Vicki.

To Daniel's gratitude, most of the attention then turned to her along with curious inquiries as to their relationship. It was also at that moment when Paul, a few beers in him by that time, extricated Daniel from the gaggle of family gossip and stories of yesteryear by offering a tour of the house. His uncle's demeanor was markedly different under the influence of alcohol. Any reticence toward candor was cast aside, which Daniel found amusing—at first.

"Good to hear you're doing well," Paul commented when they eventually reached a spare bedroom that had been converted into an office. They each took seats on opposing sides of his uncle's desk. "You certainly got a little hottie there, eh? Good show, ol' chap."

Daniel smiled thinly as he nodded. "Yeah, Vicki's wonderful, especially for putting up with me."

"Well, some guys have all the luck, right?" With glazed eyes, Paul turned to peer through the window at some point in the distance before taking another sip of beer from his fourth bottle since the brunch began. Daniel suspected that he'd had a few in him even before the funeral.

"Listen," his uncle continued finally. As he spoke, he began peeling bits of label from the bottle, a task made easier by the condensation covering the glass. "I wanted to talk to you, you know, about your mom. I'm sorry that you two didn't get a chance to clear things up before she died."

"Yeah, well, I'll deal with that in my own way, thanks." Daniel shrugged and replied in a casual tone that he hoped would dismiss the topic quickly. It did not.

"I know how she could be," Paul continued, slurred words running together at times. "It really didn't surprise any one of us when she forebidded…foreboded…wouldn't let us tell you about her cancer. That came from the same old vindictive streak she's had for like…thirty years, man."

Daniel remained silent. He wasn't sure how to respond and felt that Paul had more to say. He was correct, although he soon wished that he weren't.

"Theresa could be difficult to talk to," Paul droned on, shaking his head for effect. "She was so closed-minded. I can't imagine what it was like to be raised by her."

The conversation was taking a turn that was quickly bringing Daniel beyond his comfort zone. He felt that his uncle was attempting to manipulate him so as to elicit a specific response. With casual aplomb, he tried to block that road.

"We had our moments," Daniel said simply. "Like any other normal parent-child relationship."

Paul laughed derisively. "*Normal*?" He swallowed another mouthful of beer and pointed at Daniel. "She had serious emotional problems, ya know. The entire family knew she was in need of psychiatric help. When she was sixteen, our parents wanted to commit her, ya know, to a mental hospital. Put her away. I said no. I defended her, told them that Theresa needed a chance, ya know, to grow out of it. I figured it was just a phase."

Paul shook his head and frowned. "Your mom stayed high-strung all her life. She forced arguments with almost every one of us at one time or another. Every time something went wrong in her life, she took it out on everyone else. Christ, she held grudges for years. I can only imagine what she did to you as a kid. Ya know, easy prey."

Daniel rose from his seat and leaned across the desk. "I just buried my mother today, Paul. I understand you had issues with her long before I was born but whatever happened back then, I really don't care. *Today*, I'd appreciate it if you showed some respect."

"We heard about some of the things she did to you, ya know," Paul droned on, unfazed by Daniel's brimming anger. "You seemed to turn out okay but I can only imagine she must have fucked you up bad in here." He tapped a finger against the side of his head.

With that, a line had been crossed. With a fury he had not felt in twenty years, Daniel reached out, grabbed his uncle by the shirt and dragged him across the desk. He dropped Paul to the floor, resisting the urge to kick him in the ribs.

"Shut your mouth, you fuckin' alcoholic!" Daniel seethed. "Why don't we talk about how many times you beat your wife? I heard all about that over the years, you bastard!"

By this time, Vicki appeared in the doorway. After a moment's pause to survey the scene, she dashed into the room and stepped in front of Daniel.

"We should go," she urged. "Now."

Paul clumsily picked himself up from the floor. "Yeah, she fucked you up real good. Like mother, like son. Get outta here 'fore I kick your ass, little punk."

Daniel stepped around Vicki. "Let's take a walk outside then, tough guy. We'll finish this right now."

"She was a sick bitch and you know it," Paul growled.

Vicki placed her hands on Daniel's shoulders and began steering him toward the door. Before leaving, he turned to face Paul a final time. "Your brother, Kurt, did one thing right."

"What's that, asshole?"

"When he and Rose eloped to Florida, he turned his back on this pathetic excuse for a family," Daniel explained. "I did the same thing fourteen years ago and I was better off for it. You won't see me again."

Vicki followed Daniel for a few miles south along Interstate 97 before he pulled off at the first exit and found a small diner. After parking, Daniel unclipped his seatbelt, leaned back, and closed his eyes. Less than a minute later, there was a knock on the driver's side window. Without opening his eyes, Daniel pressed the button on the door console to lower the window.

"Are you all right?" Vicki asked as she reached in and placed a hand over his.

Daniel sighed. "Much better now, thanks. I just needed to put some distance between me and…that place."

"Understood."

There was a moment of silence, after which Daniel opened his eyes and looked at her. "Are *you* okay?

Vicki nodded. "I just never saw you that angry before. It actually scared the hell out of me at first."

Daniel lowered his gaze to the steering wheel. "Scared me, too. I don't know why I didn't walk away sooner. He's apparently an ass when he's drunk. Still, it wasn't worth letting him get to me. I haven't exploded like that in years. I almost felt like…someone else. I don't know…"

"Well, considering the circumstances..."

"It doesn't matter, it's over now," he continued before kissing the back of Vicki's hand. "Are you hungry? We didn't get the chance to eat much back there and family fights are always good for working up an appetite."

Chapter Three

Relics

The following morning found Daniel standing in the middle of Caroline Street in the Fell's Point section of downtown Baltimore peering up at an intensely bright red and yellow sign above the door to Crazy Carla's Comics and Collectibles Corner. According to the hours listed, the shop would not open for another forty-five minutes, which suited Daniel just fine. By that time, his business here would be concluded with ample time to spare for perusing the toys, comic books and games that provided an eye-catching display just inside the store's picture window. He was also curious to discover if Carla was truly as crazy as the sign so vibrantly bragged.

The true reason for his visit resided above the colorful shop. Daniel lifted his gaze to the building's second floor where a much more conservative sign indicated the office of Barry Fishman, Attorney at Law. He couldn't help but to smirk as he shook his head. *Storefront lawyer. That figures. This just gets better by the day.*

He pressed the top doorbell situated between the green wooden door of the comic book store and the steel door to the right that presumably led upstairs. He waited only a few moments before a woman's voice greeted him from the call box.

"Hi, this is Daniel Masenda, I had a nine o'clock with Mr. Fishman."

"Come on up."

Daniel yanked open the buzzing door with a sigh and climbed the steep, carpeted stairwell. Framed newspaper articles adorned the eggshell white walls on both sides, but Daniel spared them little attention as he ascended to the small square landing. To his left, a glass door bearing the same lettering as the gray and blue sign outside opened freely.

He approached the secretary's desk and introduced himself to the burly woman. Her brown beady eyes regarded him with a measure of annoyance. Daniel assumed that this was due to the fact that he was fifteen minutes late.

"Sorry, I got a little turned around once I got off eighty-three," he explained sheepishly.

She merely nodded toward the open door to the right of her desk. "You can go right in."

Daniel thanked her quietly before making his way toward the lawyer's office. He tapped lightly on the door and leaned in. The bespectacled middle-aged man behind the desk turned to face him.

"Yes, Mr. Masenda, I presume." Barry Fishman rose from his seat and extended a hand as Daniel entered.

"Mr. Fishman, sorry I'm late."

"Not a problem. Call me Barry."

The two men shook hands before Fishman motioned Daniel toward one of the two chairs flanking a small round conference table.

"I blocked off an hour for you but I doubt I'll keep you that long."

In a white polo shirt and jeans, the older man appeared all but out of place in the large, plush office of mahogany and leather furniture. Daniel estimated that the office occupied about half of what the store directly below used for retail space.

"Beautiful day out there," Fishman said as he paged through a thin manila folder. "I actually have no court appearances today so I'm playing it casual for a change." He tugged at the front of his shirt. "Might even cut out of here early and hit Camden Yards. The Orioles are playing this afternoon. OK, before we begin I need to see two forms of identification with at least one showing a photo."

"Sure." Daniel reached inside his jacket and produced his wallet. "How about two photos?" He handed both his driver's license and employee badge to the lawyer who then excused himself to make photocopies.

Daniel took the opportunity to inspect the impressive row of elegantly framed law degrees and certificates that lined the wall, extending from the desk to the conference table. Surely such an accomplished attorney could manage better than a storefront office.

"So what do you do for the township of Port Kirkland?" Fishman inquired as he slipped the copies into the manila folder and placed Daniel's identifications on the table before him. The man had a slightly whiny voice that grated on Daniel's nerves. "Mind you, I'm not at all familiar with the place."

"I'm the mayor," Daniel replied simply as he slipped the cards back into his wallet.

"Really?" The lawyer raised an eyebrow as he took the opposite seat. "Your family never mentioned that part. So, a politician, eh? How long have you been in office?"

"Just started my second term."

"So that means they either like you or there was no competition."

Daniel grinned. "A little of both. My last opponent was a lawyer."

"Ouch!" Fishman chuckled. "Please, say no more! That's why I stay out of politics. OK, two things here. First, let me express my condolences on your loss. I knew your mom for about six years. I represented her when she sustained the injury at her last apartment and we were able to settle out of court to her satisfaction. So, after her diagnosis was confirmed late last year, she came back to me to handle her will."

Daniel held up a hand. "I'm sorry to interrupt. Can you tell me a little about this injury?"

Fishman hesitated. "You didn't know about that?"

"Well…she and I…um," Daniel stammered in search of a vague excuse. When none came to mind quickly, he resorted to the truth—partially. "We hadn't spoken for a number of years, let's put it that way."

The other man nodded. "Sorry to hear that. Say no more, I understand how it can be with family, believe me. Anyway, Theresa broke her right ankle when she fell down steps that were in extreme disrepair; frayed carpet, rotted wood, the whole nine yards. Maintenance and management had been informed numerous times about it and did nothing. Tell you what, it was fixed real quick after we settled.

"Anyway, back to the here and now, what I have for you is an envelope containing two items. The first is a life insurance check for twenty thousand dollars payable to you as the beneficiary. I'll need you to sign a form acknowledging receipt of this."

As he spoke, Fishman unclasped the flap of the envelope and removed the check. He handed it to Daniel who took it gingerly and stared at it for a moment before returning it to the lawyer.

"Thank you," he said quietly. "What's the second thing?"

Fishman turned the envelope upside down above his cupped hand and shook it until a small brass key fell into this palm. He held it up for Daniel to see. "The key to your mom's apartment. The address and apartment number are also in this envelope. I'm sure you have that information already but just in case, it's here."

He slipped the check and key back into the envelope and sealed it. "The apartment manager is Sandra Merrick," Fishman explained as he pushed the envelope across the desk to Daniel. "She's expecting a call from you within the next day or two. I realize that this is a difficult time for you, Dan, but your mother's apartment needs to be cleaned out by the end of the week."

Later that day, Daniel made two phone calls from a café in Baltimore's Harborplace Mall. The first was to the apartment manager, Sandra, and the second was to Bruce who met Daniel the next morning at the U-Haul shop in Dundalk before following him to the apartment complex.

The morning passed quickly and after three hours without a break, the two men filled the moving truck with furniture, clothing and various boxes of 'stuff' — all of the detritus that accrues in the span of a lifetime. Daniel counted himself fortunate that the apartment building's dumpster had been emptied the day before. He said as much to Bruce.

"Well, at least it ain't the middle of August," his friend commented as he lit up a Marlboro. "I'd be sweating my ass off by now. You should have warned me your mom was a pack rat."

Daniel chuckled. "Yeah, I forgot about that. Amazing how some things never change. This is nothing compared to the house I grew up in. Before their divorce, my parents had a four-bedroom ranch. Afterwards, my mother moved into a two-bedroom row home. The front bedroom should have been hers; instead it was a storage room. Half the stuff should have been sold or thrown out but she wouldn't hear of it. Instead she slept on a sofa-bed in the living room for almost twenty years."

Bruce shook his head in disbelief but remained respectfully silent.

Daniel tossed the keys to him. "Why don't you park the truck out of the way? I'll take out the rest of the trash and turn the key into the office. Then we can hit the road. I want to put some miles between me and this place."

"You sure you don't want help?"

"No, take a break. You earned a free dinner today. I'll finish this myself."

Eight bags of trash and a dozen boxes later, the apartment was finally empty. For Daniel, it had been an uncomfortable, almost morbid, chore. He slid the side door of the dumpster closed, glad to be nearly finished. He reached into his pocket for the apartment key when his cell phone buzzed. Pulling it from his belt, he flipped it open as he started back toward the building. It was Vicki.

"Hey, gorgeous," he answered.

"How goes it?"

Daniel sighed. "Exhausting, but over with. I'm about to turn the key into management, then we're on our way to the self-storage near home. We might be awhile unloading. It'll be a helluva yard sale next month."

"Have you thought about dinner?"

"Only for the past hour. Someplace nice like Skipper's by the boardwalk or maybe Bertram's?"

"Bertram's is pricy."

"It's my treat."

"Bertram's it is!"

Daniel smiled. As he neared the front door of the building, he passed beneath the third floor windows of his mother's former apartment.

"Do you need help at the self-storage?" Vicki offered.

He was about to answer when he glanced up at the window. For a moment, the world around him seemed to halt. He stepped back from the building for a clearer view. He glanced over at the moving truck. Behind the wheel, Bruce sat with his head lowered, cap pulled down over his eyes. Slowly, Daniel turned back to face the window.

The boy stared down at him.

The same boy from the mirror in Daniel's dream the night his mother died. The same boy from his vision at her funeral.

That is not *me. He looks like me but it can't be me, just like that disgusting face in the mirror. They're not real. Oh, Christ, I'm hallucinating.*

"Dan, are you still there?" Vicki's distant voice beckoned from the phone.

His gaze fixed upon the window, he raised the phone to his ear. "He's in the apartment…"

"Who? Bruce?"

"I'll call you right back."

He closed the phone and dashed into the lobby. An elderly couple was just entering one of the two elevators and the other was being held up on the sixth floor. Daniel bolted for the stairwell and within a minute, found himself fumbling for the key in front of the apartment door. He thrust it into the lock and pushed the door open. He looked to the window to see the blinds lowered and closed, just as he left them.

He rounded the corner to the bedroom and nearly collided with the apartment manager. With a start, Daniel reeled back then closed his eyes and exhaled in relief.

"Sorry," the older lady said. "I thought you were finished so I came up to double check and found this."

She handed him a tattered, over-stuffed legal folder. Gingerly, Daniel turned it over in his hands. Instantly, memories thought long forgotten surfaced once more—courtrooms, lawyers, lies and accusations.

"I'm sorry about your mother," the manager said softly. "She was a good tenant. Very polite and thoughtful of her neighbors."

Daniel nodded. "Thank you."

With that, he turned over the key and departed, never looking back.

"You were quiet at dinner."

In one of the smaller upstairs bedrooms that had been converted into a home office, Daniel sat and stared at the dark tan folder atop his desk.

"Sorry," he replied softly as Vicki dropped into the small sofa along the opposite wall.

"You don't need to apologize, I'm just concerned about you." She nodded toward the folder. "So what's that?"

"Paperwork." Daniel ran a finger along the top of it, clearing a line of dust. He brushed his hands on his jeans. "About twelve years worth of legal documents including divorce papers, custody, alimony, and child support. My mom kept it all in here. It's bizarre to see this again. A partial history of my life contained in a worn, dusty folder."

"What's that writing on the back?"

Daniel spun the folder around and laughed. "Wow, I forgot about that. I wrote my mother's name on this when I was about six. I guess I figured that since parents were always writing their kids' names on everything they carried to school, I thought I would return the favor."

Vicki smiled. "That's cute."

"My mother didn't exactly see the humor in it," Daniel explained somberly.

A moment of silence passed between them before Vicki asked if he intended to open the folder.

Daniel shrugged. "It's tempting, but I think taking Memory Lane would be a wrong turn right now. Funny though, staring at this relic now, I'm reminded of a friend I had years ago that told me about this interesting exercise he devised for dealing with the past. He believed that if you had a physical object, like a letter or a picture, that reminded you of a dark time in your life, you should burn it."

"Really?" Vicki asked curiously. "Why not just toss it in the trash?"

"Well, he called it 'catharsis by fire'. The idea was that as the item burned, you imagine all of the bad memories and feelings to be carried away with the smoke, thereby releasing the pain associated with them."

Vicki raised an eyebrow. Ever the pragmatist, she snickered at the notion. "Sounds appealing but somehow I don't think it's that easy to let go of emotional baggage."

"I know," Daniel concurred. "But there's no place in my life for these anymore."

As did others in the neighborhood, Daniel had a burning barrel in his backyard for incinerating certain types of trash such as outdated financial records or other confidential documents. It had been left by the previous owners, who used it frequently. However, shortly after Daniel had moved in, the township imposed a burning ban that had been conveniently lifted only two days ago with his approval.

Daniel opened the folder and dumped its contents into the barrel. He lit a match and touched it to one corner of the folder. When it began burning to his satisfaction, he dropped it onto the pile of envelopes and folded papers.

He watched with curiosity as the flames slowly spread over the once important documents. Smoke began ascending from the barrel and Daniel closed his eyes, imaging the dark memories of those years floating away until they were no longer visible to his mind's eye and no longer relevant to him or anyone else. He drew distinct comfort from the latter, knowing that those days were long over and could no longer cause him pain.

With eyes remaining firmly closed, Daniel failed to notice the increasing volume of smoke, more than should have been generated by such a small amount of paper. A sudden breeze disturbed the air and the smoke swirled into a momentary whirlwind before coalescing into the distinguishable shape of a person. Suddenly, a thin band of the smoke began drifting toward Daniel, like an arm stretching out, slowly reaching. It stopped at his face, touching his cheek.

"Danny…"

It was a whisper, barely audible. So much so that it took Daniel's mind an extra few seconds to acknowledge it and awaken him from his meditation. His eyes snapped open and darted from right to left. He looked over his shoulder to his house to find no one there. There was no one around at all, in fact. The air had become oddly still, almost ominously so, and the smoke had all but diminished.

Daniel peeked inside the barrel to see that almost everything had been incinerated—all but the folder itself which only now was nearly consumed by the dying flames.

The last part to burn was the childish writing of "*THERESA*."

Chapter Four

Explanations

Flower baskets continued to appear on Daniel's doorstep for a few days following Theresa's funeral and sympathy cards trickled in as more friends and staff members learned of his loss. After nearly a week, however, all condolences ceased, which was why he was now surprised to find himself staring at the largest and most colorful bouquet yet.

Rotating it slowly atop his kitchen counter, Daniel recognized roses, carnations and a type of lily. The rest, while beautiful, were unfamiliar. Finally, he discovered the small white envelope tucked into the plastic prongs of its holder.

His heart skipped a beat as he read the card.

My thoughts and prayers are with you and always have been. —Love, Miranda

There was a phone number at the bottom followed by *Call me.*

Daniel read it twice before slipping the card into his shirt pocket. His first impulse was to pick up the phone that instant, but he resisted. Before calling her, he needed time to collect his thoughts. More importantly, he wanted to prepare an explanation for why he left without saying goodbye fourteen years ago, just in case the subject came up. There was no doubt in his mind that she was well past that by now. Still, it was a situation that needed closure. Perhaps no explanation would suffice and any attempts would probably come across as patronizing. Then, of course, there would be the inevitable reminiscing, the "remember whens", the intrusions of the past onto a present that wanted no part of it. No, Daniel couldn't think clearly enough right now to speak to her, maybe tomorrow. It's been fourteen years, another day won't hurt.

Besides, as of late he was far too preoccupied. Mirrors and other reflective surfaces continued their hideous reflections, some days more than others. As a result he shaved only when he could tolerate them. The nightmares of his childhood still disturbed his sleep on random nights and he had become dependent upon Vicki's company to help distract him from it all.

In fact, Vicki would be here within the hour and he had to change before they went out for the evening. Daniel resolved to call Miranda tomorrow.

Two days passed before Daniel worked up the nerve to make the call. Apprehension and excitement swirled through his stomach as he dialed her number.

"Hello?"

Fourteen years!

"Hi, I'm looking for Miranda?"

"You found her."

That sweet, airy voice. She sounds almost the same!

In the background, Daniel could hear children's voices and a television that was clearly increasing in volume, forcing his voice to do the same.

"Miranda, hi! It's Dan…Masenda."

"Danny! Wow…hey, can I call you right back?"

"Uh, sure." He recited his phone number after which she thanked him and hung up.

It was certainly not the reception he had expected. Bemused, Daniel stared at the phone in his hand before pressing the off button. He reached over to the antique end table and started fiddling with the foil wrapping on the bouquet sent by Miranda.

Perhaps he should keep the conversation brief, or would that make him seem disinterested? It was probably wise not to broach the subject of their relationship. It was so long ago, after all. *Water under the bridge, right?*

He knew that she had married about eight years ago and from the sound of things, had children. Thus, there was no value in re-treading old ground. Yes, the shorter the better.

The phone rang.

Four hours later, Daniel was still on the phone. It had turned out to be quite a lively and diverse exchange covering life, death, friends old and new, careers, depression, hopes, dreams, successes and failures, marriage and divorce—specifically Miranda's. She and her husband had made their separation legal just after the beginning of the year, staying together long enough to give their three children a happy Christmas.

Miranda's tone brightened when she spoke of them. Andrea was the oldest followed two years later by identical twins Jake and Nathan. She seemed genuinely happy for Daniel when he talked about Vicki and congratulated him on his election to mayor. It was nearly midnight when conversation ran dry.

"Before I let you go," Daniel said. "I wanted to see if you'd be interested in visiting our little shore town sometime? I'd advise sooner rather than later. The summer crowd can get obnoxious."

Miranda paused. "Well, next Saturday, Brian is taking the kids to Maine for a week for Andrea's birthday. They rented a cottage near Boothbay Harbor."

"I think we can top Boothbay Harbor."

There was a brief silence. "Well, I don't have any concrete plans that weekend, so what the hell! Recommend any hotels?"

"I have plenty of crash space here."

"Are you sure Vicki would be comfortable with that?" Miranda asked. "I wouldn't want to be the cause of scandal for the mayor!"

Daniel grinned. "Please, this town could use some controversy. No worries. I'll talk to her tomorrow. I'm sure she'll be fine with it. Look for my email with directions and just let me know what time you think you might get here and we'll go from there."

They wished one another a good night before hanging up.

Daniel exhaled as he stared at the phone for a moment longer. "Wow," he breathed. He climbed the stairs to the second floor. A small stack of mail had accumulated atop his desk since Theresa's funeral. The more important items were opened immediately while the rest remained ignored until time and mood permitted.

His conversation with Miranda left him feeling more energized than he had felt in days. Maybe the darkness that loomed over him was beginning to dissipate. If so, he didn't want to invite it back through inactivity. He began sifting through the pile of mail.

Almost halfway through, Daniel began considering the fate of the rain forests as he tossed several credit card and loan offers into the trash followed by a subscription renewal notice intended for the previous owner of his house. Finally, he came to an envelope that immediately drew his curiosity. It was handwritten, completely unfamiliar and barely legible, causing him to wonder how it even reached him. There was no return address. Inside was a one-page typed letter, signed at the bottom in the same scrawl as that on the envelope. Daniel began reading.

Then the blood rushed from his face.

While spring had officially begun two weeks ago, this clement Saturday afternoon provided the first sign of winter's welcome departure. Several shops along the boardwalk were opening for the first time this season, mainly restaurants and concession stands. The amusement park would remain closed for another month. As such, that section of the boardwalk was all but deserted save for the young couple seated at a small table in front of an ice cream stand.

Daniel and Vicki sat in close conversation, pausing only for spoonfuls from large cups of custard. After a few minutes of small talk, Daniel reached into his shirt pocket and produced a folded sheet of paper.

"This came yesterday." He held it up for a moment before pushing it across the table to Vicki.

"What's this?" she asked as she unfolded the paper.

"A letter from my father. He wants to meet me somewhere and 'clear up' matters regarding the past."

Vicki was astonished. "How did he find you?"

"Same way my uncle Paul did, through the alumni directory published by my college. Apparently, he has a friend who graduated from there over thirty years ago and looked me up in his directory." He sighed and shook his head. "I knew I shouldn't have sent them my contact info."

There was a long pause as Vicki read the letter. Daniel took the opportunity to finish his custard and toss the empty cup into a nearby trashcan.

Finally, she glanced at him curiously. "Are you going to meet him? Do you think he knows that your mom passed away?"

Daniel shrugged. "Possibly. He could've easily read her obituary in the paper." He exhaled tiredly and turned to gaze at the waves tumbling over the beach.

"More water under the bridge," he muttered.

"I'm taking a shot in the dark here but do you think you can trust anything he says?"

He pondered the answer for a moment, fighting the instinctive urge to say no. "I suppose I won't know until I talk to him. He did some terrible things to my mom and me after their divorce. He was a monster. I can't imagine any explanation that would just excuse all of that away."

"Sounds like you already have your mind made up."

"I've had twenty five years to think about it."

Vicki nodded her understanding. She seemed to sense the delicateness of the situation. Still, she pressed on. "Sorry, I'm just playing devil's advocate. Maybe he's changed and he finally wants you to know his side of the story."

Daniel did not reply. Instead, he peered silently at a spot on the table.

Reaching across to him, Vicki grasped his hand. "You never really told me much about your family. I just want to help if I can."

Daniel looked at her and in that moment knew precisely how lucky he truly was. The sun had descended beyond the amusement rides and was casting an orange radiance across the boardwalk. The light played across Vicki's hair and face and the effect was dazzling. She was the most beautiful woman to come into Daniel's life and he marveled at how deeply she cared for him.

A voice in the back of his mind pleaded with him to tell her about his bizarre experiences, starting with the mysterious ghostly boy, the scarred and bloody reflections that haunted him from every mirror, even the visions at his mother's funeral. Daniel suppressed the urge to reveal these things to Vicki all at once. She wasn't the type to believe in the paranormal and he feared her reaction. *It's too soon*, he told himself. *Maybe later.*

Rather, he preferred to lead up to it gently. He thought it better first to impart certain select details of his family history. He smiled and took her hand in his. "Walk with me."

"I always felt sorry for my mother," Daniel began, as he and Vicki strolled along the beach hand in hand. On the horizon, the sun began setting over the bay adding pastels of orange and pink to the drifting clouds. "She never had the life she deserved and it took a very costly toll on her emotionally. Her parents were of an old-school mentality where the sons were favored over the daughters. For years, she held a grudge against them for sending her brothers to college but not her. Women were expected to be secretaries or housewives.

"Then along came my father who shared that same mindset and treated her like a second class citizen. I can't imagine what she saw in him other than an escape from her parents. In the end, it was anything but. She admitted years later that she went from the frying pan into the fire with him.

"I can't say exactly when things started to go wrong between them but I do know that he wanted nothing to do with me when I was little. He hated kids; thought that raising them was the woman's job. One of my earliest memories is of my mom literally shoving him in my direction and ordering him to spend time with me. I must've been no more than three but I'll never forget that.

"About a year later, their marriage exploded. Their arguments grew more frequent and then it got physical when my dad started beating my mom, or tried to. She could defend herself pretty well. I don't remember much from back then but there were a few ugly scenes before they finally called it quits."

Daniel shook his head. "Bottom line is that they never should've been married in the first place."

"Then you wouldn't be here," Vicki said, playfully leaning into him. "And *we* wouldn't be here."

"Always the optimist." Daniel smiled wanly. "Unfortunately, my mom wasn't really able to handle being a single parent. Whenever she got angry with me as a kid, she always told me that she wished I were never born. After awhile, I began to agree with her. When I was fourteen, she finally told me that I was an accident. Later on, I attempted suicide a few times. The only reason I'm still here is that I was too much of a coward to go through with it."

He glanced out to the surf and sighed. "Whatever, that was another place, another time. It's all behind me now and obviously, my life's a lot better, especially since a certain young lady showed up."

"Oh, who?" Vicki asked in mock surprise. "Didn't I tell you that I was a jealous type?"

"Just some crazy broad I happen to be in love with."

"Hmmm, well I suppose that's okay."

Daniel rolled his eyes and smiled. He stopped walking and drew her close. "Look, I'm sorry if I'm bringing you down with all of this. That's why I never talked about it—"

Vicki placed a finger on his lips. "Stop. I asked you to open up to me and you did. With your mom passing and your dad writing to you out of the blue, I can definitely see how all these bad memories are being stirred up right now. I just want to be here for you. I'm sorry that you went through all of that."

"You don't know the half of it but that's enough about me for one day."

She hesitated for a moment. Daniel caught it and tilted his head. "Question?"

"Well, I couldn't help but to overhear what your uncle Paul was saying to you after your mother's funeral. He mentioned something about what your mother did to *you*. What was that about?"

Daniel waved a dismissive hand. "Ignore him, he was drunk. Besides, he never got along with my mom anyway. In fact, after her divorce, there were very few times when her family gave her any support at all. They treated her like an outcast."

"Why didn't you know about her cancer?"

His eyes seemed to glaze over as he looked away. "Well, we…hadn't spoken since I graduated from college. She and I had issues, many of which were never resolved, but that's a story for another time."

Vicki held up her hands. "I'm not trying to push. I was just curious."

Daniel shrugged. "Some of it's surprisingly easy to talk about, just strange considering that I haven't really thought about any of it for years. Time has faded the emotions but not the memories.

"As for my dad showing up again like this, I do have some scores to settle with him. There was this one time in college when my mom was suing him for financial assistance because he refused to provide it on his own, as usual. In response, we received a letter from his lawyer in which my dad was quoted as calling me a 'marginal student'.

"Even though I wrote him off years before, that comment really hit me hard. I admit the problems between my mother and me affected my grades during a semester or two but he judged me solely on that. What bothered me the most was when I realized that he hated me as much as he hated my mom."

"He didn't understand what my life at home was like. He didn't know what I was going through and I thought that if I had the chance to explain, he might understand. I don't know why but even after he cut me out of his life when I was ten, I still felt that I owed the bastard an explanation."

Vicki held up the letter from Gary. "Seems like now is a good opportunity. Not that you owe him anything but you might feel better and the fact that he contacted you makes me think that he has some explaining of his own. If nothing else, it may bring closure."

Daniel nodded and took the letter. "There was one oth-"

"I need to tell you-" Vicki began at the same moment. They shared a quiet laugh before Daniel signaled for her to start.

"I'm leaving for Singapore in two days."

The news caught Daniel off-guard. He looked toward the horizon for a moment. When he looked back at Vicki, he spoke with forced enthusiasm. "Oh.... So your dad's company is moving forward with the new site?"

Vicki nodded. "I'll be gone for four days, possibly five. If prospects look good and we get the green light, I'll probably return for a longer duration."

"How much longer, roughly speaking?"

She paused. "Could be a month or longer. Believe me, I'm not looking forward to the traveling and I know the timing sucks. I wanted to be here for you while you're dealing with all of these family—"

"I'll be fine." Daniel waved a dismissive hand. "Do what you have to do. If it turns out that you're away for a month, we'll manage. I know how important this project is for you."

"It could mean a huge bonus at the end of the year if all goes well. Singapore is a lucrative market right now. There's talk of India being next. An extraordinary number of industries have opened operations there. It's like the new China. I can't believe how much the business has grown in the past six years."

"Right..." Daniel replied softly.

"Sorry, I'm rambling. You had something you wanted to tell me?"

He shrugged. "Seems to have slipped my mind."

Chapter Five

Excuses

Mirrors were now the enemy.

Until this morning, Daniel had learned to endure the unsightly 'thing'—for that was what he had come to label it in his mind— and finally convinced himself with complete certainty that it was *not*, in fact, his reflection but some paranormal doppelganger sent to torment him.

He had tried talking to it. At first he had asked, then later demanded, *why*. Why are you here? What's your connection to my mother's death? Are you and the boy both one in the same entity?

What do you want from me?

There was never an answer, of course, only the sinking fear that he was taking leave of his faculties. Still, he held onto a sliver of hope that he would soon unravel the mystery behind this sadistic ordeal.

That hope was quickly fading.

For the past two days since he received his father's letter, the "thing" became even more unbearable to look at. A continuous stream of dark blood flowed from the nose and lower lip, which was split open by a gash. More blood hemorrhaged in what were the whites of both eyes. Worse, bruises were now evident on the arms, shoulders, and back of its body. That was a new development as all injuries has previously been confined to its face.

It had been more than Daniel could take. Armed with a box of lawn and leaf bags and two rolls of blue masking tape, he took one last look at the wretched sight in the mirrored doors of his bedroom closet.

For some reason, Daniel felt compelled to say something more to the thing, to give it one last chance to divulge its purpose. Instead, he yanked a black trash bag from the box, tore off two lengths of tape and went to work. After covering both doors, he proceeded to the adjoining bedroom, opened up another bag and placed it over a mirror attached to an antique oak dresser.

Downstairs in the living room, Daniel removed the decorative oval mirror that hung above two small bookcases and slipped it behind his sofa along the opposite wall. As he made his way down the hall toward the guest bedroom, Daniel paused outside the bathroom and poked his head in. Glancing at the mirror above the vanity, he sighed. *Nah, I never go in there.* He waved a hand dismissively and backed out of the doorway.

A moment later, he returned, trash bag and tape in hand. "Screw it," he muttered.

One hour and seven bags later, every mirror in the house had either been covered or removed.

"What're ya gonna do now, mother fucker?" Daniel called out to the thing. "Now what are ya lookin' at?!"

He looked up at the clock in his office as he ran a hand through his disheveled hair. "*Damn*!" He whispered. Somehow, he had lost track of time and he certainly didn't want to be late. As he entered the master bathroom, he ran his fingers over the three-day growth covering his face. Truth be told, Daniel hated facial hair, yet he dreaded what he knew he'd be forced to endure for a simple shave.

He had covered all but the mirror in the master bathroom, where he now stood. Taking deep breaths to calm his nerves, he began lathering his face with shaving cream. Running the razor over the stubble of his mustache nearly made him vomit as the "thing" mocked his movement. In the mirror, blood mixed with white cream and streaked down over its mouth, dripping from its chin.

That's what I get for being cocky.

He would not have subjected himself to this torture where he not meeting his father at Lynnhaven Mall in Virginia Beach later this afternoon. He wanted to look his best, or as reasonably close as possible under the circumstances, not merely to impress Gary but also for the sake of his job. It simply would not do to have the mayor look like hell in public no matter what the reason.

If only they could see what I see. Hell is exactly *where I am.*

Daniel had called Gary the following day after receiving his letter. His wife, Dana, had answered and was just as cold to him as she had been over twenty-five years ago. He was glad to know that some things never change. The feeling was mutual. Finally, she turned the phone over to Gary and with little small talk they made the arrangements.

Here and now, he managed to finish shaving without losing his breakfast, draped a hand towel over the mirror and stepped into the shower. Letting the warm water flow over his shoulders and back, Daniel mentally reviewed the unlikely events of the past week beginning with the nightmare on the very night that his mother died, the pursuant visions in mirrors and windows, and now the reemergence of people that he hadn't seen in over a decade or more. Surely, the odds against all of these events occurring all at once were staggering.

And now Vicki was on her way to the other side of the world.

Just getting better by the day.

Daniel realized that he had let his mind wander and brought his thoughts back to the here and now. Stepping out of the shower, he noticed that the hand towel had fallen from the mirror and the glass was completely covered in condensation. Picking up the towel, he wiped only the top third of the mirror, revealing his scalp and forehead just enough so that he could effectively comb his hair.

Maybe time for an early summer cut, Daniel mused. *Nice and short.*

Anything to spend less time in the company of the "thing".

He spent the rest of the morning considering what he would say to Gary, the myriad of questions, the man's possible responses, and Daniel's counter replies. With a wry grin, he realized that he was preparing for this meeting as he would a political debate.

Yet politics would not be the topic of today's conversation, but rather a subject deeply personal and potentially volatile. Daniel wondered whether he could maintain his composure should the discussion become heated. Under normal circumstances, there would be no question. However, recent days have taken Daniel on a strange and emotionally trying odyssey, forcing him to doubt whether he had truly come to peace with his past.

He looked at the clock. It was time to leave. Virginia Beach wasn't far but Daniel wanted to be the first to arrive at the mall and scout out the food court where they were to meet. Apparently, Gary had planned a two-week vacation in the town when he decided to contact Daniel. Thus, Dana would be with him as well as their daughter, Jill.

Daniel had never met his half sister. By now she would be in her mid twenties. Although he was told of her existence years ago, he had cared very little and had all but forgotten about her until he was reminded during his phone conversation with Gary.

Donning sunglasses and a baseball cap, he made his way down the steps to the laundry room. He reached for the knob to open the door to the garage.

"Don't fail..."

Daniel froze in place, feeling his heart skip a beat. His jaws clenched as he slowly turned to look over his shoulder. The laundry room was empty. The voice had barely been louder than a whisper but discernibly that of a child's. He walked back to the bottom of the staircase and glanced up. Seeing no one, he peeked out through the curtains covering the windows of his front door. An elderly couple walked a golden retriever across the street; two cars passed. All was quiet.

"Whatever," he muttered.

Gary Masenda had re-married five years after his divorce from Theresa. His new wife, Dana, had tolerated Daniel's presence while they were dating. As their relationship matured, however, deliberate efforts were taken to ensure that the boy would become little more than a memory. On weekends that Gary should have spent with his son, Dana had made other plans that intentionally excluded Daniel. Eventually, it had become nearly impossible for Gary to reschedule his weekends with his son, nor would he confront his girlfriend despite her obvious motives.

Dana had even gone so far as to make harassing phone calls to Theresa whenever she tried to negotiate with her ex-husband for an increase in child support. Shortly before Daniel's twelfth birthday, Dana's relentless determination had finally coerced Gary to sever all ties to the baggage of his past. In the end, the termagant had won a landslide victory resulting in a twenty-six year estrangement between father and son.

Now, Daniel peered across the food court, observing a heavyset, balding man who appeared to be the correct age, arrive with his wife and daughter. They carried on a brief conversation before the two women walked off with a wave, leaving the man to sit alone. He took a casual glance at his watch and proceeded to stare at several passersby expectantly.

It was Gary.

Daniel sighed. *This oughta be good.*

He rose from his table and traversed the circular promenade slowly, choosing a direction that allowed him to approach Gary from behind. He stopped alongside the man's chair and looked upon a father that he had not seen since he was ten years old.

Immediately, Gary stood. "Danny…oh my God." He extended a hand.

Daniel looked at it.

"The least you could do is shake your old man's hand," Gary insisted.

Reluctantly, Daniel accepted. There was little amity in the gesture. "It's been a long time since you were *my* old man." He turned away and took a seat at the opposite side of the table.

"You look great," Gary began with forced cheer. "Read about you in the newspaper, Mister Mayor. I was very proud."

Daniel remained silent.

"I also saw your mom's obituary. I'm sorry."

The younger man snorted. "Yeah, I'm sure. Let's get to the point. What do you want?"

"Not a confrontation, let me just make that clear up front," Gary replied earnestly. "I was hoping we could keep this civil."

Daniel shrugged, his tone noncommittal as he replied. "I'll do my best."

"I got this for you." Gary slid a dark blue square envelope across the table. It was obviously a greeting card.

"What's this?"

"Happy Birthday. It *is* today, right?"

Daniel stared at the envelope. "Tomorrow. I'm surprised you remembered at all."

"I never forgot."

"Could've fooled me these past twenty-six years."

Gary sighed, looked away for a moment. "When I wrote to you and asked you to meet with me, don't you think I knew that you probably hated me? All throughout your childhood, you mother took every opportunity to poison you against me—"

Daniel slammed his fist on the table. "You made that all too easy. I still remember when you came to our house to pick me up for our weekends together. There were times when you forced arguments with her, kicked and punched our door, screamed at her through the windows. She was afraid to come out of the house, let alone send me out. You were a monster and *that's* how I remember you."

Gary's jaw clenched as his son spoke. Finally, he held up both hands, palms out. "OK," his voice cracked. "You're right, I could be a real asshole back then, but I never meant to take our problems out on you."

"You mean like the time you kidnapped me for six weeks after your divorce?"

The older man hesitated, fumbling for words. "Now that—"

"Or how about all the times you moved while I was growing up?" Daniel pressed. "You never bothered to tell anyone so you could avoid paying child support. You didn't give a damn if I starved to death in that rundown shit-hole we lived in as long as you and Dana could afford to rent five bedroom homes in plush suburbs."

"If you want an apology, then you got it," Gary relented. "I'm sorry you were the victim of our battles. Look, I came here today to at least try and explain my side of the story. Can you allow me that much?"

Daniel was silent. Gary took that as his cue.

"After your mother and I were married, she started to become verbally abusive. There were times when she would talk down to me, insult me for things that no one else would even have cared about. Petty stuff, ya know? At times, she would scream at me if I didn't agree with her on something. I could do no right by her. It was as if she would go out of her way to find faults or mistakes and shoving them in my face every chance she got. It was like living with a time bomb.

"When we learned she was pregnant, I got scared. I had doubts about our marriage by then and whether I could continue dealing with this vituperative relationship. I tried talking to her about it but she always turned it into a confrontation, blaming me for everything that was wrong in our marriage.

"The first few years after you were born, the situation just deteriorated. I was miserable, I felt trapped. All I wanted to do was get away from her. Toward the end, the arguments turned violent. One time, I was working late, doing some paperwork at the kitchen table. Theresa came in and started ordering me to spend more time with you. I promised her that I would as soon as I was finished. She pulled out a wooden spoon from the drawer and started beating me with it until I went to your room. You weren't even awake, but I stayed in there for hours. I was too scared to come out.

"That was the beginning of the end. Later, I…started hitting her back. That last night we were together was the worst. I don't even recall what the fight was about. She was screeching at the top her lungs. I couldn't tolerate it so I…grabbed her by the throat and shoved her against the kitchen wall. Next thing I know, she slammed me in the head with a vase. I didn't even see her reach for it.

"I ran from the house and drove myself to the hospital. Had to get stitches," Gary waved a hand next to his right temple. "I never went home again until we put the house up for sale.

"I know I was never a model father. Even back then, it was obvious that I wasn't ready to be a parent. I know you paid the price for that in the end but I had no other choice. I had to get out."

Daniel nodded slowly before sitting back in his chair. "When I was eight years old, I saw you drive by our house one morning during the week. Mom and I were leaving for the day, she was driving me to school. You were in a different car than the Honda Civic hatchback you owned at the time. I remember it very well. It was obvious that you were spying on us but at the time, I didn't know why. I told her about it but she didn't believe me.

"A few days later, she received a letter in the mail from your lawyer stating that you were given information that she was working a full time job and as such, you wanted to cease alimony payments. Years later, I wondered how many days were you spying on us?"

Gary lowered his eyes to the table. "I don't remember. It was a long time ago."

"I still remember," Daniel continued. His voice became hoarse and he was beginning to tremble. "You see, she thought your information came from me. She thought I told you during one of our weekends together. I explained that I didn't and I reminded her that I'd seen you drive by that morning but she still didn't believe me. She had it in her head that I betrayed her.

"You can't imagine what she did to me, because of you. She almost fucking killed me."

Tears welled up in Gary's eyes, ran down his face. "I'm sorry, Danny. After I left, I never thought about what it must have been like to be raised by her—"

Daniel leaned in close, pointing an accusing finger at Gary. "You have no fucking clue how I was raised or what I went through with her. Do you know how many times she told me that she wished I was never born? So many times that I began to agree with her, you fucking bastard. I've spent almost my entire life hating you *both*, wishing you *both* dead.

"Then, when I was in college, do you happen to remember what you called me when we had to sue you for financial aid? You called me a 'marginal student'. You had no idea how much that comment pissed me off. You had *no idea* what I had to live with back then, and you had *no idea* because you didn't give a fuck!"

With each sentence, Daniel's voice rose until his last words sent the entire food court into stunned silence. Onlookers gasped as he leapt from his chair and toppled the small table. Gary froze in fear as Daniel lunged toward him, face twisted in hideous rage.

"There's no way in hell you could ever make up for all those years!"

The older man could only shrink away as Daniel knocked him to the floor with a vicious punch to the jaw. The fury that had smoldered for over a quarter century now consumed him with a power that was almost otherworldly, as if being drawn from an unknown source that Daniel never before felt.

"I've waited almost my entire life to do that," he seethed, oblivious to the spectacle he was making of himself. From somewhere behind him, several footsteps were advancing quickly. "Fuck your apologies, you bastard!"

Hands grabbed him by the arms and a face suddenly appeared in front of his. Three security guards pushed and dragged him from the food court while another assisted Gary to his feet.

"You've been outta my life this long," Daniel screamed. "Stay the hell out!"

Two of the guards escorted Daniel outside to the waiting security van while the third turned away to acknowledge a call on his two-way.

"Get your fuckin' hands off me!"

"You *will* calm down, sir, or you *will* be arrested," the third man warned. "Now, I've just been told that the other guy's not pressing charges. You're free to go after we take some information from you, but you're banned from the mall for ninety days. Understood?"

"Whatever."

Daniel rested his head on his steering wheel as he struggled to regain his composure. He was not immediately successful.

"Dammit!" He threw himself backward and pounded the wheel.

I should've kicked his fuckin' head in.

I should've put my hands around his fat throat.

I should've put a knife in his chest.

I should've…

I should…

Daniel looked at himself in the rearview mirror. The eyes that peered back were his.

And not.

They were filled with a malice that was purely his own.

And not.

The 'thing' stared back and for the first time, it smiled.

"You failed."

Daniel twisted at the sound of a voice beside him. It was the same voice he had heard earlier before he left home to meet Gary. In the passenger seat, the boy looked up at him. "You could've done worse but if you stay on this road, you'll only make it stronger."

"What the hell is going on?!" Daniel shouted. "What are you?"

"You're angry."

"Damn right, I'm angry!"

"That's what it wants. That's why it's manipulating you."

"Who wants what?" Daniel asked. His pulse was racing now and his head began to throb. "Give me a straight answer!"

The boy shook his head. "The answer has to come from you, from within you. It's the only way."

Daniel closed his eyes and ran a hand over his face. "Only way for what?"

There was no response.

There was no one to give it.

"Please tell me it was self defense. Give me *somethin'* to work with!"

Daniel rubbed the bridge of his nose wearily. On the speakerphone in his home office the following morning, the deputy mayor was sincerely perturbed. Normally, it was unusual to think of Bruce in that capacity, his appearance and demeanor certainly belied the position. This morning, however, his friend was atypically serious.

"What are you talking about?"

"I'm talkin' about page two of the Eastern Shore News where, in nice fat bold letters, it says 'Port Kirkland mayor assaults man in Virginia Beach', yada, yada, screamin', overturnin' a table, then punchin' the man with whom, witnesses say, Masenda had been heatedly conversing for several minutes, yada, yada, no formal charges have been filed."

"Exactly, so what's the problem?" Daniel asked sarcastically.

"What's the prob—," Bruce was nearly apoplectic. "I already had two council members call me demanding an answer! Your new PR guy, Parelli, got a voicemail last night from the paper asking for a comment. He's avoiding their calls this mornin'."

"It was a personal matter."

Bruce sighed. "Dan, let me start with this disclaimer. You know I'm not exactly the most politically oriented guy on the planet. With that having been said, when you're the friggin' mayor, the personal can become very public, especially when you punch someone in the middle of a crowded mall!

"Dude, I'm sorry I'm freakin' out, but damage control is not my specialty, definitely not first thing in the morning, and especially not with a hangover, and Samantha is barkin' at me every five minutes!"

"For what?"

"You name it! I can't do anything right by the old bat! For someone whose supposed to be a secretary—"

"Administrative assistant."

"Whatever! She's miserable and she makes fun of my clothes!"

Daniel smiled and shook his head. Samantha was sixty-three and had been working for the township in various capacities for thirty-one years. She was fond of pointing out that behind every good mayor there was an old bag that knew everything. During the course of Daniel's term, he had come to agree with her.

"All right, Bruce. I'll cut my bereavement time back a few days. I'll be in the office on Tuesday. If the council members want an answer, they'll have to wait until then. Tell Parelli the press gets no reply at all. We're going to let this die starting now."

"So who was the guy anyway?"

Daniel hesitated. His first impulse was to evade the question but that made him feel more like a politician than he wanted to right now. "He was my father."

"*What?*"

"I said it was personal. I'll explain it all next week."

There was a pause at the other end. "Are you okay?"

"I'll be fine. Look, I'm sorry you have to deal with this crap, and I'll apologize to the council members in person when I get back. I owe you one."

Following a reflective two-hour walk along the Matson River Trail, Daniel arrived home to find his best friend seated on the stairs leading to his front door. Bruce lowered his cell phone from the side of his head as Daniel approached.

"I've been callin' you all mornin'," he began in a voice that betrayed concern despite its thin façade of annoyance.

"I've been out and about," Daniel replied flatly.

"I tried your cell phone, too."

"I turned it off."

With a sigh, Bruce grasped the railing and pulled himself to his feet. "I just came by to make sure you're all right," he said despite Daniel's deliberate obstinacy. "And after this morning, I needed to go get a beer…or two."

Bruce reached down and lifted a flat white box from the stoop. "I brought lunch."

Ten minutes and one large pizza later, the pair sat in silence on Daniel's deck. After finishing his second beer, Bruce finally spoke. "So, if you don't mind my askin', what happened with your dad at the mall?"

Shifting bits of uneaten crust around his plate, Daniel responded softly. "It's a long and sordid tale."

Despite Daniel's reluctance to provide direct answers, Bruce seemed compelled to press on. "You never talked about your family."

"I don't have one."

"Come on, everyone has a family at one time or another."

Daniel finished the last of his iced tea and tossed the bottle into the small recycling toter at the corner of the deck. "That time has long passed, my friend."

Bruce remained silent for a moment, peering down at floor. When he spoke again, it was in a low, deliberate tone. "My father was an alcoholic, but unlike most of the stories you hear about abusive drunks, he never hit me. He never had the chance since he took off two days after I was born.

"I was the youngest of four. My mom couldn't afford to take care of all of us, so three of us got separated. By the time I was six, I'd been passed around from one family member to another until I finally ended up in a foster home under the idea that I would eventually go back to my mom.

"I was scared out of my goddamn mind." Bruce smiled thinly. "Jeff and Paula Literis. Young couple. Nice people. Almost didn't want to leave. In the end, I didn't.

"My mom worked two jobs but she still found time to visit me once a week for the first six months I was with them. I don't really remember the last day I saw her, they all sort of blend in now."

"Why did she stop coming around?" Daniel asked, his tone noticeably softer than before.

Bruce folded his arms across his chest. He didn't look at Daniel as he replied. Rather, his gaze remained fixed directly ahead as if needing something on which to focus that wouldn't stare back in pity. Daniel knew that feeling all too well. "She was killed by a drunk driver while crossing the street to get to her night job at the drug store. Hit and run. The guy ran the red light. Turned out, he was a known alcoholic drivin' with a suspended license. An alcoholic…how's that for irony?"

Daniel's jaw tightened as he absorbed his friend's story, and the pain that Bruce tried to disguise in its telling. To say that he was merely sorry seemed trite. He opted instead to remain silent.

Bruce seemed to sense Daniel's hesitation and waved a dismissive hand. "It was a long time ago and I don't think about it much anymore. Jeff and Paula ended up becoming my adopted parents and I lived with them until I was eighteen. Saw my sisters and brother all the time. Those were good years.

"Joined the Coast Guard, left when I was twenty-seven. Ended up here and been a loser ever since." Bruce chuckled as he ended his sentence.

"You're not a loser," Daniel said adamantly. "You've done pretty damn well for yourself here. Everyone likes you. You're easy to get along with and you're popular. I'd go so far as to say that you have more character than any man I know.

"A loser would still be walking around with a chip on his shoulder, always angry and taking his personal problems out on the rest of the world instead of…learning to let go and…move on." Daniel's voice suddenly trailed off.

Bruce turned to look at him. "You're not a loser either but it sounds like you're speakin' from experience." He placed his hand on Daniel's shoulder. "Also sounds like you know what you need to do."

"Why do I get the feeling I was maneuvered into a corner?"

Bruce shrugged. "What are friends for?"

Daniel rose from his seat and drew his shoulders back to a ramrod straight posture. Such body language had become predictable to many who knew him, a telltale sign of the mayor's stress level.

"Look, what I did yesterday at the mall was an embarrassment to myself, to you, and to our town. Don't think I'm not beating myself up over this one. You should have seen the stares I got along the trail this morning. I didn't know that many people read the paper.

"I'm going to work as hard as I can to climb out of this hole but I'm… dealing with something right now that's very painful and I haven't quite figured out how to handle it yet. I can't explain it right now, but I'm not above admitting that I'm scared, Bruce, and scared people sometimes behave out of character. I promise to keep it to a minimum until I get through this."

The boat captain nodded in understanding. "Just remember, you have a lot of friends and we're all here for you. You don't need to explain anything to anyone until you're ready. Besides, sulking is no way to spend your birthday. How about happy hour at Skipper's tonight?"

Daniel adopted a sheepish grin. "Ah, sorry, I already have other plans. Raincheck?"

"Uh, okay, sure." Bruce stammered. "So, what, you got a hot date?"

"Old childhood friend coming for the weekend."

He raised an eyebrow. "Really? What about Vicki?"

Daniel shrugged. "Off to Singapore to further the cause of corporate America."

"She's really missin' some key events in your life lately," Bruce frowned as he lazily slid from his stool and started toward the stairs leading to the front door. "But I have a strong feeling she'll make it up to you."

"Right…" he smiled wanly.

"Well, I'd better get back there so I can ignore even more people. I never realized how comfortable that sofa was in your office. Slept off my hangover just in time to be screamed at by our *administrative assistant*." Bruce stopped suddenly and snapped his fingers. "Oh, by the way, I almost forgot one piece of good news today. Did you hear about that anonymous donation to the ESCAPe center?"

Daniel shook his head.

"Twenty thousand dollars!" Bruce announced excitedly. "Who around here would have that much extra cash to burn?"

Feigning ignorance, Daniel threw up his hands and shrugged. "I can't possibly imagine."

Chapter Six
Reunion

That evening, Daniel found himself in the foyer of Bertram's staring anxiously through the window at a torrential downpour. The restaurant's dim lighting, intended to evoke a relaxed romantic atmosphere, also made it extremely helpful to observe happenings outside without forcing Daniel to suffer his reflection in the glass. For that, he was extremely grateful.

Behind him, a rectangular bar that seated nearly fifty occupied the left side of the place. Flat screen televisions were mounted on the ceiling at both ends while a row of four stained glass lamps hung above a central open area. A pair of beleaguered bartenders hustled feverishly to serve customers on all four sides.

Two years ago, management decided that smoking would be permitted only at the bar. As such, a glass partition was erected to separate that area from the tables and booths. A pair of short staircases at either end of the bar provided the only entrance and exit between the two sections. Matching stained glass lamps shone upon each table. In the center of the right wall, a thick wooden mantle spanned the width of a gas fireplace and was adorned with nautical themed statues and models of tall ships.

Bertram's was the most popular hang out in Port Kirkland and Daniel hoped that Miranda would like it as much as he. In making arrangements for her visit, she and Daniel had agreed to meet for dinner here, as it was conveniently located mere minutes from the highway exit. Afterwards, she would simply follow Daniel back to his house.

For the fourth time, he glanced at his watch. Miranda was almost forty minutes late. He pulled his cell phone from his belt and flipped it open. There were no missed calls.

Two white lights moved past the window as a car pulled slowly into the parking lot and turned into a space close to the building's entrance. It was remarkable timing, as an elderly couple had vacated the space mere minutes before. Pensively, he watched as the driver's door opened and a pale umbrella emerged. As it ascended above the vehicle, he focused on the face beneath it, illuminated by the restaurant's exterior lights.

She was unmistakable. Daniel exhaled in relief as he scurried to the front door and opened it just as she approached. It wasn't until she collapsed her umbrella and glanced up to thank him that recognition struck.

"Danny…" she breathed. "Oh my God!"

She threw her arms around him and he pulled her close. Fourteen years instantly melted into yesterday when they were twenty-two and fresh out of college. It seemed like a lifetime ago. Finally, Miranda pulled back and looked at him, regaining her composure.

"Sorry I'm late. The storm slowed down traffic everywhere. Hope you weren't waiting long."

"No problem." Daniel motioned for her to precede him into the restaurant. "I'm just glad you made it safely. Welcome to Port Kirkland, by the way."

They were seated immediately, at a corner table set apart from the others, and gave their drink orders to the young waitress. While Miranda ordered a strawberry daiquiri, Daniel opted for his usual raspberry iced tea.

"You still don't drink?" Miranda asked curiously.

Daniel pointed at her and smiled.

"Wow, some things never change. So is this the mayor's special table?"

Daniel shrugged nonchalantly as he opened his menu. "It's good to be the king, and the king is buying tonight so I hope you're hungry."

"I haven't eaten since six this morning. I'm ready to keel over."

"Ah, so that's your secret."

Miranda shot him a confused look. "What secret?"

Daniel lowered his menu. "To looking that good after all these years. Don't think I didn't notice that immediately."

"Oh, here we go, the obligatory flattery," she rolled her eyes and smiled. The room lit up as she blushed. "Fourteen years have been good to you, too. So what do you recommend here?"

"Well, if you're into surf and turf, they have this awesome boneless chicken breast stuffed with crabmeat. I mean it's packed in there. You won't want to eat for days afterwards. I think I ordered it the last three times I was here. Next time, they probably won't bother giving me a menu."

"Sold!" Miranda said just as the waitress returned with their drinks. After the pair ordered their meals, conversation resumed.

"Did you have any trouble with my directions?"

Miranda shook her head. "Flawless, it was just slow going because of the weather. I'm exhausted, though. Rough day at work."

"Well, my house is only about ten minutes from here so rest is not too far away. This storm is supposed to blow out of here tonight and the rest of the weekend looks perfect." Daniel snapped his fingers in sudden recollection. "I forgot to mention on the phone, I have a friend who owns a couple of charter boats and if you're interested, I arranged for a few hours out on the Chesapeake."

"Sounds great," Miranda said enthusiastically. "But you really don't need to go through any trouble for me. I'd be just as happy sitting my butt on the beach for two days with a good book."

"You can do that, too, but believe me, it's no trouble. Just want to show you some hometown hospitality."

Miranda glanced down at her drink. Her expression became solemn and she was suddenly silent.

Daniel noticed this and spoke softly. "You okay in there?"

She chuckled as she looked up at him. "Yeah, I'm fine, just tired and I think I need to get my bearings. It just occurred to me, seeing you again, that it's been over a decade since we were anywhere near each other and now here we are having dinner."

"Fourteen years," Daniel said simply before taking a sip from his glass.

Miranda paused. "So much has changed for both of us. There were moments in my life, especially after my divorce, when I wondered how it would have been if you and I—"

"I know," he interjected. "Not too many days went by when I didn't think the same, believe me."

"I didn't want to broach the topic on the phone. It didn't seem appropriate somehow. I suppose it would have been awkward."

"Some things are better discussed in person," Daniel agreed. "We should talk about it, especially if you have any unanswered questions."

Miranda shrugged. "Just one, really. I wanted to know why you left without an explanation, without saying good-bye. For a long time I thought maybe I did something to hurt you but I couldn't imagine what. Another part of me knew that you would've told me if I did. Instead, you disappeared without a trace. No one knew where you went.

"I couldn't help but to wonder if maybe you didn't think what we had was so special since you left it all behind so easily."

"It wasn't easy, Randy. It was the hardest thing I ever did."

"I know it was a long time ago. Please don't think I'm holding any grudges. I just want to understand what happened, that's all."

"That's all," Daniel repeated with a sigh. "If only it was that simple, but I'll try. First of all, believe me when I tell you that I didn't just stop loving you. I don't have a good explanation for why I left, but I can tell you that as far as regrets go…that was the most painful. I can only explain what I was dealing with at the time and let you be the judge.

"Bottom line was that my family problems became too much to bear. My home life was shifting between hostile to downright violent. It was too dangerous for me to stay there. I'm sure you remember some of what I told you when we were growing up, about the things my mom did to me."

Miranda nodded, lowering her eyes. "Yeah, actually I do."

"Well, as I got older, she resorted to emotional and verbal abuse. I think she was overcompensating for the fact that I was no longer the little boy that she could beat to a pulp whenever life pissed her off.

"The misery in that house just festered for years. First it was my mom's hatred toward my father, then her family, then me. I was the embodiment of her life's failures, being a single parent strapped with a kid. I can't tell you how many times I heard the old 'wish you were never born'. She drilled that into me until I started to agree with her.

"I didn't realize her influence on me until I was in my twenties. I saw myself becoming exactly like her. I started blaming everyone else for my problems. I was always angry, like a time bomb ready to explode. I did my best to hide that from you back then but it was obvious to me that if I didn't get the hell away from her, my life would've been ruined and I didn't want to bring you down with me. I would rather have died than drag you into that kind of life. In my mind, you were better off without me because in the end I knew I was in no shape to make you happy.

"So instead, I ran away."

"You could've talked to me," Miranda said. "We were always there for each other. Who knows, I might've gone with you."

"Hindsight is always twenty-twenty," Daniel replied somberly. "When I took off, I had no idea where I was going, no plans, no direction and no future. I couldn't put you through that.

"Look, Randy, in the end it was completely my mistake. If I'd been more mature, I probably would've handled the situation better and maybe things would've turned out differently for us. I know that's a lot of could'ves, would'ves, should'ves. I can only say I'm sorry and I have been for years."

Miranda remained silent for a moment as three waiters slipped past their table, each carrying large trays of platters or appetizers with single-handed aplomb. "You don't need to apologize. I wasn't looking for that, I was just curious, really. Now that you've explained it, let's put it behind us and move on."

As if on cue, the waitress returned with their meals. It was a welcome interruption for Daniel who needed a moment to shift his focus from their unpleasant topic of conversation. He had already wasted too much time over the past several days reexamining old wounds and sifting through emotional baggage, the burdens of which he had considered long ago jettisoned.

Tonight, he sought to forge a new relationship with Miranda and while they could never return to what they had, he hoped that she would remain in his life as a friend.

"You know, this is the second time this week I've met someone from my past at a restaurant," Daniel informed her. "Unfortunately, the first encounter ended rather badly."

"Oh, who was it?" she asked.

"My father."

Miranda's paused as she cut into her chicken. "Whoa. When was the last time you saw him?"

"I was ten years old."

"So what happened?"

He told her.

"Sorry I asked," she cringed. "I bet that didn't do much for your public image, especially on the heels of opening that youth center. Gives people mixed messages about you."

"You're starting to sound like one of our council members," Daniel remarked. "All I know is that I feel like that old cliché, 'my past is coming back to haunt me'. Present company excluded, of course."

Miranda shook her head. "Oh, I'm not offended. Hauntings are my specialty."

Daniel was immediately intrigued by her comment and sensed that it was intended to raise his curiosity. Given the bizarre events in his life since the night before he learned of his mother's death, he found himself eager to play along. If nothing else, it was an opportunity for a change of subject.

"Really? Hauntings as in things that go bump in the night?"

"Or in the daytime," Miranda nodded. "The paranormal is a hobby of mine, though I don't talk about it very often. It tends to give people the wrong impression."

"Actually, it sounds interesting. Are you one of those ghost hunters? Wait, please tell me you don't sit around a table holding séances and playing with Ouija boards."

"Well, if you really want to know," Miranda began hesitantly. "No, I don't do séances anymore and I never touch a Ouija board. They're a waste of time but yes, I do belong to a group that investigates reported hauntings mostly at private homes but occasionally a few businesses. We don't charge a fee. It's all for fun, not a job. Beyond that, and go ahead and laugh, I also discovered years ago that I have some psychic abilities. I occasionally give readings but again I don't charge."

"Wow. So no big sign out on the front lawn, 'Miranda Lorensen, Ghost Hunter'?" Daniel gibed.

Miranda smiled and shook her head. "No, I tend to keep that part of my life somewhat private, although my friends at work call me the 'ghost lady'."

"Nice," Daniel laughed. "So have you ever actually seen a ghost?"

"When they want to reveal themselves, yes," Miranda replied casually.

Daniel looked at her skeptically but in his mind, innocent curiosity was transforming into genuine scrutiny. "So what are you saying, you've seen more than one?"

Miranda nodded with a mouthful of crabmeat.

"How many would you say, roughly?"

She swallowed, took a sip from her glass and thought for a moment. "Since I was a kid? Oh, I would say over fifty. I never told you about any of this back then. I guess I was hiding something from you, too, but I was too nervous about how you'd react."

"I suppose we should've trusted each other a lot more," Daniel admitted.

"I know, it's just that I've spooked a few people in my life when I revealed my ability. As a child, it scared the hell out of me at times but as I grew older I realized that there was really nothing to fear. If you open your mind to them, they tend to gravitate to you. Some are just passing through; others have reasons for their visit."

As Miranda spoke, Daniel fell into a thoughtful, distracted silence.

"Is it your turn to zone out now?" she asked playfully.

He drew his shoulders straight as he sat back in his chair and grinned sheepishly. "Sorry." He gave a sideways nod toward the other tables. "So, do you see any ghosts in here right now?"

"Funny you should ask," she replied casually. "There's a little boy who's been peering in through the front window for the past ten minutes."

Dropping his fork, Daniel turned to look but saw only a group of four being escorted to their table. "Is he still there?"

"No. He disappeared the moment I mentioned him which is interesting, as if he knew—"

"What did he look like?" Daniel demanded.

Miranda was clearly taken aback by his sudden surliness. She answered hesitantly. "Uh, I think about seven or eight years old, dark hair. At this distance and with the rain, I couldn't discern too many facial details except that he seemed to have a bruise just below one eye.

"I told you, I see them all the time. No big deal," she waved dismissively toward the window. "I grew accustomed to it years ago. If he wants something from me, he'll appear again. Anyway, still interested in hearing about my hobby?"

"You have my undivided attention."

The storm diminished into a light sprinkle by the time the pair left the restaurant. The rumble of thunder quickly followed infrequent flares of lightning that briefly illuminated the thick clouds above. As they approached Daniel's house fifteen minutes later, the rain began to intensify once more.

Daniel parked at the curb and motioned for Miranda to proceed into the garage. Once she was inside Daniel dashed from his car into the garage, barely escaping the second deluge of the evening.

"No sense having you park out there and haul your luggage up through the rain," he explained as she stepped out of the car.

"Very thoughtful, for a guy," she winked. "But it's only one duffel in the back seat. I travel light."

Daniel retrieved the bag and pushed the button to close the garage door on their way toward the main stairs, which were immersed in total darkness.

"I thought I left this light on," he murmured as he slid his hand along the wall. Finally he found the switch and turned on the ceiling lights above the staircase. "I never leave the house at night without leaving a light on. That's a lesson I learned the hard way many years ago."

"Maybe you just forgot," Miranda suggested.

Once they reached the top step, it became instantly evident that Daniel had not, in fact, forgotten. Rather, someone else had turned off the lights in order to gain the advantage of—

"SURPRISE!"

Suddenly, the entire main floor was flooded with light as every lamp flashed on at once and several people shouted in unison. *"HAPPY BIRTHDAY, MISTER MAYOR!"*

In the kitchen, Bruce and his first mate, Joey Quint stood near the refrigerator, bottles of beer in hand. As Joey was under eighteen, Daniel made a mental note to discuss that with the charter boat captain. To Daniel's left, a few other staff members were scattered around his living room and dining nook while down the hall to the right, two of his elderly neighbors stood just beyond the guest bedroom door. They were obviously the lookout detail as the windows in the room overlooked the street and driveway.

Daniel recovered quickly and turned to Miranda. "Hey, thought you were psychic. Why didn't you see this coming?"

She tilted her head toward him and scowled mockingly. Clearly, she felt a bit awkward surrounded by a house full of strangers.

Daniel hefted her duffel bag over his shoulder as if preparing to hurl it at someone. "All right, which one of you iron-heads organized this ambush?"

"That would be me."

Vicki stepped out from behind the kitchen wall, a full sheet cake lay across her outstretched forearms.

"Oh, uh, hello." Her smile faded into bemusement as she looked from Daniel to Miranda. "I'm sorry, I don't think we've met."

"Obviously," Bruce remarked. "You're holdin' out on us, Dan-o."

Daniel refrained from wincing as questioning eyes settled on Miranda from all sides. He knew that he needed to think quickly to diffuse the burgeoning uneasiness settling over the scene. He clapped his hands together and smiled jovially. "So, I gather that the surprise was mutual?"

At that, some people exchanged glances and short laughter.

Vicki was not one of them.

"Let me start by filling you in on the plan."

After all introductions were made among the party's attendees, Daniel found himself alone in the guest bedroom with Vicki. As she folded her arms across her chest and leaned against the dresser, Daniel could not help but to notice that the mirror had been uncovered. He stepped backward until he could no longer see his reflection.

"First off, my trip was postponed. Instead, I was called to the corporate office in Boston for a day and a half. There was a big meeting to discuss a change in our plans for Singapore, but that's a whole other story.

"Anyway, on my way home I decided at the last minute to call Bruce and see if we could cook up something for your birthday. He was supposed to take you to Skipper's tonight as a ruse to get you out of the house for a few hours so we could set this up."

"Ah, well, to his credit he did try," Daniel assured her. "But I already made plans with Miranda."

"OK, well, how did this whole *Miranda* thing come about, may I ask?"

"Well, you see, it all started about thirty years ago during elementary school recess when a little blonde haired girl offered me half a peanut butter and jelly sandwich. It was love at first sight."

Vicki looked at him. Her burning gaze of earlier cooled into an icy stare.

"Tough crowd," he muttered. "Okay, fine. I'm sorry I didn't tell you about this. The truth is, Miranda and I really do go back to elementary school. We fell out of touch fourteen years ago. She heard about my mom's passing and sent flowers.

"I called her and we arranged her visit the day before you announced your Singapore trip. Believe it or not, I intended to introduce the two of you but when you said you were leaving for five days, I knew that wouldn't happen so I thought what was the point in saying anything at all? You wouldn't be around to meet her anyway."

"You could've at least mentioned it," Vicki insisted. "Look, this is your house and you can invite whoever the hell you want. In this case, though, when you have another woman staying for the weekend, somehow I think that would come up in conversation. Imagine how I'm feeling just finding out about this tonight when she suddenly pops in."

Daniel nodded in agreement but before he could respond, there was a knock on the bedroom door. As it was left ajar, they could see that it was Miranda.

"Hi," Vicki said flatly.

"I'm sorry to interrupt but it doesn't take a psychic to know that you had no idea I was coming. I was under the impression that Dan told you so I apologize for what must seem like an intrusion."

"No, it's all right. *You* have nothing to be sorry about," Vicki replied sincerely.

"It's entirely my fault," Daniel admitted. "I haven't exactly been my usual cogent self lately and I certainly didn't want the two of you to meet under this cloud of tension and suspicion."

"Oh, nice bit of political rhetoric," Vicki cracked. "What's next, plausible deniability?"

"Woman, you wound me."

"Not yet, but the night is still young."

Although Vicki was not entirely placated, everyone else seemed to enjoy themselves and the remainder of the evening passed without further incident.

It was nearly eleven-thirty when Daniel decided to retire for the evening. Most of the attendees had already departed and Miranda was sound asleep in the guest room. Vicki remained engaged in a quiet but intense conversation with Bruce for nearly twenty minutes and from her reactions, it appeared likely that the boat captain was imparting the tale of Daniel's escapade in Virginia Beach. He probably thought that she already knew.

It was just as well, she would have learned about it soon enough either from the media or Daniel himself. Thus, he wasn't concerned. Rather, he made a mental note to prepare himself for the imminent barrage of questions and chastisements in the morning. One debacle was enough for the night. It was time for a discreet exit to the second floor.

In the master bedroom, Daniel promptly closed the door and collapsed onto the bed. The excitement and anxiety of the past week was finally catching up to him. Frayed nerves that once denied him respite from his living nightmares now seemed all but drained, allowing him to drift easily to sleep.

Nearly an hour later, he was awakened by what at first sounded like an intermittent drum roll fading in and out of his consciousness. As his mind surfaced from the depths of REM sleep to a state of hazy awareness, it occurred to Daniel that the idea was preposterous. Who would be playing drums at this time of night, especially considering that there were none in the house? His eyes snapped open and immediately winced in protest at the bedside lamp that shone directly upon him.

It became clear then that the drumbeat was in fact a rumbling from somewhere *inside* the room! Without turning to look, Daniel realized that it was the rattling of the closet doors. Fear paralyzed him for several seconds, despite his mind's desperate urging to flee. At times, the shaking was punctuated by jarring thuds as if someone was pounding on the sliding doors from inside. Finally, keeping his back to them, Daniel cautiously rose to a seated position at the edge of the bed and forced himself to his feet. The door to the hall was a mere four steps away.

Where the hell is Vicki? That damn party has to be over by now!

As if sensing his escape, the sliding doors began moving back and forth with increasing vigor, tearing at the tape and dark plastic bags concealing their mirrored surfaces. Futilely, Daniel ignored what he knew was a beckoning and reached for the doorknob. In his peripheral vision, Daniel watched the plastic peel away and flutter to the carpet.

Then just as suddenly as they began, the doors slammed closed and ceased all movement. He held his breath, sweat formed on his palms. He sensed a presence watching from the mirror, felt its gaze burn into him, searing through his flesh, boring into his soul.

As if it *was* his soul.

In the deafening silence, the entity's stare beckoned, demanding his attention, and against all better judgment Daniel reluctantly turned to face his tormentor. From the right closet door the forlorn eyes of the boy stared at him pleadingly. Daniel exhaled in relief. He had expected to confront the worst of the two apparitions that had been haunting him since his mother's death.

Yet unlike his first encounter with this specter, which resembled Daniel at the tender age of eight, he felt no fear now, only a bizarre curiosity. For in this manifestation, the child's face was perfectly uninjured though it still conveyed deep sorrow.

Eager to glean some explanation as to its purpose, Daniel stepped around the bed and approached the mirror. He was fascinated to watch his own unblemished reflection behind the boy. It had been days since he had seen himself. He shook his head at the stubble-ridden, baggy-eyed stranger, telltale signs of the week's battles both within himself and with the intruders from his past. Still, it was a welcome sight.

He looked down at the boy who had been waiting expectantly. Though no words were exchanged, Daniel somehow received impressions of a desperate need and profound disappointment.

"What do you need from me?" Daniel asked, lowering himself to his knees and placing his hands on the glass. "Please tell me, or show me, and I swear I'll do whatever I can to help you. That's why you're here, right? You need my help?"

At that, the boy merely turned his back to him and looked up. Daniel followed his gaze until he was staring again at his own face in the mirror. He was taken aback to see that his reflection had remained standing.

It was not until the second blow that split the boy's lower lip that he reacted. Horrified, he watched as he, or rather his mirror image, brutally struck the now huddling child viciously about the head and back.

"No!" Daniel shouted as he began pounding on the door. "Leave him alone!"

His reflection regarded him with a derisive smirk before transforming into the sickening, mutilated visage of the 'thing'. Just as Daniel had sensed the boy's emotions, he now perceived a disgusting surge of sadistic gratification from the beast as it seized the boy and slammed his head into the mirror repeatedly until the glass was smeared with blood.

Enraged, Daniel hurled his fist into the closet door repeatedly until the upper half of the mirror shattered and shards of glass fell to the floor. He took a few steps backwards just as Vicki dashed into the room with Miranda on her heels.

"Oh, my God. Dan, what happened?" Vicki asked.

He did not acknowledge her but merely stood with his back to the women, staring at what remained of the mirror.

"Dan?" Vicki repeated as she moved around the bed to stand beside him. Miranda, not quite fully awake, remained in the doorway. *"DAN!"*

Slowly, he turned to look at her, his expression unreadable. "I'll clean it up later." He pointed toward the door. "I'm going out to get some air."

Vicki's eyes widened at she looked at the back of his hand. "Did you put your fist through the glass?"

"I didn't like the way I looked," he replied flatly.

Vicki paused for a moment, clearly trying to get a grasp of the situation. She shot a sidelong glace at Miranda.

"It's like he's in some kind of shock," Miranda said in a low voice, then to Daniel. "We should treat that hand, Danny."

"No, I'm not in shock, I'm tired. I just woke up." Daniel held his hand up in front of his face, examining the droplets of blood and broken skin that spotted his knuckles. "I'll be fine. I just need to get some air."

Vicki put her hands on his shoulders to stop him. "Dan, look at me. You're acting strange and it's freaking me out. What's wrong with you?"

"I don't know. Ask him." He nodded toward the smashed mirror before walking out of the room.

A moment later, Daniel quietly descended the stairs to the living room and turned on the floor lamp to its lowest wattage. He made his way toward the back of the room, eased aside the vertical blinds and slowly opened the sliding door. Cool air rushed to greet him as he stepped outside onto the damp wood—

—of a boardwalk spanning a section of unfamiliar beach. He froze in mid-stride and spun around. Behind him, where his house should have been, the boardwalk stretched for another two miles, ending at a stone wall that seemed to mark the beginning of several private residences.

Upon closer examination, the decking beneath his feet was not the traditional pressure treated wood or plastic composite. Rather, the entire boardwalk consisted of scored, rotted railroad ties. There were no metal tracks, but a gaping hole just a few feet away caught and held Daniel's attention for several seconds, though he couldn't understand why. It gave him a chill.

With a deep breath, he tore his gaze away from the hole and slowly turned to examine his surroundings. It was no longer the middle of the night. Clouds in varying shades of gray consumed the daytime sky, casting a dismal pallor. All of the shops were closed, their windows dark; some were boarded up. A shallow ramp led from the boardwalk to a small side street that was lined on both sides with large sedans, every one of them black. Even more peculiar was the hearse parked in the middle of the road with its back door opened wide.

If there was a funeral in progress, where were the mourners? The area was entirely deserted as far as the eye could see. To Daniel, it felt as if it had been devoid of life for decades, yet somehow he knew he was not alone—a ghost town in its truest form. To his right, a furious ocean released its anger upon the beach. He felt a light spray of salt water against his face as he scanned the horizon for ships. The effort was in vain.

With a sigh, he returned his attention to the immediate vicinity and was startled to find the boy from the mirror suddenly standing before him, within arms reach. His swollen face was mottled with bruises that severely discolored his flesh. Daniel felt nauseous at the sight of him and unconsciously averted his eyes. The apparition merely maintained its dispassionate expression, as if taking no umbrage to his blatant display of disgust. Regaining his composure, Daniel steeled himself to meet the boy's gaze.

"I don't understand any of this," he began. "What do you want from me?"

The boy extended an arm and pointed toward the beach. "Go to her."

At the shoreline, where Daniel had looked only a moment ago, lay a dark, rectangular box. Towering waves collapsed upon it, yet it remained remarkably steadfast.

"What is that?" Daniel asked.

There was no answer. The boy was gone.

He stepped off the boardwalk and trudged through the sand toward the water's edge. As he neared the box, it became obvious that it was actually a coffin. The perimeter of its lid was adorned with a familiar carving of gold flowers on a twisting vine.

It was his mother's casket.

Daniel gasped as he came to an abrupt halt, his legs unwilling to take him further. Forcing himself to turn away, he spun around as he ran a hand through his hair and shouted at the top of his lungs. "What do you want from me?"

Along the beach, the boardwalk, the shop windows, there was no one in sight. No one to provide answers, no one to help.

The surf continued to pummel the coffin and Daniel was horrified to observe the lid begin to shift as metal hinges relented to the battering. As if compelled by a force beyond his own volition, he hurried forward, desperate to prevent any further damage.

But he was not fast enough.

Within mere steps of the casket, Daniel braced himself as a massive wave rose up, towering at least nine feet above the surf. He held his breath as the wall of water seemed to hold itself in place for a moment.

As if possessing a sentient will, it hurled itself down directly upon him. It was only when the water struck him that Daniel felt the essence of the 'thing', the monster from the mirror.

As the water receded, gathering its strength for another assault, Daniel picked himself up from the sand only to find the coffin's lid at his feet. A chill ran down his spine. He staggered the few remaining steps to the casket and peered inside. It was filled with roiling salt water topped with a layer of foam such that he could not discern what lay beneath.

He dropped to his knees for a closer look when a hand emerged from the water and clutched the edge of the coffin. Daniel wanted nothing more than to scream but could utter no sound. He began to tremble. Suddenly, the body of Theresa Masenda sat bolt upright, bringing her face within an inch of Daniel's.

"Danny?" she asked, her voice little more than a whisper.

He reeled backward, struggling clumsily against the sand to get his legs under him. A moment later, he scrambled to his feet and ran frantically toward the boardwalk.

"Wait, Danny," his mother called. "Come back to me. We can save each other. You can't leave me again! Please don't leave me again!"

When he was halfway across the beach, Daniel twisted his body to look behind him, expecting to see his mother rising from her coffin, or the monstrous 'thing' in close pursuit, or any number of other horrors.

There was nothing but sand and surf.

He stopped and scanned the entire area as far as the eye could see but there was no evidence of the boy, his mother, or her casket.

Daniel turned and walked the remainder of the distance. As he stepped onto the boardwalk, he noticed that it had returned to its normal appearance of pressure treated wood planks. On the side street beyond, the hearse and accompanying cars were gone and above him, the sky had cleared and was now riddled with stars. Daniel recognized some of the constellations and their familiarity somehow comforted him.

He felt a sudden chill as a cool breeze rustled his wet clothes and hair. He leaned over to begin brushing sand from his clothes.

"Hey, come in from the rain!"

Daniel spun around to see Vicki peering at him through the sliding screen door. He was home again, the wood of his deck beneath his feet. It was then that he felt the raindrops increasing in intensity.

"Dan, please, we need to look at your hand," she pleaded. "It could be broken."

"Okay," he said simply. He looked down at his clothes as he entered the house. The sand was gone. Was it all a hallucination? Was he really there or was he losing his mind?

It occurred to him then that there was someone who might be able to provide insight in that direction. Ironically, it was yet another individual with whom he had not spoken in over a decade.

During his final two years in college, Daniel's relationship with his mother had begun to deteriorate rapidly and his home life became unbearable. Theresa realized that her only son was growing ever more independent and her control over him was waning. He had long outgrown her ability to subdue him with physical beatings so she resorted to verbal abuse in an attempt to crush his self-esteem.

It was far more than he could handle alone. His grades had begun to suffer as his emotional state crumbled. For the first time in his life, Daniel had been forced to seek counseling and in doing so, saved both his life and academic career.

Dr. Sam Michaels, one of the senior members of the Psychology department at the university, had also worked in the Student Counseling Center. His attentive manner had put Daniel at ease immediately and over the course of their weekly visits, provided a generous measure of guidance through one the darkest and most critical periods in his life. Sam had understood the pain of the confused young undergraduate far more than Daniel thought possible.

Soon after his mother's funeral, he had considered contacting Dr. Michaels but hoped that the visions would cease before it became necessary. As mayor, even in a small town, it was imperative that he tread carefully when seeking professional help of this nature. If it was discovered that he was visiting a local psychiatrist on the heels of yesterday's public meltdown, everything he had built in his life could be jeopardized. His competency could be called into question, his public image tarnished. Worst of all, he had no idea how Vicki would react. Up until now, their relationship had never suffered any significant tribulations and he wasn't eager to put it to the test over these disturbing experiences, paranormal or not.

A sentimental journey to his alma mater, however, would slip under the notice of the press and the council members.

In meeting with Sam, Daniel knew that he would be forced to sort through echoes of a past that nearly destroyed him. Though he wasn't certain if he would find all of his answers there, it was as good a place as any to begin. By confronting his past, rather than retreating from it, Daniel hoped that he might finally find peace not only within himself but also with the entities that haunted him.

Perhaps he would even discover that they were all one in the same.

An hour later, with his hand wrapped in gauze, Daniel apologized to Miranda and wished her good night. She stared at him with a serious expression.

"What is it?" he asked.

She shook her head. "Not now. I'll tell you later once I have it figured out. Get some sleep."

Vicki was still awake when Daniel climbed into bed. She put her arms around his waist and pressed her head against his chest. It was almost as if she was holding onto him for dear life.

"I wish you would tell me what's going on," she whispered. "I feel like you're shutting me out."

"No," Daniel said, caressing her shoulder. "If you just give me a little time to work through this, I promise I'll tell you everything. At the moment, there are some...strange things happening in my life that I don't completely understand and can't explain without being afraid of what you'll think."

"I *think* I can handle it," Vicki said emphatically.

"Yeah, well, that makes one of us."

Chapter Seven

Problems from the Past; Help from the Past – Part One

Despite its awkward start, the weekend proved to be enjoyable for everyone with the possible exception of Daniel. While no further nightmares plagued him, he often found his thoughts wandering back to those of Friday night.

Worse, he forced himself to suffer his maligned reflection in the mirror whenever Vicki was present. Upon questioning, he had offered a premeditated excuse for the plastic bags taped over the closet doors, casually explaining them away as 'preparations for painting'. Though she had regarded him skeptically, no further mention was made of it.

To his relief, Vicki extended a cordial, if somewhat forced, hospitality toward Miranda. Saturday morning saw sparse interaction between the two women but shortly into their afternoon tour of the Chesapeake aboard one of Bruce's boats, they gradually appeared to accept each other.

Nevertheless, Miranda departed earlier than expected on Sunday leaving Daniel feeling helplessly despondent. Despite her assurances to the contrary, he was fully aware that she felt her presence to be a source of contention. He also knew that he was solely to blame.

His depression remained with him when he awoke on Monday morning, primarily due to a sleepless night of self-evaluation. He could no longer deny that his life was spinning out of control. Unspeakable visions in the mirrors, increasingly disturbing experiences, violent outbursts, and the deliberate withholding of information from Vicki. His conduct was growing dangerously out of character and before he wreaked any further havoc on his own life or anyone else's, it was time to make a phone call and hope that his life could be saved a second time.

Just as with the neighborhood of his youth, so had the Baltimore campus of Saint Peter's University changed immensely since Daniel's undergraduate years. A seven-story building that housed the student center and expanding MBA program was erected across from the athletic field. Two of the larger dormitories were completely renovated and another was built on what had been an expansive lawn used for outdoor activities. Beside the university chapel, the original student center was converted for use by the recently established Living Arts program and housed a television and radio studio, computer lab for graphic designers, and a large art studio for painting and sculpting.

Of all the things that had changed in fourteen years, Daniel was pleased to see that the expansive concrete terrace behind the main library remained almost exactly as he remembered. Though the dark wooden furniture appeared brand new, the border of giant arborvitae still lined the patio's perimeter, providing a sense of privacy and seclusion. As such, Daniel had spent many hours here as a student, mostly when his family problems became overwhelming and he needed to collect his thoughts. To his chagrin, he had never been able to focus on a resolution to the unsolvable issues and only wasted his time in worry and self-recrimination.

Now, as he took a seat facing the rear tree line, he was reminded of one of the most frightening days of his life. In the spring semester of his junior year, Daniel had become so accustomed to his weekly visits with Dr. Michaels that he had actually enjoyed them. The pair had swiftly developed a trust and rapport that made it easy for him to speak openly about his precarious home life.

On the particular day in question, that life had taken a violent turn and finally pushed Daniel beyond the limits of self-control.

1992

Approximately an hour prior to his appointment, Daniel decided to pay a visit to the terrace in an attempt to collect his thoughts.

The situation at home was rapidly deteriorating. It seemed that upon reaching young adulthood, far less privacy had been afforded to him by his mother. Theresa had begun eavesdropping on almost all of his phone conversations and sometimes interrogating him afterwards about them. This was one prominent reason why Daniel had denied himself the pursuit of any romantic relationships, though several promising opportunities had presented themselves. He had been fully aware that his mother would've looked upon girlfriends as a threat to her dominance in Daniel's life.

Her control had already begun to erode years ago and as a result, matters grew worse. Last month, Theresa had started opening his mail and discarding anything she felt was irrelevant before Daniel came home. She had even taken the liberty of searching through his bedroom and questioning him later on his purchases of new clothes, music and most especially, books.

At an early age, Daniel had come to enjoy reading and had amassed a small and varied collection of science fiction novels since his high school days. Upon discovering them, Theresa had vehemently lectured him on wasting his money on such things.

How could Daniel explain that reading was his escape from her? Rather, he had taken a more tactful approach, explaining that books were far more preferable than such self-destructive alternatives as drugs or alcohol, which many of his schoolmates preferred. Theresa had seemed appeased by this, or perhaps she had been merely unable to think of a valid argument.

Fleetingly, Daniel had often entertained aspirations to publish a novel of his own some day. Perhaps in doing so, he would finally earn his mother's respect and approval. Yet, he could hardly focus on his dreams for the future when he was far too preoccupied with daily survival.

Suddenly, there was movement to his right as someone sat beside him on the bench. It took Daniel a moment to acknowledge the arrival of one of his fellow classmates who, upon departing Saint Peter's, would be bound for the seminary.

Ranjatu Venjay was a quiet, spiritual young man in whom Daniel had confided from time to time regarding his unstable home life.

"You present the appearance of a man with much on his mind," Ranjatu began. "And none of it very pleasant."

"As always you're most perceptive," Daniel confirmed. "I'm just a little distracted this morning."

"Let me guess. It's a woman?"

"Family problems."

"Your mom?"

Daniel nodded.

"I knew it was a woman."

They shared a momentary laugh and Daniel smiled wanly. "Very funny."

"Well, they say laughter is the best medicine."

"I need something stronger, Ran," Daniel said humorlessly. "It's reaching critical levels at home and I'm not sure I can hold together, ya know? I really don't have anywhere else to go. We're so close to graduation, I'd hoped to tolerate the situation until I could afford a place of my own. I feel like a prisoner waiting for parole."

"Maybe it's a test," Ranjatu offered.

Daniel frowned. "A test of what? Faith? Character?"

The other man shrugged. "All of the above. Every experience in your life now could be preparing you, molding you, to handle a far greater challenge down the road."

"Ah yes, the 'character building' point of view to which I've given very little thought. I'm a bit busy trying to manage the here and now to think about what's down the road."

Ranjatu nodded. "It's never easy to be objective when you're deep in the trenches of a problem. The view is always different from the outside looking in. Think of it this way, you only have control over so many things in life. Beyond that, you can only have faith that the universe will unfold as it should based on God's plan and He has one for everybody."

"Funny you should say that," Daniel said. "Looking back over the years, I've come to realize that maybe God has been protecting me—even guiding me—through all of my problems. Frankly, I can't see how else I could have made it this far."

"God gives different talents to different people," Ranjatu said. "Resilience and a strong will seem to be a few of yours and I think you'll find that they'll open doors to others you have yet to discover."

Daniel looked at his watch. He was late for his appointment with Dr. Michaels. He extended a hand to Ranjatu who accepted it hardily. "Thanks for listening. You always seem to present a unique point of view. I'll remember this conversation."

In the student counseling office minutes later, Daniel waited patiently for the secretary to finish her phone call and announce his arrival to Dr. Michaels. Instead, what she told him made his stomach sink.

"I'm sorry, Dan," she began as she hung up the phone. "I guess you didn't get the message. I called your house and, uh, spoke to your mother. Sam had a family emergency earlier today and had to cancel all of his afternoon appointments."

"Oh, no problem, I understand," Daniel replied evenly, betraying no sign that his worst fears had just been realized. Another sliver of privacy lost to his mother.

"Can I reschedule you for next week, same time?" she asked.

"Uh, yes, that'll be fine, thanks."

"Will do, and again, I'm...*very* sorry."

There was something unmistakably ominous in her apology. When Daniel arrived home a few hours later, he barely stepped through the door before realizing the meaning behind the secretary's nebulous warning.

"Counseling? You're seeing a psychologist?" Theresa seethed at him. "Imagine my utter surprise at getting a phone call from this woman about canceling your appointment. Tell me, Dan, how long have been talking to this Dr. Michaels?"

"Just a few weeks," he lied. "I just needed someone to talk to."

"About me, right?" she pressed. "You just needed to talk about me behind my back. What are you telling him, that I'm some kind of monster? Keep in mind that you wouldn't be where you are if it weren't for me. How do you expect to finish college if you're living on the street? You push me too far and that's where you'll end up!"

"Wait." Daniel held up his hands pleadingly. "There's no need for this— "

"Shut up!" Theresa screamed. "Seems to me that you've been shooting your mouth off enough lately. Did you honestly think that you would get away with this, that you could hide it from me? Eventually, I always find out what you're doing. Haven't you learned that yet?

"Don't think I didn't take the opportunity to tell his secretary what a backstabbing liar you are and have been since you were a kid!"

"To be fair, you weren't always easy to approach with issues," Daniel retorted, careful to maintain civility. "You have to admit that you didn't exactly handle life's problems very well."

"How many times do I need to explain to you that my nerves were shot back then? Have you tried to raise a child on your own with nothing? Have you suffered through a failed marriage and the stress of divorce? I didn't know where our next meal was coming from half the time! So I'm sick and tired of hearing about the past! Get over it!"

"It's not just about the past," Daniel insisted. "Let's face it, things between us haven't been perfect in a long time and I just needed to confide in someone who was qualified to help me. I have a right to that."

"I'll tell you what your rights are while you live under my roof." Theresa stepped forward until she was within arms reach. "You have no right to disrespect your mother. I told you several times over the years that what happens in this house stays here. Now, I find out that you disobeyed me by going to some stranger!

"You're no son to me and you're no better than your bastard father. May I remind you that he abandoned you ten years ago? I've always been here for you and this is the thanks I get. I would've been better off if you were never born!"

No sooner had Theresa finished her tirade then there was a flash of movement that turned the anger in her wide eyes to instant fear. There was no conscious thought behind the fingers that pressed into her throat, for Daniel's mind had been consumed with a rage that had come from somewhere beyond him.

He only wanted his mother to stop screaming, craved only her silence —permanently. Yet the craving was not his own.

End her life, end your suffering. The words had pushed themselves into his thoughts. They made sense, seemed so right, but they were not his words.

Within moments, he found himself kneeling over her prone form, watching her face turn dark violent, listening to her desperate gasps for air, feeling her claw and yank futilely at his wrists.

Reason took hold of his thoughts once more and he immediately released her. Unable to speak, he merely crawled away to the far corner of the room, eyes wide with panic. He held his trembling hands out before him, staring at them as if they were foreign objects.

"Please don't kill me..." Theresa croaked.

Your turn now. How does it feel? Daniel glanced over at his mother's coughing, whimpering form. *That's how close you came.*

As she lay with her back to him she suddenly seemed so fragile, hardly the wrathful, vindictive bully that had left Daniel beaten and bloody so many times through his childhood.

Now, he feared only himself.

"Please tell me your mother is all right."

The following day, during an emergency appointment, Daniel sat across from Dr. Michaels, a quivering teary-eyed wreck.

"Yeah, she's fine. I was just lucky she didn't call the friggin' cops. Dammit, Sam, it all happened so fast. She was screaming at me and I swear to God I tried to reason with her. Maybe she was right, though. Maybe she was right."

Michaels' brow furrowed as he asked softly. "About what exactly?"

"Oh, she's been telling me for years..." Daniel trailed off.

"Take your time. What has she been telling you?"

"That her life would've been better had I never been born."

"You *cannot* possibly believe that." The counselor took on an ardent tone. "If you do, then you're shouldering the blame for her failures and shortcomings. You're not responsible for anyone's actions but your own."

Daniel sighed. "Yeah, well, I'm not so sure about last night."

Michaels nodded his understanding. "What happened was terrible but we both know you didn't intend to hurt her—"

"I lost control," the younger man growled. "It was wrong, Sam. No matter what she says or does to me, she's my mother. I never hated her. All I want is to understand why she hates me and change it if I can."

"She doesn't hate you, Dan," the counselor assured him in a full voice that conveyed a confidence that Daniel only wished he shared. "She hates herself and just took it out on you all your life because you were an easy target. A person's environment has a definite and sometimes permanent effect on their personality and character, especially as a child. It's a testament to your strength that you managed to hold onto that decent, rational core of your identity.

"Many young people who've been repeatedly victimized often internalize it and as they move into adulthood, they automatically adopt the destructive behavior of their abusers because that's the only reaction they know. People like that often end up in therapy for years.

"From our weekly discussions, it doesn't appear that you've reached that point. The one thing that struck me about you, almost from our first session, was how you proved to be amazingly adept at self-analysis. That can be good and bad but I've been pleasantly surprised at your ability to look at what you've been through both from the subjective, emotional standpoint and then in almost the same breath, turn it around and examine it from a rational, objective point of view. Not many people who come in here can do that.

"I think you know deep down that you're not the bad guy when it comes to your relationship with your mother. You weren't the bad guy at six, or eight, or ten when your mom did all of those things to you. The only difference was that as you grew older she was forced to resort to verbal abuse because she knows all of your buttons and she pushes them until you capitulate to her. It's manipulation and it's despicable and I think you've known that all along."

Daniel nodded solemnly and lowered his gaze to the floor. "A part of me does, but it's impossible to take solace in what I know to be true because the minute I try, this looming feeling of guilt overwhelms everything. I always find myself going back to her, constantly trying to prove myself worthy of her respect and…well, whatever, doesn't matter I guess."

"Yes, it does matter." Michaels insisted. "You have no obligation to feel guilty because you haven't failed her. She failed you. I'm sorry to say it, but it's the truth, Dan. I know that you can't always help your feelings. Sometimes you can only hope that certain ones subside before they become your undoing. In other words, as long as you remain with her, you'll never break the endless cycle of abuse. It's a twisted kind of dependency. Your mother can't bear to be without you, or at the very least doesn't seem to know how to live her life without you around."

Daniel remained silent for a moment, allowing Michaels' words to sink in, pondering their implications. "She's going to find out soon enough."

Conversation among a group of passing students shook Daniel from his dark reverie. He glanced at his watch and couldn't help but to smile at the irony—just as he had been the last time he sat on this bench, Daniel was once again late for his appointment with Dr. Michaels.

Although the counseling center had moved to a new building at the opposite end of the campus, Daniel shot a glance at its original location as he stepped off of the tiny patio, past the arborvitae.

He held his gaze on the second floor window of the former Student Center behind which had been the counselor's office. A room in which Daniel had spent many an hour sharing his pain with someone he barely knew, hoping for a magic answer from an objective listener that would solve all of his family problems and bring him peace. Although he found no such 'easy out', he had been grateful for the weekly exchange that made him feel like a human being.

Daniel turned away and as he walked, he was suddenly reminded of his last meeting with Dr. Michaels just days before graduation.

1993

"This might be our final session, Sam," Dan had announced as Michaels closed his office door and accepted the outstretched hand of the undergraduate. "I wanted to thank you for doing more for my self-esteem and mental health in the past two years than anyone in my life. Before we...part ways... I wanted to get your advice one last time. I realize my life is about to change once I graduate and I don't think I can continue on with the way things have been. Problem is, I'm not sure what to do."

"You're a survivor, Dan," Michaels began as they took their traditional seats against the window. Outside, the wind disturbed the branches of the evergreens, causing them to scrape against the building. "Up until now, you've sacrificed your own welfare for your mother and in return, she's allowed you to be yourself on *her* terms.

"You've paid your dues both emotionally and physically. It's time to stop merely existing in that prison and move on to a healthy, happy life. Once you leave this campus, you'll be entering a much larger, more demanding world. I know you're far too intelligent a person to fail yourself, to fail your future.

"Dan, you're about to graduate from one of the best universities in the world. You beat so many odds to get here. You've earned tremendous respect. It'll be almost impossible for you to grow and excel if you remain in that abusive, dependent relationship. Sometimes you just have to *force* your life.

"What I'd like to see you do, as your counselor and your friend, is to use this milestone as a catalyst for change. Your greatest gifts to yourself would be to accomplish your dreams, allow the person you are inside to shine, find real love because you deserve it but most of all, be true to yourself on *your* terms, not someone else's.

"Those are my final thoughts for you."

The counselor's advice to the twenty-two year old undergraduate remained strong in the memory of the thirty-six year old mayor. Daniel knew that he had, in fact, improved his life immensely since then. As mayor, he had accomplished much for his town, surrounded himself with wonderful people, and found what he had hoped was true love. Yet the same fears and anxieties that brought him to Dr. Michaels' door fourteen years ago forced him to return today as if Daniel had made no real progress at all.

Perhaps in his strive to escape from his old life and bury the memories under a mountain of achievements and personal successes, he neglected to fix the person *inside*. If that were so, then it was a sad commentary and one that Daniel pushed from his thoughts as Michaels stepped into the waiting room.

Daniel rose from his chair opposite the secretary's desk. "Thanks for seeing me on such short notice."

"Not a problem at all," Michaels said as he and Daniel shook hands and started toward the row of offices down the hall. "It's spring break, business is slow."

Though the man's hair was now completely gray, the cut and style remained unchanged. He appeared to have gained very little weight, making Daniel wonder if the counselor still took his afternoon jogs around the campus.

"New digs I see," Daniel commented as they stepped into one of the larger offices and took seats opposite one another. "Much bigger than what you had in the Student Center."

"Yeah, we moved here about six years ago right after this building was finished, thanks in part to a bunch of massive donations."

"Ah yes, I noticed all the names of the rich people on the wall downstairs. Jeez, I remember when this was the main parking lot, but then all things change."

The counselor nodded. "They certainly do. So, how about you, Dan? I'm anxious to hear how your life has changed and where it took you."

"It took me all the way to a little town called Port Kirkland, Virginia where I've been the mayor for the past three years."

"Wow, mayor! You never struck me as the political type."

"Frankly, I'm surprised you remember me at all," Daniel admitted. "It's been a long time."

"Well, your situation was rather…unique. Most kids who grew up in the kind of environment you described were typically driven to drugs or alcohol or worse, but you stood your ground. Looks like you managed to stay on the high road.

"I even recall some of the stories you told me about your childhood. I remember loneliness and how even during your time here you denied yourself a social life. If memory serves, you intentionally didn't seek out any romantic relationships because you were afraid to bring anyone into your life at the time. Even worse than loneliness—a self-imposed isolation."

"I didn't have a choice and you have a sharp memory."

"Not to mention good notes," Michaels admitted with a sly grin. "We save them for years. So, what brings you here today?"

"Well, actually, I'm facing some issues related to that time in my life. First, I should let you know that my mother died last week after a bout with breast cancer."

"I'm sorry to hear that," the counselor said. "What was your relationship like with her before she passed on?"

"We hadn't spoken in fourteen years," Daniel replied flatly. "And she forbade the rest of the family to contact me about her cancer. It was only *after* she died when my uncle called me. It seems that she carried her hostility against me all the way to the bitter end."

"Let me guess, you moved away after graduation and this caused a rift between the two of you?"

"You could say that, but there's more."

Daniel launched into the details of his week, from his explosive reaction to his Uncle Paul, the disastrous reunion with his father, his weekend with Miranda, and all of the visions and experiences in between.

"You know, Sam, I'd hoped my past was behind me; that I wouldn't need to deal with these memories again. I'm learning now that running away from your problems and even making a new life for yourself doesn't really resolve anything. In the end, time doesn't heal all wounds."

"True, or it could just be that some people just take longer than others," Michaels' admitted. "Have you told Vicki about these incidents?"

"She was with me when I had the last one," Daniel explained, holding up his hand. Tiny scabs across his knuckles were all that remained of the events of two nights ago. "Needless to say, she was pretty upset. I haven't filled her in on the details or told her anything about the apparitions in the mirrors. I don't even know how to begin to explain any of it. Most of all, I think I'm just afraid of her reaction. I have this fear of losing her as if I slipped right back into the good old days, directly into the thick of my family problems. I had someone special in my life before I moved away. I let her go because…because I was stupid and weak."

"Those days are gone," the counselor reminded him. "Your life is here and now." Suddenly, Michaels smiled as he continued. "And by the way, it's great to hear you talk about girlfriends. Finally, after all those years of avoiding relationships! Good for you. It's a wonderful feeling, isn't it?

"Normally I would agree," Daniel replied coolly. "At the moment, it's killing me."

Michaels chuckled. "If she truly loves you, she'll stick by you but let's talk about these visions in the mirror. I have to ask, are you taking any medications?"

"No." The younger man shook his head. "I was expecting that question. These aren't drug-induced hallucinations. At the same time, I can't believe that I had a sudden mental breakdown either. I'm almost embarrassed to admit this, but after exhausting all other explanations, I believe that these events are…paranormal."

Michaels hesitated before replying. "Well, before we starting talking about ghosts, let's try to find a more…earthly reason. The first thing that comes to mind is a well-known psychological phenomenon known as stress-induced hallucinations. You've had a lot happen to you in one week. Learning about the death of your mother, the reappearance of your father, even reuniting with your childhood friend Miranda, all could easily have forced long forgotten or even repressed memories to surface. That's an enormous amount of stress piled on your shoulders in a matter of a few days."

Daniel considered the possibility for a moment, yet somehow he remained unconvinced. His first vision occurred the night *before* he learned of Theresa's demise and the events that followed. He expressed this to Dr. Michaels.

"Ah, but you said that was a dream, not a hallucination."

"But it was after I woke from that, when the visions in the mirror started."

"Maybe you were still dreaming."

Daniel exhaled and ran a hand through his hair, a telltale sign of frustration. "Yeah, maybe, that first night is a little hazy now. So much has happened between now and then."

"Have you felt threatened at all by these visions?"

Daniel shrugged. "At first, yes. Seeing your own face scarred and bloody day after day is pretty damn ominous. I'm still not sure what to make of the boy. I get the impression that he's trying to get a message to me or that he wants my help but I can't determine why or how."

"Yet you think they're related to your mother somehow because technically the visions began on the same day that your mother died, and she was also in your most recent vision."

"That about sums it up."

"Then I want you to keep me informed about your experiences over the next two weeks. I'm curious to see if these nightmares and hallucinations subside as your life returns to a normal routine. If not, then I may recommend you to a psychiatrist for treatment, which may include medication.

"On the flip side, I'm not necessarily dismissing the paranormal outright," Sam assured him. "Although I'm not exactly a true believer, let's face it, science hasn't explained everything in the known universe. We don't understand every single aspect of the human brain any more than astronomers know everything about outer space. Science hasn't yet found the cure for cancer, AIDS, or a lot of other illnesses. There are gaps in our collective scientific knowledge and in those gaps lie mysteries yet to be solved. Maybe the paranormal is one of them.

"At any rate, I suggest that you tell Vicki what you're dealing with. If you're not comfortable using the term "visions", then pass them all off as a series of bad dreams. I just don't recommend keeping this bottled up any longer."

Michaels paused, then added thoughtfully. "You know, there's something else that you might want to consider. When we talked about your past a few minutes ago you said that you didn't have a choice but to isolate yourself back then. Everyone has a choice, Dan. Your mother may be gone but it's never too late to forgive. For all we know, finding a way to do that may be the key to understanding these experiences, if not stopping them all together. Keep in mind that your past can no longer hurt you, unless you let it."

"I'd like to believe that, Sam. I really would."

Chapter Eight

Problems from the Past; Help from the Past – Part Two

He rang the doorbell and stared anxiously at the wooden 'Happy Easter' sign that hung from the wreath hook on the blue painted steel door. Miranda lived in the first of a dozen row homes on a small one-way street in Baltimore. A black wrought iron fence, about waist-high, surrounded a concrete porch and matched the antique metal mailbox affixed to the wall beside the door. Daniel pressed the button once more. Seeing Miranda's car parked in front of her house gave him hope that she might be home.

A rustling sound to his left caught his attention. He walked across the porch and peeked through the thin wire mesh of a large wooden hutch. As he did so, a gray ball of fur darted out of the enclosed section and stopped abruptly in front of him. The lop-eared rabbit looked at Daniel inquisitively for a moment before turning his attention to a pile of romaine lettuce leaves.

"That's Bullet," a familiar voice announced from behind him.

Daniel turned to see Miranda standing in the open doorway donning a faded blue t-shirt and jeans. She was barefoot and her wet hair was matted around her head.

"I just got out of the shower," she explained, sensing his mental appraisal of her appearance. "I heard the doorbell just as I turned off the water."

"I'm sorry," Daniel replied sheepishly.

Miranda waved off the apology. "Not at all. I just wasn't expecting you. How did you know I'd be home?"

"Uh, I didn't," he admitted. "But I would have waited all day."

Clearly caught off guard by the comment, Miranda drew herself to her full height and frowned in confusion. "Well, that's...very flattering. Are you okay, Danny?"

"I need your help."

"So these visions," Miranda began after listening intently to Daniel's account of the past week. "Do they tend to occur only at times of emotional distress? Before you answer, I know that you're dealing with a great deal of grief right now. I'm referring to heightened emotions like anxiety, anger, fear."

Seated at Miranda's dining room table, Daniel thought for a moment before nodding. "It seems like every time I get angry, my reflection in the mirror gets more grotesque. Although, I was feeling perfectly fine when all of this started on the night before I found out about my mom. Which is why I think there's a connection."

Miranda peered down at the table in silent thought. As she pondered the significance of Daniel's experiences, she leaned forward and began curling her lips inward over her teeth and pressing her mouth closed. It was a habit that Daniel recognized from their youth indicating intense concentration. It was also just cute to watch.

"There is a phenomenon known to paranormal enthusiasts and 'experts' called autoscopy. Simply put, it means you're seeing your own ghost."

Daniel swallowed. "And is there any meaning ascribed to this phenomenon? Do people die after experiencing this?"

"No, not necessarily. The paranormal isn't an exact science. In fact, most don't consider it a science at all and rarely are there precise answers."

"Then how do I figure out what the hell's happening to me?"

Miranda hesitated before responding. "Danny, when I came to your house last weekend, I sensed a...presence. At times, it felt like two entities but it wasn't consistent. Now, this kind of thing isn't uncommon. I felt no malicious intent so I didn't feel compelled to say anything at the time. There are spirits all around us every minute of the day. Some have reasons to make themselves known which is why there are hauntings."

"Do you think my house is haunted?" Daniel asked in a low voice. "Randy, I've been there for eight years now and never had a problem until this past week."

She exhaled nervously. "That's because your house isn't haunted. You are."

The blood drained from his face. Somewhere in the back of his mind, he had already considered that possibility but could not bring himself to openly accept it. Now, hearing Miranda verbalize it forced him to face the reality.

"You told me that you see this mutilated version of yourself in every reflective surface, not just at home but elsewhere."

"Yeah," he breathed. "And the boy shows up every so often, too. I think you saw him at Bertram's."

"It's likely that they're trying to communicate with you," Miranda suggested. "The boy and the monster *could* be the same entity but I don't really get that impression. If you'll let me, I can work with you to try and find some answers."

"How?"

"I can do a reading on you."

Daniel raised a skeptical eyebrow. "You're kidding."

"You came here for help, didn't you?"

"Well…yeah," he stammered. "I wanted to get your opinion and maybe some advice but I wasn't expecting crystal balls and tarot cards."

Miranda reached across the table. "Just give me your hand."

Daniel looked at her doubtfully before finally acquiescing. "I don't believe I'm doing this."

"You don't need to believe," Miranda replied softly before closing her eyes. "Now, don't say anything, just let me focus."

Fifteen minutes passed as the pair sat motionless. At first, Daniel merely felt foolish. As time passed, his embarrassment faded into restlessness and finally, boredom. Turning his head carefully so as to avoid disturbing Miranda's concentration, he made a hasty inspection of the room's décor. It was tastefully furnished in a rustic, country motif with a beautiful cherry wood china closet and matching dining set. Paintings of tree-lined paths in autumn, open fields, and farmlands adorned the walls while above them, a hand-carved wood chandelier completed the room's inviting appeal.

Stifling a yawn, Daniel peeked through the doorway into the living room. The orange rays of the evening sun were stretching across the wall from the window. It would be dark in about thirty minutes. Daniel could see Bullet through the window, resting contentedly in the open-air section of his hutch. As if in reaction to a sound only it could hear, the rabbit suddenly lifted its head and angled its floppy ears slightly forward.

A popping sound, like that of wood expanding or contracting, snapped Daniel back to attention. Miranda had shot forward in her chair, posture suddenly rigid. Her breathing seemed to slow and though her eyes remained closed, her clenched jaw and furrowed brow told Daniel that something was happening.

That, and Miranda's tightening grip on his hand.

She stood in the center of a small bedroom with light blue walls and a worn, bare wood floor. Though she recognized it instantly, it was not her room but that of a childhood friend. Suddenly there was a presence behind her. She turned to face the boy standing in the doorway. Beyond him was a field of pure white light, almost blinding, that *felt* utterly alive. She sensed no fear, only warmth.

The boy regarded her expectantly.

"You aren't Danny," Miranda asserted.

He bowed his head in acknowledgement. "I'm the part of him to which he must listen."

"Why?"

A trickle of blood seeped from the child's nose. "To end the punishment."

"Whose punishment?" she pressed, an awareness of fear began closing in on her thoughts.

A bruise formed under his right eye and his face immediately swelled. "I cannot keep it at bay much longer, he's grown strong from the darkness in Daniel's heart."

"Please," Miranda pleaded. She knelt before to the boy to bring herself at eye level with him. "Help us to understand what he needs to do."

"Daniel must reach beyond his pain. Only then will the suffering soul find peace."

"Suffering soul," she repeated in a whispered tone. "Please, tell me who is that? We want to help."

The boy shook his head. "Only Daniel can do this. No one else."

As he spoke, his lower lip split open and blood poured out over his chin. Miranda looked away. "It's coming. Go now," he warned. "I can't protect you."

As the boy turned from her, the field of white began fading to gray as he stepped into it and vanished.

Miranda released Daniel's hand. She was breathing heavily and a look of distress crossed her face. Without a word, she rose from her chair and went into the kitchen for a glass of water. Daniel remained silent as he watched with a mixture of concern and curiosity. He massaged his fingers, awed by the strength of Miranda's grip. She returned to the dining room after a minute, having regained her composure.

"I saw the boy," she informed him. "It was the most lucid experience I ever had in a reading." She imparted the details of the encounter to Daniel, leaving him dumbfounded.

"Do you think he meant that I need to come to peace with my estrangement from my mom?" Daniel asked tentatively. He was grasping at straws, struggling for an answer to a riddle that was beyond his comprehension, and Miranda's. "Maybe everything I've been going through for the past week was my punishment?"

She took a sip from the cold glass before pressing it to her forehead. "I don't know. A lot of people have regrets about their past, but they don't have paranormal experiences. I think there's something deeper. I want to try again."

"Now?" Daniel was incredulous. "After what you told me, are you sure it's safe?"

She was once more in the center of the bedroom and just as before, there was a presence behind her. She turned to face the man standing in the doorway. He looked like Daniel—at first. Behind him was nothing but total darkness, frigid as death itself. It *felt* utterly evil. She repressed her fear for she knew that this was the entity that the boy had tried to restrain earlier.

"You're not Danny." Miranda repeated her assertion.

The monster smiled at her derisively. "I'm the part of him to which he must listen."

"Why?"

The whites of his eyes turned blood red. "I can make him stronger, as he has made me."

"For what purpose?"

Lesions appeared on his face and hands. "Eternal punishment."

"Explain yourself," she demanded. "What are you?"

"This isn't meant for you." The creature raised its hand and made a slow downward slashing motion in the air. "But you're time will come."

Miranda screamed. Daniel jumped to his feet and stared wide-eyed as a laceration suddenly opened on her left forearm and began bleeding profusely. Daniel dashed to the kitchen and retrieved a dishtowel. He wrapped it around her arm and placed her other hand over it.

"Keep some pressure on it," Daniel instructed as he rushed her out the door and into his car.

He slumped in his padded chair in the lobby of Pace Memorial Hospital's emergency room. Miranda had been taken in for treatment two hours prior, which gave him plenty of time to review the events that had transpired during his reading and attempt to make sense of them.

During their session, Daniel had heard Miranda's side of her conversation with the boy. Judging by the questions she put to him, the entity had seemed reluctant to provide her with any useful information. Based on what Daniel had gleaned from Miranda's brief comments on the way to the hospital, most of the answers she had received were cryptic.

Despite this thickening shroud of mystery, Daniel had already formed a conclusion based on some of the spirit's statements. Fourteen years ago he walked out on his mother, left her behind, never to reconcile their differences. Now, he was being punished. That had to be the only logical explanation, if logic could, in fact, be applied to this situation.

There were no precise answers, Miranda had warned earlier. Yet, the boy's words could not have referred to anyone else. *Daniel must reach beyond his pain. Only then will the suffering soul find peace.*

"Hey."

With a start, Daniel turned his head to see Miranda's forearm wrapped in gauze.

"How bad is it?" he asked, rising to his feet.

"Eight stitches and a tetanus shot," she sighed. "Could be worse."

Daniel closed his eyes in dismay and hung his head. "Randy, I'm so sorry. I never thought it would come to this."

She motioned for him to stop talking and nodded toward the entrance. Once outside, Miranda glanced back at the doors as they closed.

"I didn't mean to cut you off," she explained. "But I sensed that some of them were suspicious about this." She raised her injured arm. "They were wondering if you did this to me."

His shoulders slumped. Even the potential of such an accusation, on the heels of the incident with his father at the mall, could jeopardize not only his position as mayor but also the personal reputation that he worked so hard to build.

"Don't worry, they weren't about to come right out and ask," she assured him as they approached Daniel's car. "You have to imagine that they see their share of battered women."

"I know," he said despondently. "I guess the thought never occurred to me."

Miranda stopped and turned to him. "That's because you're not that kind of guy, Danny."

He smiled sheepishly and opened the passenger door for her. After she slipped into the seat, he leaned in close. "So, in your educated opinion, what kind of guy do you think I am?"

She thought for a moment. "Hopefully one that'll buy dinner again for a starving gal?"

"You got it. It's the least I could do."

It was nearly eight-thirty when they sat down in the booth at a pizza shop just a few blocks away from Miranda's house and placed their order. As they waited, the pair resumed their discussion of Daniel's paranormal predicament.

"Maybe I should go back with you," Miranda offered.

Daniel would not have it. "Absolutely not!" he countered emphatically and pointed to her bandaged arm. "If that was just a warning, I don't want to know what else that thing is capable of."

They leaned back as the waitress set their drinks on the table.

"I'm not confident that you can handle this alone," Miranda said after the girl was out of earshot. "Neither of us knows for certain what you're up against."

A group of teenagers entered. Daniel let them pass their booth before responding. "I have a theory about that." He proceeded to verbalize the conclusion at which he had arrived while sitting in the lobby of the emergency room.

Miranda shook her head. "You can't assume anything. Remember what I said, *no* concrete answers. You need to be extremely careful not to misinterpret the messages you receive from the other side. That could be just as dangerous.

"Don't get me wrong. I agree that you should make a concerted effort to come to peace with your feelings about your mother and the fact that you may never find a sense of closure. I was there, Danny. I remember the stories you told me about what she did to you and I'm sure her death has probably stirred up some bad memories. These spirits, whether they're good or evil I don't know, they both seem to be anchored to your pain for whatever reason. They just haven't made their intentions clear yet."

The waitress returned with their steak sandwiches. She placed the check upside down on the table and thanked them. Daniel waited until she was out of earshot before replying.

"Well, if it's my mother's intention of ruining my life from the other side," he said. "She can rot in Hell."

Miranda pointed a finger at him. "I think that's part of the problem here. By your own admission, you've been feeling increasingly angry since she died. At least one of these entities is taking advantage of that, perhaps even fueling the fire. You need to be very careful, Dan. These spirits have attached themselves to you, each for their own specific reason.

"Now, I know you thought your past was behind you when you settled in Virginia, but it's only natural that those old negative feelings would resurface now. Maybe you haven't truly put your past behind you until you've honestly and sincerely forgiven your mother."

Daniel sat back in his seat and gave her a quizzical look. "You're the second person today to suggest that. It's easier said than done. How can I forgive her if I haven't come to peace with everything that happened between us? I thought I did, but…"

He shook his head. "I can't believe this is happening to me and I have no idea how to handle it. I don't even know where to begin!"

"Pray for guidance," Miranda advised. "You'll know what to do when the time is right."

They ate in silence for the next twenty minutes. After paying the check, it was time to take Miranda home. "Could you do one favor for a damsel in distress when we get back to my place?"

"Anything."

"Could you help me take Bullet inside? I don't like to leave him out at night."

Daniel laughed in spite of himself.

Chapter Nine

Into the Darkness – Part One

It was nearly midnight when Daniel finally returned home. Vicki's car was parked along the street in front of his house and a dim light shined from the living room window. She was seated on the sofa when he entered, her expression deadpan.

"You were gone awhile," she said, with a sidelong glance at the clock. Though it wasn't a question, the tone of her voice indicated that an answer was expected.

Sensing that something was amiss, Daniel took a seat across the room and was careful to maintain a casual demeanor. He was exhausted and wanted to diffuse any possible tension at once. "Sorry, I didn't anticipate getting home this late. I took a drive up north to see an old friend."

"Let me guess." Vicki held up a hand for silence. "Was she a blond?"

Daniel rolled his eyes and gave a short, quiet laugh. *So that's it.* "He was gray, actually, and a few pounds heavier than the last time I saw him."

Vicki was not immediately appeased. "Who exactly are we talking about here?"

"I made an appointment with my old college counselor," he explained. "Doctor Sam Michaels. He's a psychologist. I was hoping by some off chance that he would remember me.

"See, in my junior year I realized that I finally needed help coping with my family problems. I couldn't do it alone anymore and was lucky that the university had a staff of counselors. I was scared out of my mind at the thought of opening up to a total stranger but Sam put me at ease right from the start. He pulled me through those last two years simply by being a good listener and offering insight that I never would've realized on my own.

"Mostly, he reassured me that I wasn't the horrible person that..." Daniel trailed off. With a dismissive wave, he continued. "Whatever, doesn't matter. The point is, without that kind of help, I probably wouldn't have made it to graduation and *that* was not an option."

"Was he able to help you today?" Vicki asked softly.

Daniel nodded. "I think so. It was a tough one this time, like nothing we ever talked about before, that's for sure."

A few moments of strained silence passed between them before Daniel adopted a quizzical expression. "So who's this blond you mentioned?"

She lowered her head and exhaled. "Never mind. Sorry I brought it up."

Daniel knew that he was completely to blame for her suspicions. He still felt guilty for not informing her beforehand of Miranda's visit. Regrettably, his decision caused an awkward meeting of the two women and clearly caused a set back in his relationship with Vicki. A certain amount of trust had been eroded and it was now a question of honesty.

Tonight seemed like a good opportunity to redeem himself—or so he thought.

"Ah," he yawned. "Don't apologize. You were partly right. I did stop by to see Randy on the way home."

Vicki's expression turned solemn. "I see." She rose from the sofa. Turning her back to Daniel, she stood at the sliding glass doors that led to the deck.

Dammit, I screwed up again. So much for honesty.

He leaned forward in his chair, hands folded. Pushing aside mounting fatigue, Daniel spoke in slow, measured words. "Vicki, there's nothing going on between Randy and me if that's what your concerned about. Both she and Sam helped me through some dark times—"

Vicki threw up her hands. "And I suppose I'm just ignoring you? I'm not here for you now, helping you through the loss of your mom?"

Daniel stood and went to her. He placed his hands on her shoulders. "Of course, you are. I wasn't implying otherwise. You've been here for me more than anyone else. I only wanted to talk to them because they knew my background, my history. "

"What's the big secret?" she prodded. "What happened between you and your mom that you can't tell me?"

"Remember when I said that if you could just bear with me through this, I'd tell you everything?"

Vicki nodded.

"Just a little longer, please."

Her shoulders slumped. She pulled away from Daniel. "And I told you that I could handle it. I want to help you but honestly, Dan, I'm having a hard time understanding you anymore. I go away for a few days and you get evicted from a mall for assaulting your father, then you invite another woman to stay at your house for the weekend, not to mention putting your fist through a glass door!

"You do remember that you're the mayor of this little town? Much of what you do is noticed by the people out there, especially when it makes the local news."

Daniel grinned with a confidence he did not entirely feel. "I think my mayorship will survive the events of the past week."

"That remains to be seen," Vicki retorted. "And what's the real story with the mirrors? Why are they all covered up? I don't see any renovations going on."

"That's a long story."

"Of course, it is!" she smiled mockingly. "I can't wait to hear it with all the other stuff you're planning to tell me sometime in the future. I feel like I came back to a completely different person. The man I met was coherent, organized, responsible. I don't know *this* version of you and I'm not sure I want to!"

"I'm the same person, Vicki!" Daniel asserted, rubbing his bloodshot eyes. "I'm dealing with a lot more than just the loss of my mother right now and yes, there's a lot about me that you don't know but one o'clock in the morning is not the time to discuss it. Can we please just get some sleep and talk about this in the morning?"

"I won't be here," she replied flatly. "I came by to tell you that the Singapore deal is a go. I'm leaving on a 10AM flight out of BWI."

"How long?"

"Could be a year, maybe longer. Probably longer, the company found a small rental home for me. It'll probably take at least a year just to get the physical plant up to specs, the technology infrastructure, labor force, all that. I'll fly back every so often..."

They stood, looking at each other across the room. To Daniel, it may as well been a canyon. He didn't want them to part this way. In frustration, he ran a hand through his hair.

"Yeah...right," he said simply, quietly. "I guess we always knew this would be a possibility. Can you stay the night?"

She shook her head, waved a thumb toward the door. "I think it's best I go. I need to be up early."

"Fine, whatever."

Tell her you love her.

"Look, Dan, I'm sorry, I didn't want tonight to turn out like—"

"Just go, okay?" Daniel held up hand. He didn't want to hear anymore. "What's the point? You've made your priorities clear. Good luck over there. Have a nice life."

TELL HER!

Vicki nodded for moment before turning toward the door. "OK, well, I hope you do what you need to do to put your life back in order. Get whatever help you need, psychic or otherwise."

And with that, she was gone.

A wave of anger washed over him, momentarily overpowering his fatigue. He rubbed his neck as he walked toward the kitchen counter. In a sudden fit of rage, he picked up one of the stools and hurled it across the living room, sending it crashing into a floor lamp. The lamp snapped at its base and collapsed, smashing the bulb and leaving Daniel in darkness.

He dropped onto one of the other stools, leaned over the counter and rested his head in his arms.

"I almost have you, Danny."

Daniel sat bolt upright, heart pounding. The voice sounded like his own but raspier—and menacing. He looked at the clock on the microwave oven. Only a minute passed since he sat down. Did he doze off and start talking in his sleep? Perhaps it was merely the beginning of a dream.

"If only it were. Come to the mirror, Danny."

Daniel, the adult, clenched his jaw and his breath caught in his throat. He slid from the stool. "No..."

"Look at me, Danny! Look at you what you've become."

Frantic, he dashed to the opposite wall and flipped the light switch. Overhead, the ceiling lights blinked on. He glanced down the steps then around the main floor but there was no one in sight.

"Let's have 'em all on!" the voice taunted. "The better to see me with."

All lights on the floor suddenly turned on by themselves.

"Leave me alone!" Daniel screamed.

"But I'm you, Danny! Come to the mirror and see yourself..."

As luck would have it, Daniel's car keys were still in his pocket and his coat was draped over the half wall that separated the entrance stairwell from the rest of the house.

"*Danny*! You can't run from yourself!"

With a deep breath, he snatched his coat and ran down the steps so fast that he collided with the opposite wall. Seconds later, he found himself in the driver's seat of his car, fumbling for the ignition key. He barely waited for the garage door to rise completely before he threw the vehicle into reverse and raced off down the street.

His first impulse was to catch up with Vicki, but he dismissed the idea just as quickly. Doing so could only endanger her, or at the very least, complicate matters that had already become fragile. No, he would face this alone no matter what the outcome.

"Good idea, Danny. Let's keep this between you and...*you*, shall we? I'm in the backseat now. Look in the rear view!"

"Shut up!" Daniel shouted as he reached up to the rear view mirror and slapped it aside.

"Where are you going?" the voice asked curiously. Its tone was suddenly less threatening. Was that a hint of uncertainty? "You can't run from yourself."

A knot in Daniel's stomach was growing into an intense stabbing pain. His heart was slamming every beat, sending a dull throbbing through his skull. It was nearly two o'clock in the morning now as he ran two red lights on his way to—where? Where could he be safe and find peace from this evil "thing" that had suddenly found a life of its own?

Pray for guidance. You will know what to do when the time is right.

Miranda's words suddenly surfaced to the top of his frenzied thoughts. It was then that he realized exactly where to go.

"But you can't stay in there forever, Danny. I'll be waiting out here for as long as it takes."

For residents of the town, Saint John the Redeemer was open twenty-four hours until the first of June, at which point the doors were locked daily at five o'clock until just after Labor Day weekend. Vandalism inside the church, perpetrated by tourists over the years, finally forced the pastor to limit the church's hours during the summer months.

Daniel took the front steps two at a time. He reached for the first door on the left only to find it locked. Struck with panic, he tried the double doors in the middle and stifled a cry of relief as he threw them open. He hurried up the middle aisle and stumbled into a pew in the front row. The church was empty, devoid of activity save for the tiny gamboling flames of a few offertory candles in the right and left corners.

Behind the altar, a massive white marble cross adorned the wall high above. Varying from tradition, however, the crucified body of Jesus held one arm extended forward, reaching out to touch the wings of a dove. It was a remarkable sight and Daniel had always marveled at the craftsmanship.

But not today.

I have nowhere else to go and I can't handle this alone anymore. I tried and now everything's falling apart. So much from my past has come back again but why? There must be a reason. Help me to understand what's happening to me. Who is this monster stalking me?

I'm begging you. Show me what I need to do.

Daniel continued to pray for a time before exhaustion overcame him. With a mental apology to whoever was listening, he laid down in the pew. *Just for a few minutes. I just need to sleep for a few minutes…*

"Mister Mayor?"

"Mmm..."

The pastor, a gaunt man of average height in his late sixties, tugged the cuff of Daniel's jeans. "Mister Mayor, are you all right?"

Daniel opened his eyes. It took a few seconds for him to recall where he was, and why. With a groan, he reached up to the armrest and pulled himself to a sitting position. "I'm fine," he croaked. "Thank you, Father Daly."

"Do you need help? Medical attention?"

Daniel waved a hand. "No, no. What time is it?"

"Five-thirty in the morning," the reverend replied. "Can I get you anything?"

"Divine intervention would be helpful right about now." Tilting his head from side to side, Daniel stretched his neck before slowly rising to his feet. He raised his arms above his head and arched his back.

"If there's any way I can help—"

Daniel placed a reassuring grip on the pastor's shoulder, which also prevented him from stumbling on his way out into the aisle. "I'm going out to fight my demons, Padre. Got any suggestions?"

"Have you been drinking, Mister Mayor?"

Daniel frowned. "No. I don't drink although there's always a first time for everything."

He started down the aisle toward the doors with Father Daly in tow. "Are you sure you're going to be OK? How about a cup of coffee?"

"Just pray for me, Father," Daniel requested. "Maybe a little something to St. Michael."

"I always keep our public servants in my prayers. I was sorry to hear about the loss of your mother."

Daniel stopped and sighed. "Yes, thank you."

"Were you close with her? I know in today's high-stress world, it's easy for families to lose sight of what's important, to be driven apart."

"That happened a long time ago."

"I'm sorry," Father Daly lowered his head. "You know, they say the Lord helps those who help themselves. Finding inner peace takes strength. Most of the time that starts with the ability to overcome your pride and forgive others, as well as yourself. I've always thought of you as someone strong in character, Daniel. I know you'll do the right thing, you always have.

"Perhaps a walk along the river trail would help you sort things out. Whatever my problems, I find that helps me from time to time."

Daniel bobbed his head in agreement. "Good idea. Clear the old head before the big fight." He raised his fist and playfully poked at thin air. "Well, maybe I'll see you on Sunday, Padre!"

"God bless you." Under Father Daly's questioning gaze, Mayor Daniel Masenda went out to confront an enemy that existed to no one but him.

Perhaps, he realized through the thinning fog in his mind, *because the enemy* is *me.*

The sun was just beginning to shed its much welcome rays through the trees lining the Matson River trail. When Daniel had been elected mayor, the trail was only partially paved. When the budget was approved for the last fiscal year, he signed off on the paperwork to finally complete the project.

Now, he leaned on a wooden rail and stared down the hill at the brackish river that flowed from the Chesapeake. Everything around him was so peaceful, so *normal*. It disturbed him that the rest of world, ignorant of his plight, was moving forward while he was trapped in his past.

Breathing deeply of the spring air, Daniel pushed himself off of the rail and continued along the trail as it curved its way through a dense coppice of honeysuckle and short pine trees. To his left, a dilapidated concrete wall was all that remained of a cement factory demolished over fifty years ago. Beside it, an iron railroad bridge, unused for just as long, stretched across the river. Weeds and wild flowers sprouted from cracks in its rotting wooden ties. Sections of the metal track had been moved long ago, possibly to be recycled for use elsewhere.

'No Trespassing' and 'Keep Off Bridge' signs, posted at either side of the decaying relic, were all but completely swallowed by the overgrowth. As Daniel passed, he glanced upward toward the center of the bridge and halted in mid-stride.

Someone was up there!

From his vantage point and judging by the gait, Daniel guessed it to be a man. He was walking toward the opposite side, wearing black pants and a black sweat jacket with the hood pulled over his head.

Everyone knew that teenagers dared one another to cross the treacherous bridge. At least a dozen were arrested each year, mostly during the summer. Some were drunk, others strung out. Thus, Daniel wasn't terribly alarmed—until the figure climbed through the guardrail and stood at the edge of the railroad ties, peering down at the rushing water.

"Oh, my God," Daniel whispered. He patted his pockets in search of his cell phone to call the police. To his chagrin, he remembered that he had left it in his car. It was up to him to take action.

Daniel hated heights.

Nevertheless, he scaled the short hill that led up to the end of the bridge. Cupping his hands around his mouth, he yelled as loud as he could, but there was no response from the mysterious hooded figure. With a sigh, Daniel cautiously started off across the rotting railroad ties, sidestepping the most treacherous areas. To do so, of course, meant looking down through the gaps between the ties, which inspired an almost paralyzing fear as the ground fell away, revealing a one hundred foot drop to the Matson River below.

Daniel froze in place, his legs trembling. He called out once more and was again ignored. Fighting an unrelenting panic that urged him to turn back, he pressed on until he was nearly within arm's reach of the man.

"Hey, buddy!" he called. "Can we just talk a minute?"

The other man took a step forward.

"No!" All fears suddenly cast aside, Daniel lunged, one hand clutching an arm while the other yanked the hood from the jumper's head. He spun the man around and immediately regretted stepping foot onto the bridge at all.

"I've been waiting all night, Danny!"

The 'thing' smiled, revealing bloodstained teeth. Where there were once eyes, there were now only black orifices. Scars and lesions covered its face. Daniel's stomach turned as he released the monster and reeled back, nearly losing his balance.

"Don't like what you see? This is what you've become inside, Danny. As of late, your thoughts have entered a very dark place and that puts you in my company. Your blind hatred over memories that you can't let go and finally being able to strike back at those who caused you so much suffering. Feels good, doesn't it, Danny?

"But there's still one more. The one who deserves it the most."

As it spoke, Daniel's fear drained away as something in his mind snapped. He knew then exactly whom the creature was referring to. Uncontrollable rage began welling up from a place deep inside of him. The 'thing' seemed to sense this, its derisive smile slowly fading just as Daniel's face twisted with open fury. In one swift motion he barreled forward, slamming the creature in the chest with his fist and knocking it backwards into the guardrail.

"I'm not afraid of you this time, demon," Daniel roared, sending another punch to its face. "And I'll be damned if you're gonna fuck up my life anymore!"

The demon grinned. "Well said…"

In a flash of movement, it's hand wrapped around Daniel's throat. Blistered, cracked fingers tightened until Daniel could do little more than desperately tug and claw at its wrist.

"…for the damned await you, Danny."

Effortlessly, the demon propelled his victim across the bridge. As Daniel collided with a support beam, bone cracked against solid iron. He fell into a crumpled heap. Sharp pain flared through his left forearm.

Instantly, the demon was beside him. As Daniel turned to look up at it, he was met with a brutal kick to the side of his head, opening a gash on his temple. The creature lowered itself to one knee, reached down and grabbed Daniel by his hair.

Lifting his bleeding head, the monster leaned in close. "Did you really think you could hide from your past in this little town? You had to know that one day, you'd be forced to face it one last time. Of course, you probably weren't expecting it to be quite like this."

"You're not me!" Daniel spat. "You didn't come from me. What are you?"

"Call me an opportunist. Wherever there is the darkest of emotions, I'm there to fan the flames until the soul is engulfed by the inferno of its own hatred. In fact, fifteen years ago, I almost had *your* soul, Danny. Remember when you nearly strangled your mother to death? I was very disappointed when you let her go and even more so when you ran away like a coward instead of finishing the job! *End her life, end your suffering,* or have you forgotten?

"But that's all right, Danny. There have been so many others since then, and their pain was so…*delicious.* Your soul, however, will be my main course."

"Then why don't you just kill me and get it over with!" Daniel snarled.

The demon jerked Daniel's head higher until the man grunted in anguish. "Because I don't *own* your soul…yet. You're about to undertake a sentimental journey, *Mister Mayor,* with each point along the way plotted out specifically by yours truly. After which, you'll have no choice but to surrender your soul to me, and I will consume you."

"Fuck off!"

The demon scoffed. "Brave to the end." He dropped Daniel's head onto the railroad tie. Pain exploded in Daniel's skull and he closed his eyes tight against the agony. The beast rose to its feet. "I'll be leaving you, Danny, but only for now. We'll see each other again very soon, I promise."

A full minute passed before Daniel had the strength to move. With labored breathing he rolled onto his right side and with a yelp, forced his limp arm up and over his body. Finally, he pulled himself to his knees.

His tormentor was nowhere in sight.

As Daniel stood, dark clouds began rolling in from the horizon on all sides spreading like a cancer over the blue sky at a speed that seemed naturally impossible. Within seconds, they converged directly above. Instinct surfaced through his pain, urging him to move. Clutching his left arm, he started toward the end of the bridge.

He took two steps before the railroad ties collapsed beneath him. With a scream, Daniel fell through to his waist, legs dangling in mid-air. With his right arm, he pulled himself up just enough to reach across and wedge his hand in the gap between two unbroken ties. There were no metal tracks within reach. Daniel cursed as he tried to turn his body, hoping to dislodge some of the jagged wood that held him in place.

In doing so, he slipped further into the hole until his arm strained under his own weight. He realized then that he was out of options. As splinters pierced his palms and fingers, he knew he couldn't hold on much longer.

He heard footsteps behind him. His eyes widened with fear and panic finally overcame him. If it was the demon returning, there was nothing he could do. He held his breath as movement entered his peripheral vision.

Daniel noticed the small pair of sneakers first. It was then that he realized he was unable to tilt his head without immense pain. His eyes snapped up. Apparently, the demon wasn't the only vision that had taken corporeal form.

The boy stared down at him just as he had from his mother's apartment window days before. Under different circumstances, Daniel might have been fascinated by this ghost, this shadow, of his younger self. For all he knew now, the monster and the child may very well be one in the same.

"No," the boy shook his head. "We're not."

"Then help me," Daniel croaked through gritted teeth.

"I can't."

"Why not?" Daniel began to weep. "Look, there's a police station at the—"

"I want to, but it won't let me."

Daniel realized that he was referring to the demon.

"You're right," the boy confirmed with a nod. "You've given it more strength than me. I can't hold it back anymore."

"What are you?"

"You have one last chance."

Daniel's hand began to slip. "No..."

"Trust her. You're each other's last hope."

"*No*!" Fingernails dug frantically into rotting wood.

"Go to her now."

And with that, Daniel slipped through.

Chapter Ten

Into the Darkness – Part Two

Daniel stood on a worn, bare wood floor in the center of a dimly lit room. Settling cracks ran through various sections of the plaster and lathe walls like fault lines on a map. The light blue paint was dingy and faded with age. It was his bedroom, or rather that of his childhood. The wide slats of the aluminum blinds covering the window, the used dresser with the drawers that stuck, the wooden crucifix above the door, all were precisely as he remembered.

Presumably, this was the first leg on his 'sentimental journey' arranged by the demon.

He reached out to his left and touched the second hand bed that had been donated by one of his uncles when Theresa moved into the house. The dark wooden headboard was covered with chips and scratches. As he ran his fingers over them, he marveled at the fact that he was suddenly able to move an arm that had been immobile just minutes ago before he fell.

Before I fell.

The ordeal on the bridge rushed back to him. There was no possible way that he could have survived his plunge into the Matson River. There was only one explanation. A bolt of fear shot through him as he recalled the demon's words. *For the damned await you...*

Daniel started a breathing exercise that he had learned in his early teens to stifle panic attacks. It took a few seconds before he realized that he was exhaling nothing. No air escaped his lungs because no air filled them. He put a hand to his chest, then to his wrist, but there was no pulse, no heartbeat.

No life.

No way!

Reflexively, his rubbed his forehead, fighting back confusion and dread, as he tried to understand what the hell was happening. Though it seemed that he had no vital signs, he was clearly capable of conscious thought and emotion. Though how these things were possible was beyond him.

This isn't happening. It's gotta be a dream. Maybe I survived and slipped into a coma or I'm just unconscious.

Yet somehow, inexplicably, he knew that his hopes were for naught. These ghosts had been chipping away at him for weeks, calling his sanity into question, driving him to manic behavior, jeopardizing his career, tarnishing his reputation, and alienating Vicki. It was all too clear now, all of it leading up to this. His death would look like a suicide, perhaps after a nervous breakdown brought on by grief over the death of his mother.

She was behind all this. She *had* to be.

He dropped onto the bed as he considered what he had left behind. He thought of Vicki and a pang of regret washed over him. He would never have the opportunity to explain it all to her as he had promised, could never hold her again, see her smile, express his love. The barrier of death had seen to that, just as it had with his mother. Another chance lost.

Now, however, Daniel was the one on the 'other side'. Despite the demon's threats, the experience didn't resemble the traditional image of Hell as a blazing inferno filled with the shrieks and howls of condemned souls. Daniel realized upon further reflection that this Hell was of a far more personal nature. He had returned to the home of his youth, the prison from which he longed to escape throughout his childhood.

He thought of Miranda and remembered that she had mentioned being in this room during their psychic reading. An idea struck him then, restoring a shred of hope. Perhaps he could contact her somehow. *Somehow* being the operative word. He had no idea how, but he was certain that she could help him.

Daniel stretched out across the bed, remarking to himself just how *real* it felt. He gazed up at the white plaster ceiling, every hairline crack, every blemish, every patch of spackle just as he remembered them.

With a sigh, Daniel closed his eyes and pictured Miranda in his mind. In his thoughts, he called to her, over and over, but there was no response.

"Dammit, Miranda!" Frustrated, he sat up with his back against the headboard and slammed an open hand down into the pillow beside him. Rather than feeling his palm sink into the soft fabric, there was an audible smack, as something slender suddenly appeared beneath his hand. Instinctively, Daniel grabbed hold and shoved it down onto the bed with more force than he intended.

Someone screamed.

At Baltimore/Washington International Airport, Miranda Lorensen turned off of Elm Street into the free Cell Phone parking lot. There were only fifty spaces total in the lot but traffic was always moving in and out as people quickly picked up arriving passengers.

Thirty minutes earlier, Miranda's daughter had called to announce that she, along with her dad and brothers, had returned from their Maine vacation. Their plane had touched down a bit ahead of schedule which suited Miranda just fine. She had begun missing her kids shortly after dropping them off here just a few days ago.

After parking her car in the last row, Miranda reached for her purse in the passenger seat to retrieve her cell phone. A voice suddenly erupted in her mind.

Dammit, Miranda!

She screamed as a hand gripped her wrist and pushed it down to the seat. Automatically, she reached over with her left hand and tried to liberate her arm. The interior of her car began to change. Faded blue walls replaced doors and windows. Gray lining stretched farther above her head and transformed into white plaster. Looking down, she froze. The car seat was now a mattress and wooden spindles pressed against her lower back. Her wide eyes trailed up from her arm to a familiar face that smiled back sheepishly.

"Daniel!" Miranda gasped.

"Sorry, Randy," her childhood friend said quietly. He spoke slowly as he released her arm. "I didn't mean to scare you. Frankly, I wasn't even sure you heard me."

"What are you...*we* doing here?" Miranda asked as she looked around the room. "This is where I found myself during our session at my house yesterday. It's your old bedroom."

"Yes it is," Daniel nodded.

Slowly, she turned to face him and a chill ran down her spine. She feared the answer that she knew was coming. "Why are we here, Dan?"

He looked at her. He opened his mouth but couldn't utter a word at first. Finally, he took a deep breath and forced an awkward grin. "Welcome to my afterlife, Randy. I'm dead, or at least I think I am."

"No," Miranda whispered. She stared at him and shook her head seemingly unable to find her voice. Tears formed in her eyes. "Oh, God, Dan. How?"

"The monster that's been haunting me in the mirror, the one that sliced your arm open yesterday, it's some sort of demon. It's fascinated with me for some reason. Apparently, it's been keeping an eye on me for years, waiting for the right moment.

"Last night, it finally decided to take solid form and come after me with a vengeance. Needless to say our confrontation didn't end well."

Miranda looked away, her expression blank. "You were on a bridge. I can see it. You fell through."

"Yeah." Daniel nodded.

"It's orchestrating all of this," Miranda said as she waved a hand to indicate the room around them. "Everything we're seeing here. I can sense it. It's watching us."

"I'm surprised the fucker let me contact you at all."

Miranda shrugged. "Maybe it doesn't consider me a threat. After all, I can only come along for the ride. I can't affect anything here."

"No, but you can do something to help me." Daniel placed his hands on her shoulders for emphasis. "It's why I called out to you in the first place. If we lose contact, and eventually you know we will, I need you to track down Vicki and tell her…tell her I'm sorry about everything, sorry for keeping things from her, for my crazy behavior the past week. Most of all, tell her that I love her.

"We had a minor blowout last night and she's leaving for Singapore this morning. You can probably contact her through her dad's company. Will you do that for me?"

Miranda nodded quickly. "Sure. Although I'm not sure she'll believe that I talked to you like this."

There was no need to explain what she meant by 'like this'.

"Make her believe," Daniel insisted. "Please."

"I'll do my best." Miranda opened her mouth to say more but hesitated.

Daniel cocked his head to one side. "What?"

"I just wanted to tell you that I…never mind. I'll tell you later."

"We may not have a 'later'."

Miranda shifted her gaze toward the door. "Well, right now we have a visitor."

Daniel spun to find the boy standing in the doorway. He appeared exactly as he had on the railroad bridge, though this time, his back was to them.

"Hey," Daniel called. "Talk to me. What going on? What the hell's happening here?"

Without a word, the child continued out the door and walked down the hall to the left. Daniel peered up at the crucifix and held his gaze upon it. *Is this your way of showing me what I need to do?*

The sudden sound of water rushing from a faucet piqued Daniel's curiosity. He moved into the doorway and slowly leaned forward on the balls of his feet, peeking into the narrow hallway. Ahead of him, a white and brown railing spanned the length of the hall overlooking the steep staircase to the first floor. On the wall to his right, the curved tarnished metal of a light fixture hung loosely from its round base. *We never did fix that.*

A strip of light shone from the bottom of the bathroom door, while to his right, the door to his mother's bedroom was wide open.

Theresa Quinn-Masenda stood just outside, staring in his direction.

Daniel froze in awe, both at seeing his mother so young *and* at the brimming fury in her eyes. She appeared to be no more than twenty-six years old; exactly the age she was when she divorced Gary. That would put her son at five.

"Danny!" she roared as she stormed down the hallway. His eyes wide with fear, Daniel stepped back into the bedroom as she passed without a hint of acknowledgment. Instead, she threw open the bathroom door and barged in just as the boy finished brushing his teeth. He was holding a large glass bottle of mouthwash in his trembling hand.

Theresa glared down at him. "Did you go into my room after you came home from school?"

"No," Danny replied diffidently.

"Don't lie to me," she warned. "Some of my things were moved around and I know I didn't do it."

The boy merely stared at her, speechless.

"Dan, what going on?" Miranda asked.

"Something that happened in my childhood," he replied simply.

Daniel was reminded of the vision he experienced at the church during his mother's funeral. Then as now, he looked on at this living memory being played out before him by those who apparently were unaware of his presence. As such, he was fully aware of what was to come.

Theresa grabbed the boy by his hair and swung him around violently. The glass bottle slipped from his grasp. It shattered on the floor, green liquid splattering over the white and gray tile.

"You know what happens when you lie to me!" She drew back and punched him in the face, twice. Blood began trickling from his nose.

Daniel swallowed and his breath caught in his throat. His fingers curled until his knuckles were white. Heat rose into his face partially from sheer anger, but also from embarrassment.

"I didn't go in there!" the boy screamed pleadingly.

"Then who did?" She pulled him close. Reflexively, Danny winced in pain and placed a hand atop his head where Theresa maintained a firm grip.

Tears ran down his face as he answered timidly. "I don't know."

She stared at him, her expression one of bloodlust. Finally, she shifted her gaze to the floor. Twisting Danny's head around, she forced his eyes downward. "Look at the goddamn mess you made!"

"I'm sorry," he whimpered. "I'll clean it up."

"Damn right you will," she replied. "Starting right now." Lowering herself to one knee, she forced her son onto the floor, pressing his face into the spill. "Lick it up!"

The child began sobbing loudly.

"Shut up and do it!" she commanded. "I want to see your tongue on the floor now!"

Theresa released him and stood, drawing herself to her full height. Relieved that his torment was finally over, Danny began pushing himself up from the floor. He rose no more than six inches before Theresa stepped on the back of his head and slammed him to the tile once more. The boy yelped in pain.

Across the hall, Daniel staggered back against the doorjamb of the bedroom, lifting a hand over his mouth in shock.

"Dan, listen to me, this isn't real." Miranda stepped in front of him in a vain effort to gain his attention.

"It *is* real, it happened to me." Daniel gently pushed her aside.

"But it isn't happening *now*," she insisted. "It's just a vision conjured up by the demon. You have to fight it! Dan, listen to me! Turn away. Ignore it!"

Though he knew she was right, Daniel couldn't help himself. He stepped away from Miranda and moved closer to the bathroom, stopping just outside the door. Tears blurred his vision. He wiped them away and forced himself to watch.

Under the tread of Theresa's shoe, the boy struggled to turn his face sideways. In doing so, his lower lip scraped against a shard of broken glass. Blood seeped into his mouth and across his chin.

"You're going to learn to be more careful, if I have to kill you," Theresa seethed. "Now, lick it up!"

In fear for his life, the boy had no choice.

Sickened, Daniel finally turned away unable to bear witness to this maleficent re-enactment. It was his earliest memory of Theresa's brutality and had ignited the spark of hatred that would grow over the years eventually to devastate their relationship.

Just then, a telephone rang putting an end to her vicious assault.

"Get up!" Theresa barked before hurrying out of the bathroom and down the steps. There was only one phone in the house, located on an end table in the living room.

While his mother answered the call, Daniel risked a glance into the bathroom. Danny pulled himself up, red and green dripping from his chin. He stood before the sink. His reflection in the mirror was exactly as it had been in Daniel's dream on the night that Theresa died.

Miranda went to Daniel. She gasped at the sight of the boy as he washed the blood and mouthwash from his face with trembling hands. While his nose had stopped bleeding, his lip had not and he pressed wet paper towel to the wound. Below his right eye, the skin was bruised and discolored from striking the tiled floor.

Daniel reached for the boy's shoulder but his hand merely passed through it.

"It doesn't seem like we can interact with them," Miranda said needlessly.

"You should put some ice on that eye," Daniel suggested, his voice hoarse. His words went unheard.

As if on cue, Theresa started up the stairs carrying an ice pack. The phone call had apparently deflated her anger. Her expression was forlorn as she walked right through Miranda and handed it to her son. Miranda shivered.

Yes! I remember what happened! Daniel waited for Theresa to confirm his recollection.

"That was Uncle Carl that called," she began solemnly. "Apparently he hired a plumber to come over today and inspect the furnace which meant that he had to go to each radiator in the house and bleed the air out of them. He didn't tell me in advance, of course. I guess since he owns the place, he didn't think he had to.

"They had to move some of my things out of the way to get to the radiator in my room. I'm sorry, Danny. Don't worry about the broken bottle, I'll clean it up."

She began crying as she dropped to her knees and wrapped her arms around him. "I'm so sorry. I've been under so much stress lately. My nerves are just shot thanks to your father. I didn't get a support check from him this month and my lawyer is trying to track him down.

"I didn't mean to take it out on you." She leaned back and looked at him, forcing a smile through her tears. "You know I love you, Danny."

The boy nodded silently. Fear was still evident in his eyes.

As Theresa proceeded to treat his injuries, Daniel leaned against the wall beneath the hallway light. "And so it began," he muttered.

On a dark, rainy summer afternoon there was no better place for a six-year-old than in front of the television. While visiting his grandparents recently, Danny's grandfather had introduced him to reruns of old shows including *Star Trek, Hogan's Heroes, The Avengers, The Twilight Zone* and a few others.

Danny became hooked and at every opportunity since then he tuned in faithfully, joining Captain Kirk and his crew as they overcame another seemingly insurmountable galactic threat or sneaking about with Colonel Hogan and his wisecracking band of pretend prisoners thwarting the bumbling Nazi menace in their own country. He was fascinated, even at his age, by those insightful tales of the bizarre hosted by Rod Serling and wondered how Emma Peel and John Steed always managed to brawl with the bad guys without moving a hair out of place. If only it worked that way in the schoolyard.

Daniel remembered how much he had missed his grandfather at that age and had wished that the constant arguments between Theresa and her parents had found a peaceful resolution so that he could have visited them more often. Vaughn Quinn had always made it a point to spend as much time as possible with his grandson whenever they were together. The pair had enjoyed long walks around the neighborhood during which he would regale Danny with engrossing tales of yesteryear. Somehow, Danny had never found them boring, even on the second or third telling.

Then one day, he had come home from school and suddenly Theresa was ranting about her parents, calling them liars and troublemakers. She had ordered him to ignore them if he crossed paths with them in public. His mother had frequently demanded that Danny show loyalty by hating the same people that she did and he acquiesced. Disobedience had painful consequences.

Presently, Daniel wondered why the demon had chosen to conjure this particular moment in his childhood. Everything certainly seemed peaceful enough. Sitting on the floor of the living room with his back against the coffee table, his younger self was absorbed in a Cary Grant movie playing on a small used television that Theresa had bought from a co-worker.

There was a knock at the front door. Danny jumped to his feet and walked over to the two double hung windows that looked out to the porch. He peeked through the blinds to see Miranda leaning against the railing.

"Who is it?" Theresa bellowed from the kitchen.

"Randy Lorensen," Daniel replied. "She's a friend from school. Can I go out and see her?"

"Sure. Just stay near the house, you hear me?"

"OK," Danny acknowledged, before opening the door and stepping outside.

Daniel turned to Miranda with a wry smile.

"What?" she asked suspiciously.

He nodded sideways toward the porch. "Your turn to see yourself as a kid."

Miranda moved to the window and peered out. "Oh, God, pigtails. This is too weird."

"Now you know how I feel."

A moment later, Theresa summoned her son back into the house. He asked Randy to wait outside. As Danny entered, Theresa calmly ordered him to close the door.

Daniel looked on broodingly as he tried to recall what had happened on this day. The memory was vague. Gauging the boy's expression, it was obvious that he sensed that something was amiss, but Daniel the adult was hard pressed to determine what could possibly have transpired in the last minute to perturb his mother.

The eight-year old closed the door behind him and joined her in the middle of the living room while Daniel and Miranda looked on.

"Why do you think I called you back in?" Theresa asked.

Danny looked at her, unable to provide an answer.

"I see," Theresa nodded. Without another word, she reached out and pulled him close, wrapping her arm around his throat. "Take a good look around the room. It should be very obvious."

In unison, both Daniel and Miranda looked around in search of something broken or missing.

Think! Why the hell did she do this to me? Daniel came up empty.

The boy's breathing became raspy and his face reddened.

A commercial playing on the television caught Daniel's attention. "It's the TV!" he shouted.

"I guess you don't pay attention when I tell you things," Theresa remarked through gritted teeth. Spittle formed on her lips as she spoke. She increased the pressure on her son's throat. He began gagging. "You force me to do these things to you because you never learn."

"Just because of the TV?" Daniel screamed. "You fucking bitch!" His tantrum was futile as he was an unseen spectator, unable to intervene in events that were already set in the stone of his past.

"I'll give you a hint." The woman spun, jerking Danny around to face the television.

Realization struck him. "Off…" the boy wheezed.

Theresa bowed her head close to his. "I'm sorry, what was that?"

"You goddamn monster," Daniel seethed as Danny pointed to the screen.

"Very good!" Theresa chimed mockingly. She dropped her arm and Danny fell to his knees, panting. With her foot, she shoved him onto his side so that he was looking up at her. "I'll bet *now* you'll never forget to turn off the TV before you leave the room." She walked off and returned to the kitchen.

Miranda looked to Daniel but he turned away, embarrassed at yet another painful moment from his childhood laid bare for her to see. He felt violated, exposed, and strangely even ashamed. *Why should I feel that way? If anyone should be ashamed, it's that abusive bitch!*

He looked out through the front window and his jaw dropped. Randy was peering in, hands cupped around her eyes. She had witnessed the entire incident, something that he never knew until this moment.

"Now, I know why you didn't wait for me on the porch," Daniel said without averting his gaze from the girl. "I came out a moment later and you were gone."

He watched as she backed away from the window and fled in apparent fear.

"Sorry, I was scared," Miranda replied in a quiet voice. "I didn't know what to do. I never saw anything like that before, except on TV. You know, those after school specials when they would do a show about child abuse, but I do remember running home and telling my mom."

"Really?" he said. He turned just as Danny finally got to his feet and switched off the television. "I'd love to hear how *that* conversation went down."

Daniel skirted past the boy and dashed out the door, with Miranda close behind. He started up the street after the girl until a sharp pain exploded in his right temple and flared through his skull. Clutching his head with both hands, Daniel doubled over in agony.

"Dan!" Miranda put her arms around him as he sank to his knees.

Impossibly, the bright clear sky above them suddenly darkened into night. A pair of headlights approached as a small white Datsun 210 turned the corner and slowly passed. He recognized it instantly as his mother's car though he had not seen it in over twenty-five years.

Oddly, she parked the car across the street despite the open space directly in front of their house. Daniel watched as Theresa pointed toward the home and spoke to her son for a few moments. The car windows were closed, preventing Daniel from hearing the conversation.

While the boy remained inside, Theresa left the vehicle and crossed the street to the house. As she passed under the streetlight, her face was illuminated for only a second, but long enough to show her troubled expression. Puzzled, Daniel stood up, with some help from Miranda, and made his way back down the street to the house. The pain in his head had subsided to a tolerable level.

He stopped at the porch steps and looked up. Bright light shone from every window in the house. Daniel frowned. He remembered that his mother habitually turned only one light on before going out at night. She would never have allowed such a waste of electricity.

Then again, she would never have left the front door wide open either.

Of course! Daniel's stomach turned as he whispered. "The robbery."

On a cold March night in 1979, Theresa had taken her son out to the movies to see *The Great Train Robbery* only to come home and find their own house ransacked. It was the only time when she had forgotten to turn the living room light on. The house had been in complete darkness making it an obvious target for burglars.

The sad irony of that night never faded and had fueled his mother to take extreme measures later.

Daniel lowered his head and muttered. "Oh, I think I know where this is going."

He looked back at Miranda only to find that they were no longer standing on the sidewalk outside of Daniel's childhood home. Rather, they were now in the cramped backseat of a small hatchback.

It took a moment for Daniel to become oriented to the sudden change of surroundings. The car lurched ahead then stopped. From behind the passenger seat, Daniel leaned forward for a closer look at the driver. "You gotta be kidding me."

"Where are we?" Miranda asked as she craned her neck to look into the passenger seat. Recognizing the boy in the passenger seat, she pointed to him. "Hey, look, it's you again."

"From mother to father," Daniel said incredulously as he sat back. "So the plot thickens. Randy, meet my dad, the asshole. He vanished out of my life when I was about ten. You know, new wife, new life. Before that, I remember that he used to take me here once in awhile after picking me up from my mom's."

"So what happens next?"

"We'd usually go to a nearby park to eat and just hang out for a few hours."

Gary Masenda pulled up to the drive-thru lane at McDonald's. As he waited to place his order, he turned to his eight-year old son in the passenger seat and pointed to his brand new sneakers. "Did your mom buy you those?"

Danny nodded.

"They're nice. Must've been expensive."

His son remained silent. Gary pulled the Honda Civic up to the speaker and recited his order.

"How about a strawberry milkshake?" he asked the boy.

"Yeah, can I?" Danny smiled, bouncing his feet enthusiastically.

"Sure," Gary replied, tousling his son's hair. He leaned out the window and finished ordering. As he rifled through his wallet for the total, he continued questioning the boy. "So is your mom working now?"

"Don't answer that," Daniel, the adult, growled from the back seat. "He's just pumping you for information." Then, to himself he muttered. "Shame I had to wait twenty-five years to knock you on your ass, old man."

The boy shrugged off his father's question.

"Does she have a job that she goes to everyday?" Gary pressed.

"No," Danny replied. "She's always there when I get home from school but she does baby-sit once in awhile."

"Ah, right." Gary nodded as they moved ahead toward the pickup window. "Does she get money from your grandparents?"

Danny pondered that for a moment. "Well, they bought us a new washing machine."

After getting their order, Gary drove over to the local playground where father and son took their food to one of the empty picnic tables. "Finish your lunch before you go off to play."

They ate in silence for a few minutes before Gary resumed his interrogation. "So if you're mom isn't working, how do you think can she afford to buy you those expensive sneakers?"

"Oh, fuck you!" Daniel bellowed. He was standing beside his father on the bench, looking down at him with venom in his eyes. "What the hell do you know? When was the last time you bought any clothes for your son, ya bastard!"

"I don't know," the boy said.

Gary sighed deeply.

"What's the matter, old man?" Daniel asked as he stepped off the bench. It was a rhetorical question, of course. "Not getting the answers you're looking for?"

"What's this all about?" Miranda asked.

"My...*father* wanted nothing more than to stop paying alimony and child support. He tried everything to get out of it but if he could somehow prove that my mom was gainfully employed, he could take her to court to stop paying at least the alimony."

"So he tried to manipulate you into giving up information." Miranda said. It was not a question. "Jeez, devious little creep."

Daniel sighed. "Well, if our demonic friend is directing this show the way I think he is, wait until you see what tactics dear old dad resorts to next."

Miranda frowned. "I can't seem to get a sense of what's to come. It's like my psychic abilities are being impeded."

"Well, the demon did say that this show was meant only for me. It should get interesting from here."

For the fourth consecutive morning, the yellow Chevy Impala parked at the top of the one-way street pulled away from the curb. It cruised slowly past the first row-home on the block before picking up speed.

"You and I seem to be spending a lot of time in back seats of old cars," Miranda commented as she turned to Daniel.

"Just like old times," he replied distractedly as he watched Gary lean over in the driver's seat to peer out through the passenger side window. Daniel followed his father's gaze to watch his mother and younger self emerge from his childhood home. He craned his neck to continue staring at them through the rear windshield as the car accelerated.

"Did you see that?" Daniel asked Miranda.

"We've been seeing the same thing four times in a row," she replied, clearly annoyed. "Your dad drives this obnoxious yellow car down the street just when you, the *other* you, and your mom are coming out of the house."

"Yeah, but I remember this day in particular because I made eye contact with him. This was the day I noticed him!"

"What's going on? How many times does he drive by here and did he get a new car? If so, he had crappy taste."

Daniel shook his head slowly, keeping his gaze fixed on his father, his stare boring a hole in the back of the man's head. "This is one of those situations where you had to be there to believe it."

"I seem to be here," Miranda reminded him with gentle sarcasm. "This may be a surreal recreation of moments from your childhood but I'm along for the ride, so I think that qualifies."

Daniel smiled wanly and leaned his head back as he launched into his story. "Pathetic as this is going to sound, Mr. Scumbag here apparently took a week off from work to spy on my mom. He obviously rented or borrowed a different car to do it."

"Who uses a bright yellow car to spy on someone?" Miranda asked rhetorically. "So why was he spying on your mom?"

She nearly jumped out of her seat as Gary spoke up. "Four days in a row dressed in professional clothes," he mumbled to no one in particular. "You can't tell me she doesn't have at least a part-time job, lying bitch. I'll be on the phone to my lawyer as soon as I get home."

"If only you knew the consequences of what you're about to do," Daniel said in a low, seething voice. "Though I wonder if you'd even care."

"This is about the alimony again," Miranda suddenly realized.

Daniel sighed. "As a kid, I didn't put the pieces together until... something else happened later on. I tried to tell my mom but she didn't believe me."

"What exactly happened later on?"

Daniel didn't reply nor did Miranda press him. They rode the rest of the way in silence. An hour later they found themselves in an unfamiliar neighborhood.

"This place familiar to you at all?" Daniel turned to Miranda. Her eyes were closed but she did not appear to be asleep. Her breathing was controlled, deliberate.

"Randy?"

After a few seconds, her eyelids fluttered open. She stared straight ahead.

"Are you okay?" Daniel asked.

"I've been trying to break through this barrier that the demon created to block me from seeing what's to come," she explained "I'll keep trying but it's like everything we're seeing is a projection. We haven't traveled back in time. All of this is happening now but it feels two-dimensional as if we're watching a movie. I can't sense anything around us but emptiness."

"Let me know if anything changes."

Miranda and Daniel remained with Gary as he returned the rental car and walked three blocks to a small café where he met his new fiancée, Dana.

"How did it go?" she asked. Daniel remembered her short sandy hair and thick-framed glasses.

Gary took a seat opposite her and grinned in a way that made Daniel's skin crawl, which was odd considering his present condition. "I got her," he replied in a low voice. "She was dressed in office attire every day I drove by. You don't wear that just to take your kid to school and come home."

"Are you sure they didn't see you?"

Gary shook his head. "Not a chance."

"Wrong!" Daniel chimed in as he dropped into a chair between the two.

"So now what?" Dana asked curiously.

Miranda nodded in her direction and whispered. "Dan, who is she?"

"Around this time, she was my dad's new wife-to-be, Dana Olsen, a.k.a. Supreme Bitch," Daniel explained. "This conversation oughta be good."

Gary leaned back confidently in his chair, hands folded behind his head. "I'll call my attorney this afternoon and tell him what I know."

"And *how* you know it?" Dana placed a hand up to the side of her face, thumb and pinkie extended, mimicking a telephone. "Yes, hi. I took four days off from work, rented a car, drove to another state and spied on my wife to find out whether she has a job or not. Do I have a case?"

She lowered her hand to the table and pointed at Gary. "You can't really think that'll hold up in court."

He shrugged. "What do you want me to say, Dana? I can't afford both alimony and child support. I'm goin' broke."

"If you tell him what you did, you'll look like a scumbag," Dana warned.

"See?" Daniel slammed his fist on the table. It quivered visibly upon impact but no one seemed to notice. "What did I tell you, Mr. Scumbag!"

"The last time you were with Danny," she continued. "Didn't he mention that Theresa was working part-time?"

"Baby-sitting," Gary scoffed. "That's all. Why?"

Dana took a sip from her coffee as an idea formed in her head. "Well, all you need to do is inform your lawyer that during your last weekend with your son, he told you that your ex-wife has a job."

Gary frowned. "He's an eight-year old. How reliable would that be in litigation?"

Dana began counting on her fingers. "First of all, he lives with her, so he would know. Secondly, you wouldn't exactly be lying. He did tell you that she was working—"

"Baby-sitting!" Gary repeated in exasperation.

"*And,*" Dana persisted without missing a beat. "It's a hell of a lot better than admitting to spying on your ex-wife. Some guys who've done that ended up in jail for murder. You see it on the news all the time."

Daniel's eyes went wide. "You conniving bitch! You're setting me up!" He looked at his father. "You let this wench push you into making me a scapegoat! That's even worse than if it was completely your idea! I don't believe this bullshit!"

Daniel closed his eyes and cradled his head in his hands. "I just want to scream."

"Before you do that, I need to talk to you."

He sat bolt upright. "What?" He shot a glance at Gary only to find that he had been replaced by Theresa and to his left sat his eight-year old reflection. The café had transformed into the kitchen of his childhood home. *Back again…these transitions are freakin' me out!* Daniel frowned as he looked behind him. Miranda was gone.

"I said, before you start your homework I need to talk to you."

Danny laid his pencil atop the table and turned his full attention to his mother.

"I bought something today." She lifted her hand from beneath the table.

In it was a gun.

Specifically, a black .38 caliber Smith and Wesson revolver with a wood grip. Daniel's expression turned pensive as his eyes fixed on the weapon. Conversely, his younger self was in awe.

"This is for home protection, do you understand?" Theresa continued. "You are not to touch this. It is not a toy. The gun and the bullets will be stored in separate places in the house and I'm not telling you where. All you need to know is that I have it just in case, God forbid, I ever need to use it.

"And you're not to tell anyone that I have it, especially your father. Is that clear?"

"Okay," Danny replied simply.

"Good." She turned the gun over in her hands. "All I want to do is keep you safe. If those bastards break in here again while we're home, this gun will be the last thing they see."

"Don't put me through this," Daniel whispered. "God, I don't think I can stand to watch that." As he stood to leave, the sharp pain in his head returned, accompanied by another just below his chest. He stumbled into the living room and dropped onto the sofa. His breathing became forced and he let out a strangled moan as the pain intensified.

There was movement elsewhere in the house, but Daniel ignored it as he flopped over onto his side. His attention was consumed by his own suffering. As if drained of energy, he suddenly felt weak and his eyelids grew heavy.

And for a time, Daniel Masenda faded away.

"Wake up!"

Consciousness slowly returned to Daniel, yet his mind didn't immediately process external sounds. He was preoccupied with his own condition. He was no longer in pain. This was a good start. His eyes fluttered open and focused on the paisley upholstery of the sofa. He closed his eyes again as he was reminded of his whereabouts. Daniel was uncertain how much time had passed since he collapsed but the house was now in total darkness save for the meager glow shining down from the second floor. He looked around for Miranda, called out to her, but she was still nowhere to be found.

Randy, where are you?

"I know you're not really asleep so stop pretending!"

The shouting was coming from upstairs. It was Theresa's voice, irate as usual. Daniel righted himself until he was sitting properly. Once he was confident that his legs were under him, he stood and made his way to the top of the stairs. The first thing he noticed was the puff of smoke drifting from the open doorway of his bedroom. Frowning in confusion, he peeked in to see Theresa pulling a cigarette from her mouth with one hand, ashtray in the other.

It was a rare sight. Daniel could only recall two occasions when his mother had smoked and at the time, he found it surprisingly out of character given her ardent criticism of the habit. She had rationalized it as 'stress relief', but if there had been one thing consistent about Theresa, it was her propensity for self-contradiction.

Do what I say, not what I do, Daniel mused as he entered the room.

"I was talking to Mrs. Hartman down the street," Theresa was saying as Daniel entered. He stepped around her to see Danny sitting up in bed, barely able to keep his eyes open. "She just happened to mention that you and a friend were playing in the backyard after school."

According to the alarm clock atop the dresser, it was eleven forty-five. There had been random times when his mother woke him late at night to vent about her problems, interrogate him about his father, or generally chastise him. As such, the scene playing out before Daniel now was not an uncommon event.

"Do you remember when I told you not to let anyone in the house when I wasn't around?" she asked.

"We weren't in the house," Danny replied wearily.

Theresa took a drag from her Lucky Strike, turned, and blew the smoke at her son's face. "How do I know that?"

The boy turned away and coughed. She dropped the cigarette into the ashtray and grabbed him by the chin, snapping his head forward. "You look at me when I talk to you, boy! I told you no one is allowed in this house when you're here alone. Did I not?"

She rocked Danny's head up and down in agreement. He was far too frightened to speak or move now. "Do you realize what I go through as a single parent? I work two jobs, take care of you and run this house all by myself, go to court to battle your deadbeat father who keeps moving to avoid supporting you, but do you make my life any easier? Of course not."

Slipping her hand from his chin, she took one last drag, again exhaling the smoke in his direction.

"We really did stay in the backyard." Daniel repeated his assertion of nearly thirty years ago, not that it would do any good now. He leaned against the dresser in resignation, eyes downcast. He still couldn't fathom why he was being made to return to these distressing moments in his childhood, or when they would finally come to an end.

I remember this day very clearly because I told Miranda that I couldn't let her in the house and she was very understanding so we stayed in the yard. For Christ's sake, she was only here for twenty minutes anyway!

Theresa held up the smoldering butt of the Lucky Strike. "Maybe I should put this out on your face, you little bastard." After a moment, she crushed it into the ashtray. "But I wouldn't want to leave a mark. People would notice that and ask questions now wouldn't they? Besides, you have plenty of those elsewhere, don't you? That's what happens when you don't listen. So, I think that as punishment for your constant disrespect, you don't deserve a bed to sleep in tonight." She grabbed him by the front of his t-shirt and dragged him across the covers.

"No!" Danny cried, squirming in her grasp. "I'm sorry, I'm sorry!"

His mother slapped him repeatedly across the face and head. "Don't you struggle with me! You're going to learn to do what you're told!"

Daniel cringed as the boy dropped to the floor with a thud.

"If I were you, I'd stay down!" Theresa snarled. "Because that's exactly where you're spending the night. On the cold, hard floor with no pillow and no covers if that's what it takes to teach you to respect your mother! You force me to do these things to you. Do you think I enjoy it? I don't need this aggravation!"

During her tirade, Daniel slid down the side of the dresser to the floor, his eyes downcast as yet another frightening moment in his childhood played out before him. He folded his arms across his knees and lowered his head.

"You have no idea," she continued. "How much I wish I never married that son of a bitch and how much I wish you were never born. God knows my life would be so much better without either of you.

"I could have gone to college, had an education, got a real job making real money but instead I let my fuckin' parents brainwash me. Oh they sent my brothers to college but women were meant to be good little housewives and secretaries. I should never have listened to their bullshit! If I didn't I wouldn't be stuck in this rundown dump with you! I hate them and I hate you for being nothing but a fuckin' burden to me!"

"I'm sorry." Daniel and Danny spoke in unison.

The boy's voice began to quiver. "I didn't know..."

"Didn't know what?" Theresa snapped.

Danny started to cry. "I'm sorry about all that."

"Shut up! What do you care? You make me sick, and don't think that you're just going to climb in bed the minute I walk out of here." She stepped over him and flipped off the light switch before stretching across Danny's bed. "I'll be spending the night right here. If you wake me up by so much as sneezing, I will beat you up and down every inch of this house. Now quit your damn crying and go to sleep."

"Stop this," Daniel whispered, before screaming at the top of his lungs. "Just stop this! Why the hell are you doing this to me?"

No one answered. The house fell silent.

Perforated moonlight shined through the blinds, washing over Danny's prone form on the floor. He was shivering, partly from the cold, mostly from fear. He was dressed only in a t-shirt and pajama pants.

Daniel removed his jacket. "I don't know if this will help considering you can't even see me." He sat down beside the boy and draped it over him, covering his upper body.

Barely an hour passed when Daniel picked himself up from the floor and walked to the window. He opened the blinds, expecting to gaze at the stars but instead found himself momentarily blinded by the bright glare of sunlight. In confusion, he turned to look behind him. The bed was empty and his jacket lay flat on the floor where Danny had been.

According to the alarm clock, it was now four-thirty in the afternoon. Time seemed to be little more than a tool in this bizarre realm, its purpose a mere prop in the depiction of these dreadful incidents from his past.

After retrieving his jacket, he cautiously descended the stairs. At first, it appeared that no one was at home until Daniel heard a pair of muffled voices. He followed the sounds to the basement where he found Danny accompanied by two other boys. Instantly, he recognized Nathan and his younger brother Paul, who had moved into the neighborhood nearly five years after Theresa and Danny. All three were engrossed in the model train set that had been a birthday gift from Danny's grandfather. It was laid out atop a large makeshift plywood platform supported by four sawhorses. The wood had been spray painted green and was populated with various miniature buildings, people, and landscapes. Some of them had been antique even in 1979.

Oh, wow... Daniel was elated to see it again, far more detailed and intricate than he recalled. Sadly, it would only be a few more years before Theresa would force him to disassemble the entire display as the platform was eventually used for additional storage space.

"I remember it, too."

Daniel spun to find Miranda approaching from the front of the basement. "I thought I lost you," he said. Relief was obvious in his voice.

"You did," she confirmed. "We lost contact. I think our demonic ringmaster has had enough of me. I woke up back in my car, extremely disoriented. It took me a few minutes to find you again."

"I ended up back here," Daniel said. "On the day my mother bought her gun."

At the rear of the basement, the double metal doors that led out to the backyard were wide open and Daniel could see Theresa sweeping the patio. The aroma of freshly cut grass permeated the air. Judging by the children's t-shirts and shorts, Daniel guessed that it was late spring. They were still discussing teachers and classmates in the present tense, evidence that the school year had not yet ended.

"I think I'm starting to see what's happening here," Miranda informed him anxiously. "And maybe even *why*."

"Really?"

The phone rang in the living room above and Theresa disappeared from the patio. Less than a minute later, she called down from the top of the basement steps.

"Guys, your mom called. She wants you home for dinner."

Danny turned off the controls and the locomotive came to a halt on a bridge that stood several inches over a painted blue river. Daniel's brow furrowed as he leaned forward for a closer look at the bridge. There was a jagged edged hole in the center as if something had punched through the plastic railroad ties. It was a detail that he didn't recall from childhood but seemed oddly familiar as if it belonged there as much as the nearby church and walking trail that paralleled the winding river. There was something inexplicably ominous about the scene. Though he couldn't pinpoint why, Daniel suddenly felt uneasy at the sight of it.

"Dan," Miranda said. "What's wrong?"

He drew back from the platform and shrugged casually. "Nothing. You know...just good to see all this again."

Outside, Danny waved good-bye to his new friends as they departed through the chain link gate that opened to the sidewalk. He hurried back to the basement to resume the train's circuitous trek through the grassy mountainsides and plastic towns. As the caboose cleared the bridge, Daniel took one last look.

The hole was gone.

Motioning to Miranda, Daniel felt compelled to get out of the basement. "You had something to tell me. Let's talk upstairs."

They arrived just in time to see Theresa toss a stack of mail atop the dining room table. If there was only one thing he learned during his experience in this realm, it was that everything happened for a reason. As such, he suspected that there was something pertinent among the envelopes and grocery store circulars that he was meant to see. He gave them a quick scan. There were four envelopes, partially overlapping one another. The first two were bills, the third a credit card offer.

The fourth was a letter from Gary's attorney.

Damn it! He moved away from the table toward the living room, his stomach sinking. "I knew this was coming," he said in low voice. "Fuck no. Don't do this to me. I don't want to relive that."

"Now what?" Miranda asked.

Theresa poked her head into the basement doorway. "Everything all right down there?" she asked.

"Yeah, I'm fine!"

Not for long. Daniel thought. Tautly, he observed Theresa as she picked up the letter. It was only a matter of minutes now.

"What the hell is this?" she grumbled, reaching for the letter opener. It did not take long to find the answer. Blood seemed to drain from her face as she read. "Oh, no. Oh my God, no. Danny, get up here!"

"I should've run out the back door," he muttered. Then to Miranda, "You witnessed all of my dad's questions about my mom's finances, all of his spying and plotting. Now you're about to see the result. Hold onto something."

As the youngster emerged from the cellar, Daniel dropped onto the sofa and lowered his head, wishing that he could vanish from existence.

"I'm going to ask you something and I want the truth," his mother began. "Did you tell your dad that I'm working full time?" Danny thought for a moment.

"It wouldn't have mattered what answer I gave you," Daniel said. "You already had your mind made up. I was taking the fall."

"I don't get it," Miranda said.

Finally, the boy shook his head.

"Think!" Theresa pleaded, here eyes moist with sudden tears. "Did he ever ask you if I was working?"

"Yeah, but I said no. I said that you were home all the time."

"Well, somehow he knows and he wants to stop paying alimony!" She was screaming now, arms flailing frantically. "I'm barely scraping by as it is! The only way he could've found out is if you told him. Now I want the truth!"

"I'll tell you the goddamn truth!" Daniel leapt to his feet and marched toward his mother, stopping within mere inches from her face. "None of this was my fault! This wasn't my battle but you both used me as a fucking pawn!"

"Dan, what's happening?" Miranda asked.

"Fine, I know a way to make you talk, you little bastard." Theresa threw the letter to the floor and stepped around her son. Danny merely turned to watch his mother as she returned to the dining room table and began rifling through her purse.

Though his face betrayed no expression, the boy was frozen in fear. Daniel knew this because he remembered standing there nearly thirty years ago, heart pounding, bracing himself for some unknown punishment for an unknown offense. The only difference was that Daniel knew what was about to come in the next few seconds. Yet that knowledge provided no comfort. Instead, he found himself even more frightened now than he had been then.

As boy and man looked on, Theresa found what she sought and lifted her hand from her purse.

Damn it, no. Please, God…

"Danny?"

Randy Lorensen stood just beyond the cellar doors and peered curiously down into the basement. Just a few moments ago, she stopped to talk with Nathan and Paul from whom she learned about Danny's exciting birthday gift. Rather than knock at the front door, she decided to surprise him. Yet there was only silence, no telltale sounds of an active train set and no response to her beckon.

Quietly, she made her way down the short flight of steps. Though the rear of the basement was dark, overhead lights illuminated the rest of the room ahead of her. Still, Danny was nowhere to be found. Randy stood by the platform, awed by the elaborate diorama. Though the locomotive was stopped on its way into a tunnel, traffic lights and storefront signs flashed in random patterns on the little town's main street.

"Think!"

Randy started at the piercing sound of Theresa's voice. Her breath caught in her throat as the woman continued shrieking, presumably at Danny. The girl then realized that they were directly above her. While her mind urged her to run, fear kept her motionless. The floorboards snapped and creaked as heavy footfalls moved over her.

"No, please! I didn't say anything to him! Please don't kill me!"

Randy shuddered as she recognized Danny's voice, pleading for his life. *Run*! She moved away from the platform toward the cellar doors but halted in mid-stride. If her friend was in danger, how could she leave him? Then again, what could she possibly do to help? At the very least she would tell her parents and this time, make them do something. Before she did, however, she had to know exactly what to say.

Randy drew herself to her full height as she turned and gingerly crept up the stairs to the first floor. As she approached the top step, she held her breath and pressed herself flat against the wall. Theresa and her son were both shouting at one another, their words overlapping such that Randy couldn't determine what it was all about. She was scared now and tears began streaking down her face as she craned her neck around the doorjamb. They were no longer in the dining room. Randy turned her body and dared a glance toward the front of the house. She breathed an inward sigh of relief at seeing Theresa's back toward her—but nearly screamed as she watched the woman seize Danny by his throat and shove him against the front door with a sickening thud.

Theresa raised her other hand, pressing the barrel of a gun against the side of her son's head, burrowing it into his temple.

"No, please! I didn't say anything to him! *Please don't kill me*!"

Daniel Masenda could tolerate no more. "God dammit, why are you doing this to me?" Tearfully, he closed his eyes and turned his back on the horrifying scene, the defining moment that forever shattered the relationship between mother and son. He fell to his knees and pressed his hands against his ears in a vain attempt to mute the desperate screams of his younger self.

"Dan, listen to me!" Miranda crouched down beside him, put her hands on his arm. "Listen to me! Shut it out! Shut it out of your mind! I know what the demon's trying to do! I figured it out!"

Miranda tugged at his arm but Daniel recoiled from her and began punching the floor as Danny screamed at the top of his lungs, pleading for his life, only to be cut off by Theresa's choking grasp.

"Don't make me pull this trigger, boy!" She barked. "The truth is the only way out of this!"

"*Shut up*!" Daniel yelled. "*Shut the fuck up*!"

Miranda moved directly in front of him. "Dan, you have to listen to me. This is exactly what it wants from you. I've broken through! It all makes sense now. Remember what the boy said, you need to 'end the punishment, only then will the suffering soul find peace'. This isn't just about you, it's—"

Suddenly Miranda began to fade. She became transparent before his eyes.

"I can't stay here any longer!"

"Randy? No!" Daniel eyes widened. "Find Vicki, please! Tell her everything. Tell her I'm sorry! Tell her I love her!"

"Where is she?"

"Try the airport! Randy? *Randy*!"

The hideous visage of the demon flashed into his mind. It was indeed his reflection as it had been from the beginning. Daniel knew this now and with that knowledge came intense sorrow. All of his dark, monstrous emotions clawed their way to the surface of his soul until they consumed him like a cancer. Hatred, bitterness, regret, vengeance. His reflection had been the truth that lay hidden, ignored for fourteen years until the death of his mother released the inner demon that would no longer be denied.

Finally, his self-control relented to the anguish and at the top of his lungs, Daniel Masenda roared.

"Try the airport!"

"I'm already there."

Breathing sharply, Miranda awoke from her trance. After regaining her composure, she reached down to unclip her seatbelt only to find that she couldn't. Suddenly, her car door locked. Frowning in confusion, she pressed the unlock button to no avail. Fear began rising in the back of her mind as Miranda tugged the door handle in vain.

The seatbelt strap crossing her chest shot upward and wrapped around her throat. Miranda's scream of panic was instantly choked off as her fingers clawed at the tightening strap. She felt herself shoved forward into the steering wheel seat before being thrown flat on her back as her seat reclined sharply.

"I told you, your time would come, woman."

It was the voice of the demon. Miranda remembered it vividly from the previous night. Her eyes darted in every direction, but there was no one in sight.

"You can't help him now. You can't help either of them. They're both *mine*!"

Chapter Eleven
Final Chance

There was silence.

Daniel opened his eyes, slowly moved his hands away from his head, and stared at the unmarred white surface beneath him. The interior of his childhood home had vanished, supplanted by a seemingly boundless empty void. He couldn't discern floor from wall, wall from ceiling. There was no depth, no height, merely a glowing white infinity that defied his comprehension.

He rose to his feet and turned completely around, taking in the nothingness, searching for a seam, a blemish, the hint of an entrance or exit. There were none. Daniel began walking and continued for what may as well have been hours. Without a sense of direction, he could have walked in complete circles, or the length of ten city blocks, or he may never have moved at all.

The only certainly was the increasing feeling of loneliness. Perhaps he had finally reached his Hell.

"You were never alone," a soft voice called out from everywhere. "And this isn't Hell."

Slowly, Daniel realized a presence behind him. He spun to face his mother.

For the first time in fourteen years, mother and son looked upon one another in a place beyond time and reality.

She stood ten feet away, ten miles away, as young as she had been through the tormenting visions from Daniel's youth. Yet now she looked upon him not with the hatred with which he had become accustomed, but with pity—and was that a touch of fear?

"We can talk to each other now?" Daniel asked.

"Of course," Theresa said.

"Well, then I guess it wasn't enough, everything you did to me back then," Daniel began, his tone scathing. "You had to completely ruin my life *now*, sending that thing to kill me—"

"Nice to see you, too," Theresa interrupted, maintaining a calm, light tone. "If it helps, I never wanted to ruin your life and I definitely never wanted to kill you."

"Really? Well, you didn't exactly get off to a good start! You know, I think we had a similar discussion before I left home. I asked you why you did these things to me. Do you remember the bullshit excuse you gave me, as if I was supposed to just buy it? As if it would make everything all right? *Do you remember*?"

Theresa nodded somberly. "Yes."

"Then tell me again! Once more for old time's sake!"

"I said that my nerves were shot."

"So you spat in my face, stomped my head into the floor, pulled a gun on me all because your nerves were shot?" Daniel pointed an accusing finger. "That's not good enough! Why did I have to suffer for *your* misery? Why did I have to pay the price for *your* bad decisions in life? Give me a damn good reason, *right now*!"

Theresa held out her hands plaintively. "There was no reason in the world why you should've had to go through that. I admit you deserved better. Danny, I know how much you hate me and why. What I did to you was despicable. At the time, I was immature and filled with rage at your father, not to mention my own family. I had no experience at being a parent, let alone a single mother. I was twenty-five, divorced, and broke. Most of all, I was scared, Danny.

"My own parents scorned me after the divorce. The entire family was riddled with infighting and backstabbing. I had no friends to rely on because I closed myself off from the world."

Theresa began sobbing as she spoke. Her voice trembled as she continued. "Without any emotional support, I took out my problems on the dearest person in my life. I never realized the damage I was inflicting on you both inside *and* out, never took into consideration the consequences of my words and actions. I was too bitter to think about the future, it was always about surviving one day to the next.

"After you left, I spent a long time hating you, but as the years dragged on I finally faced the truth. Blaming you was really just a way of deflecting my own guilt for everything I did to you. Of course, by then it was too late to tell you. I blew it. You were gone and I had no idea where to find you. I desperately wanted to see you again because I knew I pushed you away."

Daniel exhaled and turned his eyes to the white surface below. As he listened to his mother's confession, he struggled to hold onto his anger, reluctantly giving way to remorse and sadness. When he spoke again, he kept his tone civil. "OK, so answer this. Why did you forbid the family from contacting me when you were diagnosed with cancer? You didn't even want me to know when you…when you died."

Theresa nodded. "Another mistake born out of bitterness. There was a part of me that couldn't bear to let you see me like that and another part that didn't think you would care. By then, we knew where you were. Paul found your name on the Internet when you were elected mayor.

"You might find this hard to believe but even though I never told anyone, I was happy and proud to hear that you were doing well."

A dull throbbing started in Daniel's head as she spoke. He massaged his right temple as the pain intensified. Nevertheless, he remained focused. "My mom is dying of cancer and she didn't think I would care. Did it ever occur to you that during those fourteen years I might've taken the time to think about everything, too? At the risk of turning this into a therapy session, I still battle with my own guilt for turning my back on you and for a long time, I closed myself off from the world, too.

"So I can sympathize but the fact is I had to leave! I had to get the hell out or risk becoming just like you. I was already starting to see it happen. It really hit home that day I almost strangled you when you tried to stop me from going to counseling in college. At that moment when I had my hands around your throat, I wanted nothing more than to see you dead. You only had yourself to blame! When you kick a dog enough times, eventually it's gonna bite you back and that's exactly what happened.

"And then to top it off, despite every beating, every insult, every ounce of self-esteem you kicked out of me, you demanded respect and loyalty. When you didn't get it, you started dictating my life, invading my privacy, taking away my freedom like a fucking warden!

"If you wanted respect, you went about it the wrong way, but you know what the worst part is? Even knowing all of that, knowing that what you did was wrong, somewhere deep down I still felt like that 'little bastard' that you used to call me. Congratulations, you really did a number on me, mother dear."

"You needed to get that off your chest, I understand." Theresa approached him slowly. "But none of that matters anymore. It's in the past. You need to—"

"It matters to *me*!" he retorted. "I need you to know this. All I ever wanted was a normal fucking life, to be treated like a human being!"

"I know—"

"No you don't! You never knew that when I was a kid, I was convinced that I must've somehow deserved what happened. After all, you were my mother. I didn't know any better. Why else would you have done these things to me?

"I tried so damn hard to prove myself to you, to show you that I was worthy of your respect and approval, but no matter what I did it was never good enough! You just beat me down again and again.

"I would've done anything to just get you to love me." As he uttered that last sentence, Daniel finally broke down into tears. "Goddammit!"

Theresa reached out and placed her hands on her son's shoulders. "*I know*, Danny. A part of me knew it then, too, but I was too steeped in my own selfish needs to care about yours. Look, you're my son, and I love you. I always did. I'm sorry I didn't show that more often but there were good times, too. It wasn't all bad. Carnivals and circuses, movies, days at the park, trips to the beach."

Daniel scoffed. "Yeah, any day when I wasn't afraid of you was a good day."

Theresa folded her arms, her expression annoyed. "Anything else?"

When Daniel remained silent, she continued. "Why should the bad times hold more weight, more importance for you, than the good times? At the risk of sounding like a therapist, the demon has made it so that the darkest memories are fresh in your mind, forcing you to focus solely on them.

"I'd appreciate it if you'd let me have a turn." Theresa held out her hand. "Come with me."

Daniel wasn't certain if he wanted to continue reliving any more moments from his childhood yet he knew that his mother had a valid point. At the very least, he owed her the chance to state her case. With a deep breath, he took her hand.

And colors began to bloom out of the white nothingness surrounding them.

"Back again."

Daniel turned to look around the living room of his childhood home. Everything was as it had been just minutes—years?—ago, except that something *felt* different. For starters, the room was oddly dark. The white aluminum blinds covering the two double hung windows were closed, permitting only thin bands of light between the slats.

Further, there was a strange silence, or perhaps a *strained* silence would have been more appropriate.

On the couch, Theresa and Danny sat beside one another, looking much the same as they had since the beginning of this ethereal odyssey through Daniel's past. As usual, the scene was permeated by an almost tangible atmosphere of tension and fear. It was then that Daniel realized the difference. This time, it was not the boy who was scared.

It was his mother.

"Weird seeing myself like this," Theresa commented from beside Daniel. The pair stood across the room from their younger selves, near the bottom of the stairs.

"Tell me about it." Daniel mumbled. "What's going on? It's quiet as a morgue in here."

"There's a reason for that," Theresa replied solemnly. "Just watch and listen."

Rising from the couch, Danny's mother stepped over to the window. Slowly, she parted two of the slats just enough to peek out into the street. After a moment, she suddenly yanked her hand away and turned her attention back to her son.

"Your dad's here," she announced in a low voice. "But I don't want you to go out there just yet."

"Why not?" the boy asked.

Theresa exhaled audibly before explaining. "He's very angry with me and I'm afraid that he might take it out on you."

Across the room, Daniel scoffed. "Look who's talking." He shot a sidelong glance at his mother, but her expression remained fixed on the scene playing out in the living room. If her feelings were hurt by his remark, she didn't allow it to show.

From the street outside, the persistent blaring of a car horn signaled Gary Masenda's growing impatience. Normally, Danny had always waited on the front porch for his father's arrival. After a full minute, the incessant noise ceased, but was followed by the slam of a car door. A moment later, the front door shook under the force of several solid blows.

"Open the fuckin' door!" Gary shouted. "I know you're in there! I didn't drive all this way for nothing!"

Daniel shot a glance at the boy on the couch. He sat rigid, jaw clenched as he stared at the front door. Such body language in times of stress had remained with Daniel all of his life until it became an involuntary reaction. He had never given it much thought until now as he forced himself to relax his shoulders.

"Don't worry, that bolt lock will hold," young Theresa assured her son, though the quiver in her voice betrayed her confident façade.

"If I have to pay more to support the two of you," Gary continued, accenting every third word with a violent pounding on the door. "I want to see my son or I'll take *you* to court next time, you stupid bitch! Now open the goddamn door!"

"Danny, go upstairs," Theresa pointed to the steps, her tone low but firm. "Right now."

Slowly, the boy stood and made his way across the room toward Daniel and his mother. Automatically, each took one step away from the other to permit the boy to pass, though it was unnecessary as the people in these flashbacks were non-corporeal and, as Daniel learned early on, could pass through him as if *he* were the ghost haunting *their* world.

Daniel started at a sudden crashing sound from the front porch, followed by the slamming of the wrought iron gate. Danny stopped mid-way up the steps to watch as Theresa finally picked up the phone to call the police.

Twenty minutes later, two officers stood on the front porch as Theresa detailed the events of the past hour. In her hands, she held the black metal mailbox that Gary had knocked from the front wall of the house.

Daniel observed his younger self as he sat on the steps and watched it all through the storm door window. He nodded his head. "Now I think I remember this. It came back to me as soon as I saw the mailbox, not to mention the dents along the bottom of the front door."

"At the time, I'd just sued your father for an increase in child support...and I won," his mother explained. "Gary actually exploded at me in the courthouse. His own lawyer had to drag him outside to shut him up. He was incredibly violent when he was young."

"That's all right," Daniel snarled. "What goes around comes around."

"If you're referring to your meeting at the mall, I happen to know that you regretted what you did almost immediately after."

"Doesn't matter. In the end, he had it coming."

Theresa shook her head. "Two wrongs don't make a right. You really need to learn to let go. Do you remember what else happened this same weekend? Where we went the next day? Maybe this will brighten your outlook."

Like clockwork, Saint Gregory's had hosted its annual church carnival during the second week of May and somehow, it had always worked out so that Theresa and Danny found themselves able to attend at least one night.

For Daniel, it had been a rare and welcome respite from the stress of home life. He remembered how relaxed his mother had seemed while they were there and how much of a relief that had been to him.

One night without worry.

Here and now, Daniel stood in the center of it all, the unobserved observer, surrounded by food kiosks, game stands, flashing lights, rock music, and most importantly, the rides. To his left, the Pirate Ship swung back and forth like a pendulum, gaining momentum that would eventually propel the gondola to a vertical position at each end of its arc.

Beyond that, the Chair-O-Planes spun like a giant blue and gold top, twirling children and adults alike in a high-speed circle as it tilted on its center axis. Directly ahead, however, the Ferris wheel towered above all else. It remained Daniel's favorite ride. The experience of seeing everything from a bird's eye view had always been exhilarating.

"Funnel cake would be good about now."

Daniel turned to see his mother approaching from behind him. "Or cotton candy, or a Sno-Cone," he added. "I definitely remember this. The church in my town holds a carnival every July. It reminds me of this one."

"I know," Theresa grinned. "You still ride the Ferris wheel."

Daniel returned the smile. "Yes I do."

"So let's ride this one, for old time's sake."

Daniel raised his eyebrows. "I didn't think we could interact here in this...wherever we are."

"Not with the people, but you're standing on the grass, right? Since you've been *here,* you've walked up and down steps and sat in chairs. Don't think about it too much, just go with it."

Theresa nodded her head toward the Ferris wheel. "Shall we?"

"But aren't we here to watch our past selves?" Daniel asked as they began walking.

"They're off having a good time at the moment," his mother waved dismissively. "We'll have plenty of time for that later."

Five minutes later, the pair was lifted skyward, confined in a white metal seat that slowly rocked as they ascended.

Riding a Ferris wheel in the afterlife, Daniel mused. *This is insane.*

When they reached the top, the wheel abruptly stopped and the seat lurched forward. Looking down, Daniel frowned. They seemed far higher than they should have been. The church grounds appeared to be a mile below—and utterly deserted, as were the other seats on the wheel.

He turned to his mother. "What's going on?" He demanded. "What is this?"

"I thought you might enjoy a private view." She held out her hand toward the horizon.

Daniel gazed out at the distant landscape, taking in the river, the walking trail, the railroad bridge. After a moment, his eyes widened as he realized that this was not the town of his childhood.

It was Port Kirkland.

"I think this is where you say, 'I can see my house from here'," Theresa quipped.

Her attempt at humor was lost on Daniel who slipped into a ponderous silence, eyes fixed on the railroad bridge.

"Why am I seeing this?" he asked finally.

"It was on your mind."

"I was thinking about the life I left behind."

"And the people?"

Daniel nodded. "What else can I see?"

"Name it."

"Vicki."

"Of course." Theresa looked beyond Daniel to the right toward the horizon.

He turned to follow her gaze until he was staring at a massive window that spanned a wide section of the second level of a building approximately one hundred feet away. He looked down and was surprised to find that the Ferris wheel was now sitting atop an open area of macadam between what appeared to be two concourses. It dawned on Daniel that they were now at Baltimore-Washington International Airport. He instantly recognized the three intersecting runways far off to the left.

He returned his attention to the window of the terminal's Observation Lounge. In the center of it, Vicki stared out at him. Daniel felt his heart jump, which he fleetingly noted was rather odd given his current condition.

"Can she see us?"

"No. Nothing's changed, Danny, we're still just an audience in a movie theatre. The actors on the screen can't hear or see us."

Daniel then noticed dark figures moving about behind Vicki. "What are those shadows?"

"Just other people going about their business in the terminal."

"Why are they only appearing as silhouettes?"

"Because they don't matter to you," Theresa replied flatly. "Only she does."

He wanted to shout, to find some way to get through to Vicki, to hold her in his arms and feel himself in hers. Instead, he could only watch until she turned away from the window and blended in with the rest of the shadow people.

"I thought you'd want to see her," Theresa said. "To know that she was safe. The demon had no interest in her."

"Yeah…thanks." Daniel lowered his head and sighed loudly. *The demon?* He sat up with a start and turned to his mother. "What about Randy?"

With a sudden jolt, the Ferris wheel continued on its course and they began descending. Daniel looked down once more to find that they had returned to Saint Gregory's carnival.

"What about Randy?" Daniel repeated, his tone mixed with anger and alarm.

Theresa shook her head. "I don't know. I can't find her."

"Can't find her? I thought I could see anything or anyone I wanted?"

"I'm sorry, Danny, I'm limited on what I can do. You asked earlier about watching our past selves. There's something down there that might interest you."

They reached the bottom and stepped out of the car onto the metal deck. As they proceeded down the ramp, Daniel happened to look up and spotted Danny near one of the game stands. He was surrounded by four other kids, three of whom were much taller. By the look on Danny's face, it was clearly a confrontation.

Daniel hurried over as the four closed in on their prey. He recognized two of them instantly though he couldn't recall their names. At the time, they both had a reputation for trouble.

"You here by yourself?" the tallest one asked. As Daniel recalled, he had always been the ringleader.

"No." Danny answered simply.

"I don't see anyone else," one of the other goons chimed in. "Who ya here with, asshole?"

"Me."

All four heads looked up to see Danny's mother approach from behind him. They each took a few steps back.

"Is there a problem?" she asked, glaring at each of them in turn before settling on the tallest.

All four looked at each other and shook their heads, avoiding her burning gaze.

"Danny, why don't you wait for me by the water pistol game?" Theresa placed her hands on her son's shoulders and gently moved him to the right. "I'll be there in a minute."

Without a word, the boy obeyed, never looking back.

As Daniel watched the scene play out from about six feet away, he remembered being too scared at the time to even *want* to know what happened after he walked away.

Theresa spun on the gang of four. "If I ever see you near him again or even hear that you were near him, I'll put a goddamn bullet in every fuckin' one of you."

"We didn't do anything, we were just talkin'," the ringleader said in a tone of mock innocence.

Theresa stepped within inches of the boy. "Do you normally talk this close? Shut the fuck up or you'll be the first one I take down, asshole." She held up a hand, thumb and forefinger extended in the familiar gesture of a gun and pointed it to the side of his head.

"Bang."

With a smirk, she started off after Danny, looking back once for effect. By then, the four were scurrying in the direction of the parking lot.

"Wow," Daniel said, just as a twinge of pain shot through his left forearm. He began to massage it with his other hand. "Always wondered why I never had problems with those losers again."

"I tried to protect you as best a mother could."

Theresa stepped around from behind him. As she did so, the colors and sounds of the carnival faded away, returning them to the white void. "Of course, those were only two examples that I hoped you might remember. There were other times."

Daniel was not convinced. "Sorry, but don't you think that seems just a bit hypocritical?" He shrugged as he continued. "I mean, what does it prove? Don't get me wrong, I was grateful that you spared me from potential harm inflicted by *other* people but that doesn't negate or excuse the things *you* did to me.

"Protecting someone from abuse by others doesn't give *you* automatic license to abuse them yourself."

"I never thought it did." Theresa's shoulders slumped. "But I take your point."

She turned away from Daniel for a moment, obviously trying to come up with another angle from which to convince her son that she had done her best for him. He knew that she was trying and though he was not yet persuaded, he would certainly allow her every opportunity. Besides, where else could he go?

With a deep breath, she straightened her shoulders and faced him. When she spoke, there was a new and startling urgency in her voice. Clearly, she was determined *not* to fail. It struck Daniel that there was something else, some deeper reason than mere argument's sake as to why his mother was so desperate to prove herself.

"It's come to my attention that we're running out of time," she began. "But let's step back for a moment, away from the topic of abuse and violence since those are the *only* memories that you've been forced to rehash since you've been here. I shouldn't have taken that approach and I'm sorry about that.

"Instead, there's one common factor among all good parents, something basic and instinctual—sacrifice. Ask yourself this, Danny, did I ever abandon you even at the worst of times? Did you ever go hungry? Was there ever a time when you were sick and I didn't take care of you?"

Slowly, Daniel shook his head as embarrassment began to creep into his thoughts, weakening his earlier defiance. He replied quietly. "No... to all of the above."

His answer seemed to give his mother momentum as she continued. "You were dealt a lousy hand and I admit I didn't make the situation much better. I did some horrible things. You were made a victim by both Gary and me and believe me, I lived to regret that but when it came down to it, you were never second to anyone else in my life.

"But don't take my word for it."

The house was enormous.

Or so it had seemed to Daniel when he and his mother had visited throughout his childhood. Even then, he had thought that it seemed out of place, situated as it was just down the street from the cramped, narrow row home where he had grown up.

Some neighborhoods were like that, with new construction clashing against the older, and typically more modest, residences. In fact, Port Kirkland was no exception. It dawned on him now that such familiarity might be precisely why he had felt so comfortable there, why he never moved on even when he could have afforded to and why he stayed there long enough to be elected mayor.

Long enough to die there, he brooded silently.

The wondrous house in which Daniel now found himself had belonged to his great Aunt Penny. She had been his grandmother's sister and one of the few members of the family with which Theresa managed to get along. A shrewd business woman who had worked her way out of poverty, Penny had also been Theresa's landlord.

All of these memories flooded Daniel's mind as he stood in what was essentially the central foyer of the first floor. He spun at the sound of a deep, melodic chime from the grandfather clock in the far corner. He stepped closer to it, the face of the clock at eye level. He realized that he had never really *looked* at it before, probably because the last time he had been in this house, he couldn't have seen the clock's face even standing on his toes. The entire house seemed so much larger then, like a mansion.

The ring of the doorbell interrupted Daniel's reminiscing. A moment later, the floorboards in the hall above him groaned and creaked as someone scurried toward the staircase. Daniel moved away from the clock to stand at the bottom step. Looking up, he smiled as his Aunt Penny made her way down toward him. She had been dead for at least twelve years, but here and now, she was still the lively, energetic fifty-something that Daniel remembered.

Penny glided past him and into the sitting room where she opened the door to Theresa. Judging from her clothes and youthful appearance, Daniel estimated that the time was the late 1970's. Upon seeing her, he turned around to look behind him, fully expecting to see the spirit of his mother standing somewhere in the foyer or on the stairs, but she was nowhere to be found.

Apparently, this vision was meant for Daniel alone.

"Come in, sweetie, come in," Penny was saying as Daniel turned his attention back to the sitting room.

While his mother may have looked younger and thinner than Daniel ever remembered seeing her, she was clearly exhausted and troubled. Her expression was extremely somber and her eyes bloodshot.

"You look spent, dear," Penny said. "Sit down, please."

Theresa nodded as she dropped onto the sofa and rubbed her eyes. Penny took a seat in a familiar oak rocking chair that Daniel swore had to have been an antique even then.

"I haven't had much sleep these past two weeks or so," Theresa explained. "Danny's just now over the measles. It's been sheer hell."

"Oh, my Lord." Penny shook her head. "How is he now?"

"Better. Hasn't had a fever in about a week and the rash is a day or so away from clearing up completely. Doctor said that he should be able to go back to school on Monday."

"God bless you both," Penny shook her head. "Like I always say, it's a great life if you don't weaken."

"Yeah," Theresa whispered as he rubbed her eyes. "Anyway, I came by to deliver the rent check." She pulled a small white envelope from her purse and handed it to her aunt. As she did so, her stomach began to rumble and Theresa doubled over, hand against her stomach.

"Are you okay?" Penny asked. She bounded from the rocking chair and took a seat on the sofa beside Theresa.

Concerned, Daniel quickly moved to stand in front of them, although he knew that there was no way that he could help.

"Yeah, I'm fine," Theresa answered finally. "I just need a bite to eat."

"Well, you just come out to the kitchen and I'll fix whatever you want. When was the last time you had a decent meal?"

"Truthfully, I haven't eaten in two days," Theresa replied as she and Penny moved past Daniel through the foyer.

"*Two days*!" Penny and Daniel said in loud unison, both taken aback.

"When the hell did this happen?" Daniel asked, knowing full well that there would be no answer.

"I haven't been able to afford a lot of food this month," Theresa explained. "Gary hasn't sent a support check. He moved again and no one knows where he is. My lawyer is trying to track him down.

"I've been making sure that Danny gets three meals a day. Besides, I can stand to lose a little weight. It's just hard to make up different answers when he asks why I'm not eating. I think he knows something's wrong, but I don't want him to worry. He's just a kid. He wouldn't understand."

"Children understand more than we realize," Penny replied.

"Either way, I'm dealing with it. It's no problem if I go for a day here or there."

"It damn well *is* a problem!" Daniel retorted.

As Theresa took a seat at the kitchen table, Penny slid the envelope toward her. "You keep that. You can pay the rent when the money is better."

"No," Theresa shook her head. "That's okay, thank you, but this isn't your problem. I want to pay my rent. I appreciate the fact that you had a house available for us, but I don't want to be a charity case."

Penny folded her arms across her chest. Daniel remembered that she had a tendency to do that when she was about to become adamant. "You're not a charity case, you're family and I care about you both. Besides, true charity begins in the home, with one's own family."

Tears streaked down Theresa's face. "That's more than I get from my mother."

"I've known her longer than you, sweetie. Carolyn had it the easiest of the four of us. She was our mom's favorite. She married a man who took care of her every whim. She had no idea what it was like to be a single parent."

"How did you do it?" Theresa asked.

Penny shrugged. "Sometimes, I think it was sheer grace of God. A pinch of faith and a dash of hope, mix in a lot inner strength that you didn't know you had. You're sort of forced to be strong."

Tears ran down Theresa's face as she shook her head. "I don't know….I don't know if I'm strong at all."

"You stood up to an abusive husband, you made it through the divorce, you're raising your son alone," Penny reminded her, counting each point on her fingers. "Give yourself a little credit, dear, you're doing all right so far."

Theresa started to cry. She began to speak but her voice quivered. She struggled to catch her breath and wiped her eyes with a paper napkin from the kitchen table. "I'm not ready for this," she whispered. She cleared her throat before continuing. "I never imagined that I would end up like this. If I'd known that everything was going to fall apart, I would never have married that bastard. I was hoping for so much more out of my life. Now I have nothing."

"You have a son, and he has you," Penny reminded her. "It'll be just as tough for him without a father around all the time. Think about what he's going through, and *will* go through down the road. Children always suffer the most in divorces.

"I understand your life isn't what you expected, but if you do your best for Danny, teach him discipline, dignity, and responsibility while encouraging his interests, you'll be rewarded. Right now, you're stressed out, tired, and scared. Believe me, I know where you're at. I've been there. People think life was simpler thirty years ago but really, it wasn't. I struggled and starved more often than not when I was your age.

"I don't have to tell you that part of being a good parent is sacrificing for your children and not resenting them for it. For some people, that can be the hardest part. They take their anger out on their kids as if it was their fault. Don't let that happen. You both deserve better."

Theresa nodded. "I'm doing the best I can. I just feel like my nerves are shot after everything I've been through the past six months. The divorce, Gary kidnapping Danny, my own parents turning their backs on me just because they disapprove of divorce. I'm tired of it all, Aunt Penny. Tired of worrying, tired of going hungry, of chasing down Gary for the goddamn child support every time he pulls a disappearing act. Most of all, I'm tired of the anger, the fighting, the hatred. All I want is a peaceful life."

"You and Danny are always in my prayers," Penny assured her. "I have faith that you're going to be okay, no matter what happens, but you can't make it on an empty stomach. Why don't you bring Danny over tonight for a home cooked meal? I could use the company."

Theresa smiled wanly. "As long as we wouldn't be imposing."

Penny waved dismissively. "Not at all! It's the least I can do."

"Thank you for being there for us. I appreciate the support because I can't keep going on like this. Something's got to give and I'm afraid of what'll happen when it does."

"I knew we were poor back then, but I never knew you went hungry. Why didn't you tell me?"

In the infinite white expanse, mother and son faced one another. Theresa exhaled a long, slow breath as she shook her head.

"Would it have done any good if I had? You were five years old. What could you do? Even at that age, you started to learn what it meant to worry. You were scared of me, of your father. I hated to see you like that, although I know that my behavior made that seem, as you said, hypocritical."

With each passing vision that Theresa had conjured up for him, he had begun to see her less as a monster and more as someone to be pitied.

Daniel couldn't help but to feel his anger toward her replaced—no, *redirected* would be more appropriate. He was enraged at the circumstances and situations that singled him out to be the victim of an abusive, dysfunctional family. He despised the suffering that he and his mother had endured throughout his childhood that forced them to live—no, *exist*—like animals in a cage.

To Daniel, those years had seemed like some sadistic psychological experiment to see just how much bad luck two people could endure, how far they could be pushed before violence became the only result. His mother was not entirely innocent, of course, but Daniel knew now that the blame was shared among everyone who should have known better.

"I'm out of time to show you anything more," Theresa said, folding her hands in front of her. "I hope it was enough to convince you."

Daniel shrugged, holding his hands out in front of him. "Convince me of what? I don't even understand the real reason why I've been put through all this! All the demon told me was that he was preying on my dark emotions and that eventually he would own my soul. He wasn't exactly clear on the specifics.

"Do you have enough time to explain exactly what the hell that *thing* really wanted? And what about all the crazy stuff that's been happening to me over the last several days? The visions, the dreams, the little boy who looks like me?"

"Think of it all as a competition."

Daniel adopted a perplexed expression. "For..."

"For you," Theresa said bluntly. "The apparition you saw of yourself as a child was supposed to represent your good, innocent side. I had hoped it would be able to communicate with you without scaring you.

"Unfortunately, the demon was trying to stop me. Whenever you saw the boy in the mirror, with bruises on his face, the demon was winning the battle. As he told you himself on the bridge, his goal was to take control of you and encourage feelings of bitterness, anger, and hatred toward me, your father, everyone around you. When he was winning, your reflection in the mirror became more grotesque than when you had those emotions under control.

"Your reactions to your uncle Paul and your father were just practice. The demon was manipulating you, pushing you further into darkness, and each time you allowed your anger to prevail, he grew stronger.

"In effect, it and I were at war ...over you."

"What do you mean, *practice*?" Daniel asked. "Practice for what?"

Theresa paused. Clearly, she was trying to find the words to describe ethereal concepts that Daniel couldn't possibly comprehend. "There's little time left to explain. If you stay here too long, you'll be stranded here. I'm sorry you were forced to relive those horrible memories but what you witnessed was…my punishment.

"I've been sentenced to relive those incidents over and over again for eternity."

Daniel was speechless. He ran a hand through his hair as his mind raced to accept all of it. A supernatural battle, with Daniel as the pawn! The irony was astounding. He had not escaped a damned thing fourteen years ago. He was being used yet again! Were he not so stunned by this impossible situation, he may actually have been enraged but that seemed fruitless here. As it was, he only wanted to find the answer, bring this to an end and move on to…*where?*

"So what do you want from me?" he asked finally, pushing any further speculation from his mind. Meanwhile, the pain in his left arm returned and was rapidly becoming unbearable. He began massaging it as his mother continued.

"I need you to listen very carefully, Danny. The demon was sent to ensure that I would never escape my punishment. By manipulating you into despising me, he hoped that you would never grant me the one request that would set me free."

"And what is that?"

"It's said that a soul can't move on until it comes to peace with any, shall we say, loose ends of its earthly existence. See, the only way that I can find rest now is through your forgiveness. So I'm asking you, Danny, actually I'm…begging you. Can you forgive me for everything I did to you?"

Daniel took a deep breath as if about to speak but remained silent, holding his mother's gaze for several seconds. Finally, he lowered his head and took a few steps back. He started pacing. *Her punishment certainly fit the crime, but for eternity? Could I deal with that on my conscience? Does that mean that these entities would torment me for the rest of my life and beyond? In the end, would I end up just like her?*

Theresa adopted a pensive expression, able to do nothing more than wait for an answer that would decide her eternal fate. The child that had once been her victim was now her judge, jury, and executioner. Her only son had become her only hope.

"So." Daniel came to a halt and turned to face her. "The stakes are high and time is short…at least for me."

Though it wasn't a question, Theresa nodded anxiously.

"Right, and yet even with all you were up against as a single parent, how much you sacrificed for me, you're asking me to absolve years' worth of abuse in a single moment."

Daniel closed his eyes and rubbed his forehead. Strangely, he was starting to get a headache. "God, I really thought I'd put all this behind me years ago. I thought I was over it until that 'thing' came along."

"But you know I'm right."

The voice wasn't Theresa's. It came from behind him and judging by his mother's lack of reaction, she hadn't heard it.

Slowly, Daniel turned to find himself facing a full length mirror.

"Don't you get it? She doesn't care about you!" His reflection said. Daniel looked over his shoulder at Theresa but she was gone. In her place stood another mirror.

"She's just being nice because she wants something from you!" His reflection's right eye was swollen shut, the skin around it a sickening purple. "She made you this way!"

Daniel turned his back on it but to his right, another mirror appeared. In it, blood streamed from the boy's nose. A blackened scab ran down the middle of his split lip. Tears streaked his face. "I'm scared. Please make it stop. It hurts. She won't stop hitting me."

"Oh, Christ," Daniel whispered. He realized then that he was starting to tremble. His fists clenched.

"She did this to you." The demon's voice came from everywhere.

"Yes," Daniel nodded. "Yes she did."

"Then how can you possibly let her get away with it?"

Daniel spun to face himself in the mirror. For a moment, he merely stared at the demon. *My demon.* It had attached itself to his pain, thrived on his bitterness, drew strength from his hatred. Daniel let it happen. The boy had been right days ago after Daniel's violent confrontation with his father. *That's what it wants. That's why it's manipulating you.*

Slowly, he approached the mirror, stopping just within arm's reach.

For the first time, the demon seemed unsure of itself. It couldn't anticipate what would happen next. "Are you listening to me?! How can you forgive her?!"

"Because I'm better than that," Daniel replied coolly. "I'm better than you."

With his full weight behind it, Daniel sent his fist through the glass, dead center into the demon's chest. Its eyes widened in shock. A black liquid oozed from the mirror where Daniel had struck it. The demon threw its head back and howled, whether in pain or the anguish of failure Daniel didn't know.

Nor did he care. He knew that he had won.

Daniel continued to pummel the mirror until the glass exploded, shards flying in all directions. He closed his eyes and allowed a smile.

Glass struck his face and hands but left no marks. Finally, the demon's scream abated and Daniel opened his eyes to the infinite white void.

"We're both better than you," he whispered.

"Danny?"

Daniel looked around. There were no more mirrors. There was only his mother. Clearly, she hadn't witnessed the demon's final, desperate attempt to corrupt him. He was glad of that. The violence was over. It had to be, for both of their sakes.

Daniel shook his head and let out a short laugh. "Sorry, I was uh, I was just thinking. I'm getting too old for this crap, you know. I'm climbing towards forty. God knows I've carried this baggage for more than half my life. If I live twice as long, I suspect it'll only get heavier.

"And I must be dense or something because I've had a few people talk to me about forgiveness lately and obviously it went in one ear and out the other. Truth be told, I'd always hoped for the chance to reconcile our differences. When that opportunity seemed lost, every dark emotion that I thought I'd outgrown just resurfaced again—the same rage, the same hatred from fifteen, twenty years ago. There's no way I can continue to live like that...and there's certainly no way in Hell I wanted to give that 'thing' out there the satisfaction of claiming another soul, yours *or* mine."

Daniel curled up one side of his mouth in a half-smile. "Besides, far be it from me to condemn anyone to eternal damnation. I don't think that's within the purview of *any* mayor." He reached out to his mother; put his hands on her shoulders. "Despite what you did, at least you never abandoned me. When I was sick, you took care of me. When we were poor with only enough food for one of us, you gave it to me. I know it, mom. *I know it*. In between the rough times, you taught me responsibility, honesty, dignity. For better or worse, I became the person I am today partly because of you. I suppose that says something.

"And you *are* my mom...for better or worse." Tears welled up in his eyes as he spoke. He pulled her close. "So how can I not forgive you?"

For the first time in fourteen years, and for the final time, mother and son embraced somewhere in the middle of eternity.

"Although, honestly, I didn't think the afterlife would be this painful." Daniel suddenly realized that he was unable to move his left arm now. Sharp pain surged through his forearm.

Theresa reached up and touched his right temple. "That's because you're not dead." She pulled her hand away. Blood covered her fingertips. "The pain you're feeling is that of your mortal body. They're working to save your life as we speak. It's time for you to return.

"Just do one more thing for me. Wherever life takes you, focus only on the good inside yourself and others. You've always been one to worry far too much over the problems in your life."

"Problems need to be resolved," Daniel insisted. "It's what my entire life's been about. It's all I know."

Theresa shook her head. "But not to the exclusion of all else. You have so much going for you now, and an even brighter future. There are so many wonderful people in your life that care about you. Don't alienate them by retreating into yourself. Most of all don't push Vicki away. Tell her what's in your heart. Tell her everything. I like her, Danny, she's wonderful, but she just needs a chance to grow and learn to balance her career with her life.

"And while we're on the subject, I want to tell you that I'm sorry about what happened between you and Randy years ago. It's good to know that you found each other again, with impeccable timing no less. She has an amazing gift."

In spite of the pain surging through his head and arm, Daniel let out a short laugh. "This is all strange talk coming from you."

"I learned too late," Theresa admitted. "I don't want to see you make the same mistake. Please, don't continue to let the past hold you back. All problems eventually find solutions though they may not be immediately clear. It's just the way of things."

Theresa leaned forward and kissed her son on the cheek. "I love you, Danny, and I am so incredibly proud of you."

Daniel's vision became blurry. A wave of extreme fatigue overtook him and he staggered. "Mom…"

"Thank you, my son, for saving me. For saving both of us. Now… *LIVE*!"

He slipped further into the jagged wooden hole until his right arm strained under his own weight. He realized then that he was out of options. As splinters pierced his palms and fingers, he knew he couldn't hold on much longer.

He heard footsteps behind him. His eyes widened with fear as panic finally overcame him. If it was the demon returning, there was nothing he could do. He held his breath as movement entered his peripheral vision.

Daniel noticed the small pair of sneakers first. It was then that he realized he was unable to tilt his head without immense pain. His eyes snapped up. Apparently, the demon wasn't the only vision that had taken corporeal form.

The boy stared down at him. "The demon is gone now. We won, thanks to you."

"Then help me," Daniel croaked through gritted teeth.

He felt himself slipping. His hand lost its grip.

The boy reached out and caught it.

Somewhere on the other side, the demon released an anguished, bone-chilling howl before fading into absolute silence.

The sound echoed in Miranda's psyche and she felt its presence slip away into nothingness. She knew the demon was defeated and that Daniel had won, but it provided little comfort.

By now, the seatbelt had sliced into her throat, a trickle of blood seeped between her fingers as she tugged in vain at the strap. Fleetingly, she considered the irony of it, a device intended for protection would be the instrument of her death.

Tears streaked down her face as she gasped for the last few breaths of life. Images flashed through her mind. Her children. Her ex-husband. Her father smiling down at her a decade before his death. *Will I be with you again soon?*

Suddenly, he was there. Standing above her, no more than thirty years old, his moist eyes conveyed remorse and pity as he held out his hand. Miranda reached out to grasp it, ignoring the smears of red across her fingertips.

Dad, I miss you so much. Help me, please. Take me away from this.

Her father leaned closer until she could feel his hand closing around hers. Then he stopped abruptly and turned slightly to his right. Time seemed to stop as her gaze followed his. Her eyes widened as the mysterious boy from Daniel's visions appeared between them. He grasped each of their wrists and moved their hands apart.

What are you doing?

With a nod of understanding, her father smiled warmly. He lowered his hand as the boy released it.

Dad? Dad, no, please! Don't leave me again!

Shaking his head, he waved farewell and faded from view, leaving only the boy to gaze down at her with a peaceful smile.

Strangely, Miranda began to feel relaxed, her panic diminishing as she lay back and found herself able to breathe normally. *Are you an angel?*

As she peered deeper into his eyes, Miranda realized that the pressure around her throat was gone. The seatbelt had suddenly loosened. With trembling hands, she slipped it over her head and pulled herself up. Slapping the unlock button, Miranda threw her car door open and propelled herself out. She fell to her knees in front of the boy, choking and coughing as she breathed rapaciously of the cool air.

"Thank you," she choked.

"I know where she is," the boy said as he pointed toward the airport terminal. "You need to hurry, there isn't much time."

With that, he was gone.

After a moment, Miranda slammed her car door closed and started off toward the terminal.

Someone called her name the moment she emerged from the revolving door. She halted in mid-stride to see her ex-husband, Brian, and her three children waving for her attention near the luggage carousel. She approached them in a hurry and her two boys darted ahead to meet her halfway. She leaned down and hugged them both.

"Did you have a good time?" she asked.

"Yeah, we went out on this huge fishing boat," Jake replied excitedly. "And Andrea caught this huge fish on her birthday!"

"Yeah, and Jake got seasick!" Nathan added, for which he received a solid punch in the arm from his twin brother.

"Shut up!" Jake barked.

"That's enough, you two," Miranda pulled them apart. She rolled her eyes. "Boys will be boys."

"We want to go to McDonald's," Nathan declared.

"Oh, really?" Miranda glanced at Brian who immediately threw up his hands.

"It was three against one," he explained with a mock scowl. "I didn't have a chance."

Miranda held up a hand. "Actually, that might just work out. I need to find someone, a friend, before her flight takes off."

Brian frowned as he pointed to the bandage around her forearm. "Are you all right?"

"It's nothing, just a flesh wound."

"And your throat?"

"Look, it's a long story and I'll tell you about it later but right now—"

Miranda caught sight of the boy entering a nearby elevator. After stepping in, he turned and looked directly at her just as the doors closed.

"—I gotta run. I'll meet you back here in about a half hour, okay?"

On the second level of the terminal, Miranda dashed out of the elevator, nearly colliding with two well-dressed businessmen, each with cell phones pressed against the sides of their heads. With a whispered apology, she weaved her way around them, glancing right and left in search of the phantom child.

Dammit, where did he go?

Nervously, Miranda began twirling a lock of her long hair between her fingers. *Relax…think! Vicki's going where? Singapore, right!*

On her way to the airport, she had seen a billboard for Singapore Airlines but had paid little attention. However, for some reason, even that fleeting glance left an indelible impression. Miranda stepped back, out of the way of traffic, and began scanning the walls for a directory or map of the terminal. She knew the name of the airline, now where the hell are they boarding? She chose a random direction and started off, counting on the hope that airport management was kind enough to post maps near the restrooms or at the junctions between concourses.

As luck would have it, her eyes were instantly drawn to a color coded sign between the rest room doors a few steps ahead. A quick scan of the map revealed that Singapore Airlines boarded at Concourses A/B. Miranda sighed in relief as there would have been no way for her to continue along the corridor into Concourses D and E. Only ticketed passengers were allowed beyond Concourse C.

Miranda backtracked until she reached a line of fast food shops stretching from Concourse B into A. There were people everywhere. They all blended together, backpacks, duffel bags, wheeled luggage passing to and from. Miranda began to panic. She hated crowds. She could feel their emotions sometimes—fear, worry, frustration, anxiety, anticipation. At times, it gave her a headache. There was no possibility of finding Vicki in this throng of travelers.

Time. How much time? For all Miranda knew, Vicki could have been gone by now. *No, the boy led me up here for a reason. Ghosts don't waste people's time. There's always a purpose to their actions.*

A flight status screen had to be close by. Miranda surmised that Singapore Airlines probably had only one departure per day, if that, and if Vicki was here this early, then that time was probably fast approaching.

Miranda retraced her steps back toward Concourse C and stopped just outside the Observation Gallery. There were several screens in the gallery, and Miranda hurried to the closest one, impatiently waiting as arrivals and departures scrolled up a few lines at a time.

After a moment, she shook her head and began twirling her hair again. She turned away from the screen and took in her surroundings. The crescent-shaped gallery allowed for a massive panoramic view of three of BWI's four runways. An aviation exhibit consisting of cross sections of commercial planes, a complete cockpit and other artifacts clearly made the gallery a popular hangout for commuters. Under better circumstances, Miranda might have been more interested in it all.

Outside, the mid-morning sun reflected from the nose of a departing place and glided across the top of its fuselage as the craft climbed skyward. Miranda held up a hand to block out the blinding reflection.

Then she saw her. Vicki was seated at a table, her back to the window.

Oh my God!

Miranda rubbed her hands together, took a deep breath and slowly made her way over.

"Vicki?"

With a start, the other woman looked up at the sound of her name. "Miranda…what are you doing here?"

"My ex-husband flew back from Maine with the kids," Miranda explained. "I'm meeting them here."

"Really." Vicki nodded toward Miranda's arm. "What happened there?

"Nothing. Listen, can I talk to you for a moment? It's about Dan."

"Oh?"

"It's important. Please."

Vicki checked her watch then motioned for Miranda to take the seat opposite her.

With a deep breath, Miranda began. "Dan…contacted me earlier today. He asked me if I could try to catch up with you while I was here. He wanted me to tell you that he's very sorry for his behavior as of late and he feels terrible for keeping you in the dark. He, um, wants you to know everything that he's been keeping inside—"

"I have a cell phone," Vicki interrupted. "He could have called me this morning."

Miranda hesitated, trying to find the right words. "Well, not really."

"Not really?"

"I, uh, sorry, this is really hard. I came here to tell you that Dan is…"

Something stirred in Miranda's consciousness, a small voice beckoning for her attention. She looked across the Observation Gallery just as the boy turned away from the window and smiled.

"…alive?" Miranda said finally. "Oh my God! YES!"

"What?" Vicki asked.

"What?"

Vicki rolled her eyes, clearly annoyed. "You just said that Dan is alive."

"He's alive, yes!" Miranda repeated exuberantly. "Of course, he's alive. Why wouldn't he be? If Dan is nothing else, he's certainly…alive."

Vicki looked at her suspiciously. "Is he okay? Did something happen to him?"

"He's fine...I think," Miranda assured her. "Look, Vicki, he really needs you. Can't you postpone this trip?"

As if on cue, the PA system announced that her flight was now boarding.

"Look, I know you think you're trying to help," Vicki said as she rose from her seat. "But if he wanted to talk to me, he should have called. I can't postpone. This Singapore deal has been years in the making."

"So has your relationship with Dan, if I'm not mistaken."

Without a word, Vicki powered down her laptop and closed the lid. Miranda placed her hand on it. "Isn't there anything I can say or do to convince you?"

"I have a flight to catch, *now*." Vicki slipped the laptop out from under Miranda's hand but not without losing her grip and sending it crashing to the floor.

"Dammit!"

"Let me get that," Miranda offered as she crouched down to pick it up.

"Just leave it alone!" Vicki growled.

As both women reached for the computer, Miranda brought her hand down over Vicki's.

They looked up at each other.

Then the airport disappeared.

Miranda was gone. Vicki stood alone in a small bedroom of pale blue and white.

"Miranda?" she called out. The silence absorbed her voice. It was absolute. A chill ran down her spine and her breath was visible in the suddenly frigid air.

"What the hell is this?" she whispered.

As if in response, the thickly painted white door opened slowly, revealing a narrow hallway. Pulling her jacket tightly around her, Vicki held her breath as she stepped nervously from the room. There was sobbing coming from a bathroom to her left. She slowly made her way over and stopped just inside the door, avoiding the small drops of blood scattered across the floor. Some of it was mixed with a green liquid that smelled of mint.

Across from her, a man sat on the floor, his face cradled in his hands. He was wearing a white t-shirt and simple gray sweatpants, both stained with blood.

"Dan?" Vicki asked. "Dan, is that you?"

The man lowered his hands and slowly raised his head. Vicki's stomach lurched at the sight of his swollen, bruised face. Her mouth fell open and tears formed in her eyes.

"Dan, oh my God." Her voice cracked as she spoke. "What happened?"

The man rose to his feet and approached her. Vicki shrank away against the wall. The coldness of the ceramic tile penetrated her skin, her bones, her *soul*. She shivered and began to massage her arms.

It was then that she realized that she was naked.

"This is who I am," the man said as he drew near.

"You're not Dan." Vicki shook her head and started to cry. "Oh my God, leave me alone!" She began sliding down the wall to the floor, desperately covering herself with her arms and hands. She had never felt so violated, so vulnerable. She was paralyzed by the suddenness of her fear.

"Yes, you feel it now," the man said. Whatever this creature was, it was more monster than human. "As Dan feels."

He reached down and grabbed her shoulders with bloody hands. She screamed as he pulled her up and spun her until she was facing the mirror above the sink. Vicki tried to pull away but could no longer feel her legs, her arms, any part of her body, as images flashed across the glass.

Danny at the age of five, his bloodied, tear-streaked face brutally pressed into the cold, wet tile of a bathroom floor and forced to lick up spilled mouthwash under the tread of his mother's heel.

"Oh, God!" Vicki gasped as another wave of nausea overtook her. It took her a moment to find her voice again. "What are you doing? *Stop it!*"

"They can't hear or see you," the monster informed her casually. "These events are set in the stone of Daniel's past, they cannot be altered."

"But you're *not* Daniel," Vicki reasserted, her tone conveying far more courage than she felt. Still, it was time to question the monster. "So what are you?"

"I am his pain," it replied. "A side of him that you chose to ignore."

"What?"

Vicki felt the cold hands of the monster on her bare shoulders as he turned her, more gently this time. The bathroom wall to her right melted away as if dissolved by acid. In its place, an old wood framed double hung window materialized in the middle of almond stucco. The smooth, cool ceramic tile under her feet suddenly transformed into coarse concrete, warmed by the afternoon sun behind her.

"What's in there?" she asked. The monster did not answer.

Cupping her hands around her eyes, Vicki peered through the window into a small living room. Straight ahead, she could see an end table and the side of a couch upholstered in hideous brown and white paisley.

As she gazed to the right, her eyes widened and she drew back for a moment until she remembered that she was invisible in this—wherever this was. Danny and his mother were in the room, standing before the television. Vicki cringed as the woman wrapped her arm around his neck in a strangle hold. She twisted the boy until he was facing the window and Vicki cringed as his face turned a deep purple.

"Why does she keep doing these things to him?" Vicki asked.

Again, the monster remained silent.

Though she knew the effort would be futile, Vicki wanted to scream, pound on the window, *anything* to save the boy's life! Finally, his mother released him and he fell to the floor with a thud. A moment later, Vicki breathed a sigh of relief when the boy reached up and turned off the television.

She backed away from the window and turned to face the monster. "Why are you showing me these things?"

"So that you understand him."

"I thought I did."

"Please don't kill me!"

With a start, Vicki spun at the panicked shriek behind her. She was inside the house now, standing in the middle of the living room. By now, she was no longer embarrassed by her nudity, no longer afraid of the monster. Her only concern was for Danny as she watched his mother press the muzzle of a gun against his head.

As he screamed and begged for his life.

"I didn't say anything to him! Please don't kill me!"

Vicki stepped back, speechless, tears streaking her face, able to do nothing but shake her head for there was nothing she could do.

"Why?!" she asked. "I want an answer right now! Why did she do all of this to him?"

"The reasons are complicated," the monster replied. "They would be foreign to someone who comes from affluence."

Vicki inhaled sharply. "Then show me, damn you."

And the monster opened her mind.

Opened her mind to Danny, the pawn in a war between ex-spouses, blinded by their hatred for one another, leaving their son the sole casualty.

Opened her mind to the pain of a child nearly destroyed as much by words as by the blow of a fist, pain that lived on inside to adulthood, buried by time, resurrected by death, enflamed by an evil force bent on finishing the job, extinguishing both the abused and the abuser.

"That's who he is. Didn't you know?"

The monster was gone. She looked at her battered face in the mirror, covered in black and blue. Streaks of red ran from her nose.

"Dan…" Vicki whispered as tears streaked her face, thinning the blood that dripped onto her breasts. She fell to the floor, curling herself into a ball beneath the sink. "Why didn't you tell me?"

They were in the airport once more. Vicki didn't remember getting back into her seat. There was a tapping beneath her. She looked down at her laptop. *How did that get there?* It took another moment to realize that the sound was the drops of her tears—and blood—on the computer's lid. She held a hand up to her nose. Her knuckles came away red.

"What the hell just happened?" She asked, visibly shaken as Miranda quickly handed her several tissues.

"That was everything that Dan was too ashamed and embarrassed to tell you."

"How did you do that?"

Miranda shook her head. "I'm not really sure. That's never happened before. Psychics can't just transfer their experiences to another person's mind simply by touching them. It doesn't work that way. I'm sorry about that." She looked over toward the Observation Gallery windows where, for a moment, she thought she caught a glimpse of the boy just before he faded from sight. "Though I may have had a little help on this one."

"No offense, but I never believed in psychics," Vicki informed her, though the firmness of her tone had diminished either because she was still dazed by the experience or because her stubborn streak was beginning to falter. She threw the tissue away in a nearby trashcan and applied another.

"Yeah, I figured that out when we first met," Miranda said flatly. "Still, believer or not, you saw why Dan's been in so much pain. The question is, now what?"

Vicki said nothing as she looked from Miranda to the last few people being ushered down the boarding tunnel to the plane. She looked down at the tissue. There was no blood. She tossed it away and sighed heavily. She had finally stopped shaking and almost completely regained her composure.

"My dad's gonna kill me."

Vicki rose from her seat and zipped up her jacket. She slipped her laptop bag over her shoulder and lifted the handle on her wheeled suitcase.

Miranda stood and pushed in her chair. "Where are you going?"

"Back to town. Look, I don't know what just happened or how and I'm not sure I want to, but thank you for sharing it with me. Of course, now I feel horrible."

"Why?"

Vicki sighed. "Dan and I didn't exactly part on the best of terms last night. This Singapore deal has been stressing me out. I'm afraid I developed a case of tunnel vision and his problems took a back seat."

"I'm sure he understands that," Miranda assured her. "You know, even if you take a back seat in someone's life, at least you're behind them all the way."

"What's that from?"

Miranda shrugged. "I just made it up. Come on, I'll walk you down. You can meet my kids, maybe even help me figure out how to explain all this to them."

"Do they believe you're psychic?"

"They think I'm nuts."

"I can't imagine why."

Chapter Twelve

Rescued

When Daniel awoke, the first thing he realized was that he was lying on his back. There was motion—horizontal, drifting. The landscape glided past. Was he floating in the river? No, he wasn't wet. There were voices, jumbled, talking over one another. Slowly, he opened his eyes and squinted at the mid-day sun, burning brightly in the cloudless sky above. There was a dull ache in his right temple.

"I think he's comin' round," someone announced.

Is that you, Bruce?

"Don't try to move, Mister Mayor," another voice instructed.

He gazed down toward his feet and noticed a clear plastic cup over his face. There was air in the cup. He breathed deeply of it. He realized then that the cup was an oxygen mask. There was pressure across his forehead and left wrist, keeping his swollen arm immobile. He was strapped down!

"Take it easy, sir." A stocky woman in a white short-sleeved shirt leaned close to his left. "You're gonna be just fine."

"Dan, it's Bruce. I just want you to know I'm here." Daniel shifted his gaze to the right to see a familiar face hovering over. "And you look like hell."

There were arms reaching down near his shoulders and legs, pushing him along. He was on a stretcher, being rolled along the river trail. There were flashing lights from police cars and crackling voices from radios.

"He held me there," Daniel whispered, his breath momentarily steaming the inside of the oxygen mask. No one seemed to hear him. For some reason, it was important to him that they did. Daniel tapped his fingernails against the aluminum side handles. Bruce clasped his hand. "He held me there." Daniel repeated the cryptic statement.

"Yeah, okay, I can't wait to hear all about it."

Even through his delirium, Daniel knew that his friend had no idea what he was mumbling about. Still, Bruce nodded energetically as he gently lowered Daniel's arm. The boat captain gave him a pat on the shoulder. "Time to go, buddy. These folks are gonna take good care of you. I'll see ya soon."

Daniel was suddenly lifted. The trees and sky gave way to stainless steel and glass as he passed through the double doors into the ambulance. There was talk of shock, x-rays, possible dehydration. Someone's arm was badly swollen and bruised. *Who, me?*

It was his last thought before he fell back to sleep.

By the time Daniel finally re-entered the world of the lucid, he was again on his back but this time within the safe confines of a recovery room at Shore Memorial Hospital. Dr. Ronald Faderman, an osteopath, informed him that in addition to the fractured ulna in his forearm, the mayor suffered only a cracked rib and a minor laceration on his right temple.

"But look on the bright side," the doctor said cheerfully. "No internal bleeding. All told, you're damn lucky to be alive. If you'd fallen through those railroad ties, you'd likely be dead."

Daniel's brow furrowed. He had two distinct memories of his fate on the bridge and his mind struggled to reconcile them. "I did fall through," he muttered.

Dr. Faderman shook his head. "Nope. They found you on the bridge, or should I say *in* the bridge."

"He held me there…"

"I'm sorry?"

"How long was I up there?" Daniel asked.

The doctor flipped through the papers on his clipboard. "Well, according to the police report, they estimated only about twenty to thirty minutes."

"What?" The mayor was incredulous.

"That's what the report says." The doctor turned the clipboard around to face his patient. He pressed his finger to the paper beside the time estimate.

Daniel raised his head to read it. He exhaled and dropped back onto the pillow. "Felt like days."

Faderman gave an understanding nod. "Traumatic events sometimes do. So, here's the deal. You can go home later today. I just want to keep you here for another three to four hours for observation. I'm going to prescribe something for the pain. No driving and no strenuous activity for the next six to eight weeks.

"The stitches on your head can come out in a week and the cast on your arm in about four weeks. The cracked rib will heal on its own in about six to eight weeks. It is not serious enough to warrant any invasive procedures. Your lungs are undamaged, so you'll be all right so long as you take it easy."

"Will do, Doc," Daniel assured him.

"In the meantime, you have a few visitors who are eager to see you."

Minutes later, Daniel found himself surrounded by familiar faces around his bedside including Frank Parelli, Director of Public Relations, their administrative assistant, Samantha, and of course, Bruce.

"I think the main thing we're all wonderin'," Bruce began. "Is what the hell you were doin' on that bridge in the first place."

Daniel adjusted the bed's controls to elevate his upper body to a slight incline. He stopped as soon as his rib complained. "I saw someone up there," he explained. "Young guy, black sweat jacket, black jeans. He climbed over the rail and acted like he was going to jump."

"Why didn't you call the police?" Parelli asked.

"I didn't think they'd get there fast enough," he replied. "Besides, I… left my cell phone in my car back at the church."

"So did the guy jump?" Samantha asked wide-eyed. "Should we have the cops drag the river?"

Daniel shook his head. "No, as soon as I fell through, he ran off the bridge toward the trail."

"Jeez," Parelli said. "That's crazy. No good deed goes unpunished."

"So what did you guys tell the cops?" Daniel asked. "I guess they're waiting for a statement."

Parelli waved dismissively in the general direction of the window and replied in his usual rushed manner, giving the impression of someone who took everything a little too seriously. "I'm supposed to call Lieutenant Kane as soon as you're ready to talk but you're the mayor, so just take all the time you need. I'll keep them off your back."

"Our biggest concern is that you recover," Samantha asserted. "We want to see you a hundred percent healthy."

"Here, here," Bruce agreed. "By the way, I volunteered to give you a ride home later."

"Thanks," Daniel smiled wanly. "I'm looking forward to my own bed, or sofa or lounge chair. Hey, speaking of rides, my car keys were in my coat pocket. Can someone go to St. John's and drive my car back to my house for me?"

"No problem," Parelli nodded. "I'll get someone on it right away."

"Did anyone call Vicki?" Bruce asked suddenly.

Everyone looked at each other with blank expressions.

"She's on her way to Singapore," Daniel said somberly. "Her flight should be taking off in about an hour and a half. Never mind, I don't want to call her now. She has enough stress without worrying about me. I'll get in touch with her later when I'm in better shape."

He looked at the trio. "So, you guys think you can handle it without me for six more weeks?"

Samantha aimed a thumb at Bruce. "You mean I gotta put up with this air head for six more weeks?"

"Watch it, grandma!" The boat captain sneered at her. "Isn't there a retirement home waitin' for you?"

Daniel rolled his eyes and dropped his head back onto his pillow. Parelli took his cue to intervene and ushered the pair out of the room.

"At least they dress better there! Don't you have anything but Hawaiian shirts?"

"This ain't Hawaiian, ya crazy old broad!" Bruce tugged at the front of his shirt. "Hawaiian shirts don't have sharks on 'em. You keep pickin' on me and I'll feed you to 'em, if they'd eat a stale old bird like you."

"How about tucking it in, you always look like a lazy bum!"

"You don't tuck in this kinda…"

As the door closed, Daniel wondered if either of them would still be alive in six weeks.

By the time Daniel arrived home, his SUV was already parked in his driveway.

"Damn, that was quick, Frank," Bruce commented as he pulled up behind it.

"There better not be a scratch on it," Daniel grumbled as he struggled to unbuckle his seat belt with one hand.

His friend regarded him with a mock frown. "How could you tell?"

"Shut up!" Daniel barked as he opened the passenger door and swung his legs out.

"Need any help there?"

Gingerly, he slid down out of his seat to the pavement and closed the door behind him.

"OK, guess not. Is there anythin' you need at all? I'm going straight to my boat from here so I may not be available until later tonight unless it's an emergency."

Daniel smiled wearily. "No, I'll be fine, thanks. I think what I need most right now is some time by myself, clear my head, you know?"

Bruce nodded. "Sure, I understand. Just take is slow, okay? Don't do anything I wouldn't do. In fact, I wouldn't do anything at all which is my favorite thing to do."

Daniel reached into the window and shook his friend's hand. "Thanks, man. I'll talk to you later."

With a parting wave, Bruce backed his truck out of the driveway and drove off. After retrieving his mail, Daniel tucked it under his arm and collected his keys from his unlocked car. He closed the driver side door and halted upon noticing the reflection of a small boy in the window. He breathed a sigh of relief at seeing the Super Soaker in his hands and realized that it was merely Teddy, his neighbor's son. The tot was standing on their second floor balcony watching him just as he had last week.

Daniel could not help but wonder whether the little cherub desperately longed to be a sniper when he grew up. He was certainly off to a good start. The mayor shook his head as he turned and pointed up at Teddy. "Don't even think about it, kid!"

Whether out of fear of the man's burning gaze or pity for his condition, the boy lowered his weapon and shrank away from the railing.

Once inside, Daniel shrugged off his jacket, as it had been loosely draped over his shoulders at the hospital. He tossed the mail atop the kitchen counter and took a step toward the phone to check his voicemail. He stopped himself with a mental '*hell with it*' before heading upstairs. With a great deal of effort and a few pained expletives, he undressed and stepped into the bathtub.

After soaking for nearly thirty minutes in relaxing warm water, Daniel dried off and stepped over to the sink. He began wiping the condensation from the mirror but after one pass across the top, he stopped himself and lowered his hand.

"Forget it, I'm not going through that again."

It was a balmy, cloudless afternoon when a slightly unkempt Daniel finally stepped out onto his deck wearing gray sweatpants, t-shirt and baseball cap. He didn't care how he looked. All he wanted was to relax in peace, alone with his thoughts. With drink in hand, he stood at the railing and took in his surroundings, his senses embracing the sights and sounds of his town.

Below, children played and frolicked in nearby backyards while adults tended to grills and picnic tables. He gazed out upon the calm ripples of the Matson River a short distance away. Boats of various sizes and colors lazily drifted in and out of his field of view while a team of bicyclists raced across the river trail.

Daniel fixed his eyes on the trail for a moment longer. Although it was well out of sight, his thoughts turned to the railroad bridge. He lowered his head and let out a long breath. He was grateful to be alive. More importantly, reconciliation with his mother provided a salubrious closure and left him with an almost tangible feeling of triumph. Together they had defeated the demon at its own game, allowing mother and son to find peace in a way that Daniel could never have imagined. Now, he only wanted to pick up the pieces of his life and move forward.

"You will."

He spun at the sound of the boy's voice behind him, cringing at the sudden pain in his midsection. For a moment, the boy was merely a reflection in the sliding glass door until he stepped through onto the deck. It suddenly dawned upon Daniel that there was something markedly different about this ghost of his younger self. He noticed it earlier on the bridge but had been far too terrified at the time for his mind to register it.

The child's face was perfectly unblemished by bruises or scars and for the first time since he began appearing to Daniel over a week ago, he was smiling.

Daniel carefully lowered himself to one knee, bringing him at eye level with the boy. "I suppose a major thank you is in order."

"For?"

"Saving my life back there on the bridge."

"You had as much to do with that as I," the apparition replied. "Your ability to ascend beyond the darkness within saved the both of you."

Daniel nodded. "I understand that now. Just tell me, who exactly are you? Where do you come from?"

"I thought it was obvious." The boy reached out and placed a hand against the center of Daniel's chest. "It's where I've always been and always will be."

The boy inside the man. "Of course," Daniel whispered as he cupped his hand around Danny's. "Will I ever see you again?"

"Just look in the mirror and you'll know who you really are."

With that he was gone, leaving Daniel to peer at himself in the darkened glass door. He rose to his feet and stepped closer to the door. As he ran a hand gently over his face, Daniel let out a short laugh. Despite the bandage covering his right temple, his reflection was once again his own.

Daniel leaned forward, pressing his forehead against the glass as a wave of relief washed over him. He closed his eyes and laughed quietly.

"Mister Mayor, you never looked better."

After three failed attempts to contact Dan both at home and on his cell phone, Vicki decided to stop at the docks on her way into town. She hoped to catch Bruce at work on one of his charter boats, preparing for the upcoming season. Perhaps Dan would be with him or at the very least the captain might know of his best friend's whereabouts.

Hurrying past the privately owned sailboats and cabin cruisers, she noticed movement aboard the *Salty Ace II*, Bruce's newest and largest boat docked beside her smaller, elder sister. His back was turned to her as she approached.

"Avast ye, matey!"

With a start, he turned and for a moment was clearly taken aback at the sight of her. "Vicki, hey there…you!" he responded, in awkward recovery. "What brings you here, li'l lady?"

She shrugged as she stepped to the edge of the dock and glanced down into the water. "Well, I was on my way back home and I thought I'd just swing by and say hello."

"Oh. Dan said that you were on your way to Singapore."

"I decided to postpone it at the last minute," Vicki explained. "You wouldn't happen to know where he is by chance?"

"He's at home," Bruce replied simply. "In fact, I just came from there."

"Really? I called there a few times and there was no answer."

"Uh, well, he's probably asleep. The old boy isn't exactly a hundred percent."

Vicki frowned. "Oh? What's wrong with him?"

The boat captain turned away and began fiddling with a fishing reel that he had been reassembling when she arrived. "I'm sorry, what was that?"

Vicki was beginning to get the feeling that his answers were intentionally evasive. She repeated her question slowly, enunciating each word.

"Well," Bruce began, avoiding her gaze entirely and giving the impression of someone backed into a corner. "Dan was in a minor accident early this morning."

Vicki's eyes bulged. "What kind of accident? A car accident?"

"No, no!" Bruce shook his head. "He, uh, fell…through some… lumber."

"*What*? Where?" she demanded. "Bruce, tell me what happened, all of it."

"I don't exactly know the whole story—"

"All of it, Bruce!"

"Okay."

He proceeded to impart all that he knew of Daniel's ordeal on the bridge as described by the mayor at the hospital earlier in the day. By the time he was finished, all color had drained from Vicki's face.

"Just so I'm prepared, how badly was he injured?" she pressed.

Bruce exhaled and in his best casual tone, replied. "Well, he just fractured a bone in his forearm and got a tiny li'l cut on his head." He held up a hand, thumb and forefinger barely a half-inch apart.

"Is *that* all?"

"And he…cracked a rib."

"Anything else?"

The boat captain thought for a moment. "Lotsa splinters."

Vicki Harlan rolled her eyes as she turned and ran toward the parking lot.

"We would've called," Bruce shouted after her. "But we thought you were on your way to Singapore!"

She found him asleep in a chaise lounge on the deck.

His left forearm, wrapped in a cast, lay across his chest while taped gauze covered his right temple. Aghast at the sight, Vicki stood over him and shook her head.

"Oh my God," she breathed as she knelt down beside him. She removed the empty glass from his right hand and placed it atop a nearby table. Gently, she leaned over and kissed him passionately on the lips.

A few seconds passed before Daniel's eyes fluttered open. He uttered a quiet moan that grew louder in proportion to the widening of his eyes. He raised his uninjured arm reflexively and grabbed her shoulder.

Vicki rocked back and adopted an expression of pity. "What am I going to do with you?"

"Several things come to mind," Daniel replied after catching his breath. "None of which I'm in any shape to do right now."

She sighed. "How can you make jokes? You look terrible!"

"If only you could've seen me the way I did these past several days." Daniel ignored her perplexed frown as he tapped his cast. "It's a long story—"

"I heard some of it from Bruce," she said flatly. "I just couldn't believe it. You could've been killed! It seems like every time I go away lately, you end up doing something crazy!"

Daniel snickered. "I know how it looks but that wasn't the intention, believe me. This wasn't some desperate attempt to make you feel guilty for leaving. None of this was ever about you. My mother's death brought me to a very weird place but I'm happy to say that it's over now. I told you last night that someday when I was ready, I'd tell you everything. I'm ready now. Just sorry that I made you feel like you were on the outside looking in. That'll never happen again."

Vicki reached out and touched the side of his face. "Don't worry about it. I'm sorry I got upset. If it makes you uncomfortable, you don't need to tell me anything—except that you love me."

Daniel turned his head and kissed her hand. "I love you."

She kissed him again. "The feeling's mutual, Mister Mayor."

They shared a momentary laugh before Daniel groaned at the sudden pain in his chest. "Sorry, it hurts to laugh. In fact, it hurts to do anything."

"Well, I'm glad that I didn't go home and unpack. Seems you need a resident caretaker for the weekend."

It was Daniel's turn to be puzzled. "That's right, aren't you supposed to be on a plane?"

Vicki nodded. "Yeah, well, change of plans. I asked dad to send someone else more…interested." She paused. "Besides, I ran into a certain friend of yours at the airport—"

"Let me guess," Daniel held up a hand. "Was she a blond?"

Despite herself, Vicki smiled and nodded. "Yeah. She, uh, has a remarkable gift, that one. I *think* I could get to like her."

"You feeling okay?" Daniel asked with a mock frown.

Vicki leered at him playfully. "Who's the one all busted up?"

"Just checking! So, you canceled your trip for little old me?" Daniel asked. Randy had come through for him…again. He couldn't wait to call her. Maybe even invite her back soon. He knew that the air between his two favorite women was much clearer now.

"Well, I found myself doing a little unexpected, um…*soul searching* until I finally decided to call it a day. Then when I couldn't get in touch with you on the way home, I took a chance that you might be hanging out with Bruce on one of his boats. He alluded to the fact that something happened to you, but I had to practically drag the details out of him."

Daniel snickered. "If I know Bruce, that must have been hilarious."

"Like hell it was!" Vicki retorted. "I was so upset, I ran like the devil to my car—"

Suddenly, the mayor cupped his right hand over her mouth and looked from side to side. "Don't say that word!"

"Whaah worr?"

"Devil!"

Her brow furrowed in confusion. "Why nah?"

He exhaled as he lowered his hand. "You're going to think I'm insane after I tell you what really happened to me over the past two weeks."

She leaned close once again. "I'm already convinced that you're crazy. I'm just glad you're still alive to talk about it."

By this time, the sun had begun its descent beyond the horizon, casting a pastel glow of pink and orange across the sky. Locked in an embrace made somewhat awkward by Daniel's condition, the pair failed to notice the youngster watching them from behind a quietly moving sliding glass door—until a torrent of water struck Vicki on the side of her head.

"Hey! What the hell?" She pulled away from Daniel and fell backward onto the floor of the deck. As she wiped her face with her sleeve, she glared across the narrow gap between Daniel's house and his neighbor's. Directly across from them, the kid with the Super Soaker giggled victoriously.

Daniel rolled his eyes. "Oh yeah. Vicki, I'd like you to meet Teddy. He has a rather unique way of introducing himself, but that's okay because this time, I'm prepared. You see, the kid has the Sneak Attack model which is pretty good, but—"

He reached down with his right hand and from beneath the chaise lounge, produced a massive blue and orange contraption.

"—I have the Hydroblitz and you're goin' down, son!"

"Wait!" Vicki chimed in as Teddy's jaw dropped. "What about me?"

Daniel thought for a moment. "You know what? You're absolutely right, gorgeous. After all, you're the offended party *and* you have two good arms." He thrust the Hydroblitz toward her and she eagerly snatched it from his grasp. "Do us both proud, soldier."

He closed his eyes and leaned his head back. "Now, you two have a blast. I need to get some sleep."

"Here?" she asked incredulously. "You'll be caught in the crossfire!"

"No problem, it's all drip dry."

Epilogue

Six Weeks Later

Daniel sat patiently behind a table at a steak house in Baltimore's Harborplace Gallery. After a few minutes, he looked up from his twiddling thumbs just as Gary entered the restaurant. He rose from his seat and held up a hand to draw his father's attention. Daniel remained standing as Gary approached.

"I'm not going to need a bodyguard this time, am I?" The older man asked sardonically as they took their seats.

Daniel shook his head and smiled wryly. "No. That was a different person. He's gone now."

"What's changed?"

His son looked away for a moment, catching a glimpse of his reflection in the mirrored surface of a nearby pillar. "I learned to let go."

"I see," Gary nodded. "Honestly, I was surprised when you called."

Daniel shrugged. "Yeah, well, I felt the need to apologize. I thought maybe we could try this again."

"I'd like that."

Finally, a waiter appeared to take their drink order. As he departed, the men continued their conversation.

"I've been doing a little soul searching of my own," Gary went on. "Maybe in the end, I deserved a punch in the face. Looking back, I was a lousy father and no excuses or rationalizations can make up for that. It's left me with years of regret. I just wanted to believe that my son wasn't entirely lost to me."

"I'm still here," Daniel said simply. For the first time in twenty-five years, father and son shared a smile.

"So, how's Dana?" Daniel asked in an attempt to lighten the mood.

"She's doing well," Gary replied with a curt nod. "You know, she reminded me the other day that you never met our daughter, Maria. She would be your half sister. I think the two of you would like each other. She has quite a stubborn streak like someone else I know. Maybe someday, you know, if you have time, we could..."

"I'd like that," Daniel said quickly.

The waiter brought their drinks and the pair fell silent. As he sipped his iced tea, Daniel peered up at the ceiling mounted television in the far corner while Gary rotated his glass atop the table. Finally, he leaned forward in his chair.

"So, what should we talk about?"

Daniel met his father's gaze. "Anything but the past."

ONE

The farmer's fist hit my face for a third time, and now I fell to the ground. Blood clouded my vision, and a piece of one of my teeth lay loose on my tongue. As I tried to stand, a boot impacted my head. I screamed despite myself and opened my eyes, squinting against the bright sun in the Virginia sky. Through a red haze I saw what must have been the same boot, raised, about to stomp on my face. I inhaled, feeling broken ribs, and willed myself to roll out of its path.

"Leave him," said a voice.

"Leave him?" demanded another. I decided it belonged to the owner of the foot. "I'm gone kill the sumbitch!"

There was a scuffle as my assailant was pulled away. He protested with much enthusiasm and vulgarity.

"We're gone kill him all right," said the owner of the first voice, "but let's leave him so's he knows it's happenin'."

I was hauled to my feet by two men who turned me to face the mob which had descended upon me. To my surprise, the first face I saw was that of a woman, red and inflamed with rage. She stepped forward.

"In Harrisonburg," she said, "they's women that asked to form their own regiment to fight them that done this to us. If women can fight, what's wrong with you?"

My lips were swollen from the blows. I was moved to vomit by the taste of my own blood, but I managed to croak, "Our Lord commanded us to love our neighbor as ourself."

She spit in my face and turned away.

"String 'em up!" shouted a man behind me. They marched me toward a tree.

A week ago, I had been in Baltimore, at the home of Philip Meigs, childhood playmate and member of the Society of Friends. I traveled frequently to Maryland. The Fairfax meeting, in which I'd been a member since birth, was a part of the Baltimore Yearly Meeting, and Meigs lived in the city, where he was an investor in Hopkins and Brothers. Phillip had attended school with me, also training as a physician, but had not found success in medicine. I attributed this to his apparent lack of interest in the suffering of his fellow human beings. I had always assumed him to have a good heart, and I suppose one always assumes one's childhood friends do, but he hid it well. His lack of tenderness did not prevent him amassing a small fortune as a businessman.

This October of 1864, however, had brought hardship on the business of Johns Hopkins and his brothers. Purveyors of "Hopkins Best" whiskey — although Johns was a Quaker, and most southern Quakers detested the use of spirits — they purchased their stock in the rich Shenandoah Valley. Dealing in various wares from wagons, they accepted corn whiskey in trade. This he re-bottled and sold in Baltimore. His trade led to his expulsion from the meeting, but he maintained it was legitimate business, even though his own uncle accused him of "selling souls into perdition."

Perdition on earth, however, was where his suppliers had recently found themselves. The Shenandoah, in the wake of the Union's General Sheridan, was a smoldering ruin. Over 2000 farms had been burned to the ground, all the crops destroyed, the livestock seized or killed.

"It's a damned frustrating setback for our business," Philip said as cut into his steak, stopping briefly to ask his butler to reprimand the cook on its temperature. "Those bastards drank, stole or drained all the whiskey, and left the cornfields a black smear on the earth. I doubt our suppliers will be able to rebuild. I don't know where we're expected to find another source of stock."

"Nor where your former suppliers are to find a new source of income?" I asked pleasantly.

He shrugged. "Hardly my concern, is it?"

I felt my jaw tighten. Philip's attitudes often infuriated me. When I lost my temper with him, as I had often over the course of our relationship, he never failed to make sport of me. I'd learned to control my outbursts, more or less.

"They *are* fellow human beings, Philip," I said.

"Obviously they are. And it's unfortunate that they happened to live in an area of such strategic importance that it had to be routed by the Union forces. But what else was the army to do, eh? The Shenandoah was used repeatedly as a staging ground for attacks on Washington and Maryland. They had no choice — "

"Christians always have a choice," I said, too loudly. "Making war is never necessary."

"The majority of the nation — two nations, if the rebels are to be believed — is not in agreement with you, Shep."

"With us," I corrected him. "They are not in agreement with *us*."

Again he shrugged. "I suppose. Though I don't see how we're to break the South of slavery, other than through war."

"Do you believe this war will break slavery?" I asked.

"It cannot help but, if the North wins. They will not allow the South to continue this practice which gives them such an economic advantage."

"Philip, it irritates me how you speak of the evil of man against man — brother against brother — as if its only consequences were financial ones."

"One must be practical, Shep — " He threw down his fork. "I cannot eat this damned steak!" He exclaimed to his butler. "Take it away and ask the silly woman if there is something she does know how to prepare in a state that a human might consume!" He turned to me. "Though how one's digestion is to function in the presence of Dr. Autrey and his oozing emotions is beyond me," he said scathingly.

"I'm only asking you to show some compassion, Philip. As a physician, and a Quaker, one would think you'd have a little."

He sighed. "You do make me tired, Shep. I am merely considering how the events around us affect me and my livelihood. Is that wrong?"

"Only insofar as you fail to see how you might be contributing to the suffering of others."

"And how am I doing that?" he asked.

"By failing to join your brethren in combating the evils of both war and slavery. Before this conflict erupted, you did nothing to help bring about a peaceable end to what the Southerners call their 'peculiar institution.'"

"You mean I didn't endanger my household by taking in fugitives," he said sourly.

He knew that I had sequestered four negroes who had escaped their masters in my own home, and seen them move safely on to the North in a quest for their freedom.

"My household was in little danger, I assure you. But better that I, a single man, be in danger, than leave the burden to fall to a family with children."

"You live in the country," he said. "I do not. It's far more difficult to hide an escaped slave in a crowded neighborhood such as mine."

"Nor have you offered any medical aid to the casualties of this war," I pressed on. "As so many of our fellow doctors, and our fellow Friends, have done."

"I am not a practicing physician, Shepherd."

"I wonder if you are a practicing Christian, " I said.

He threw down his napkin. "Ah! I see. Now I am to be threatened with expulsion, like Mr. Hopkins, because I do not meet your standards of piety?"

"I would not move to have you expelled," I said.

"You damned well better not! Were I to lose my standing with the Friends, my business would suffer!"

"Oh, in the name of God, is that all you can think of?" I shouted, flinging my own napkin across the table. Philip swallowed, taken aback for once by the violence of my tone.

Embarrassed by my outburst, I stood to leave. I began to make my apologies, however insincere, for my breech of etiquette.

Philip raised his hands in a calming gesture. "Now, Shep. Let us not allow our tempers to color our friendship. I understand that you feel strongly about what is happening in our land. I... simply do not... show my feelings as easily as you do."

I sighed heavily. "With that I would agree."

"Please sit down. We'll have some sherry. I have a fine amontillado in the cellars, I believe. It will calm you."

He called for the delivery of the spirits while I composed myself. When we were alone again, I said, "Philip, please forgive my outburst. It's just that you seem so... indifferent to human suffering."

"It's just that there's so much of it," he countered. "What can one man do?"

"One man can do what he can," I replied. "Your... associates in the Valley. You could show them some Christian charity. I have no doubt that they are hungry, homeless. In such conditions, disease flourishes, and more violence."

"And what would you do to stem the tide?" he asked quietly.

"Many Friends have set up hospitals and shelters," I said. "Offering comfort to the wounded, the dying, the bereft. You could go there — "

"I would be shot by the Union troops were I to go near the Shenandoah!"

"Unlikely," I said. "Safe passage can be arranged, especially for doctors. And Quaker neutrality is... grudgingly accepted."

He shook his head. "You are having sport with me, Shep. You do not believe for a moment I could go and — "

"I do!" I insisted. "I believe any man of conscience would go and offer aid — "

His face lit up with interest. There was no good intent in him then, I was sure. "Would you go yourself?"

"Of course!"

"To the Shenandoah? Tomorrow?"

"I — yes. As soon as I could make preparations — "

"I do not believe it."

I met and held his gaze. "You think my convictions so shallow, after all these years?"

"I believe even you are too practical to walk into such danger."

"I will prove you wrong, then," I said. I started, once again, to stand and leave.

Philip smiled his most predatory smile. "I do believe you're serious!"

"I am."

"Well then... perhaps we could discuss... a small wager?"

Of course, laying money on a proposition — any proposition — was enough to secure Philip's interest. Those of my faith do not believe in gambling. It inflames the lust for profit which distracts us from the more noble impulses which our Lord called upon us to follow. In this case, however, I felt moved to accept Philip's wager. If a small sin on my part would draw my errant comrade into a moral venture, was it really a sin?

Because of course, Philip would not take my word where money was concerned. Once I had agreed that I would pay him a sum of fifty dollars were I to fail to go to the Valley and spend full two weeks there, aiding the afflicted, there was no way he would remain home and take me upon my word that I had fulfilled my part of the bargain. No, with money on the line, he was willing to travel with me.

So it was, days later, that we had arrived in Virginia and joined in relief efforts near the ruined town of Winchester, where one of the few standing homes had been converted to a makeshift hospital. Here wounded soldiers were treated. Here, also, those left homeless as Sheridan had cut his fiery swath through the Valley came in search of food and shelter.

On our second day there, a woman arrived with six children, the oldest being a fourteen-year-old boy who looked about ten. He was thin and small for his age, not malnourished, just slower than average in his physical development. The father, I was told, was a soldier in the Confederate Army. He had gone off to war six months previous, and they'd had but one letter from him. The smaller children proudly told me that Daddy was a brave soldier, gone to Washington to kill Abe Lincoln, but the eyes of the mother and the oldest boy told me that they believed Daddy was dead and buried in an unmarked grave somewhere.

Their home, like so many others, was gone. Burned to the ground. They had only the clothes on their backs, and those not much to speak of. But the mother, herself a Quaker like so many in the Valley, fell in with me. She nursed the wounded and helped find beds and floorspace for the refugees. The boy likewise attempted to help, but was largely occupied with supervision of his young siblings. I find that the young have a natural proclivity to be helpful to their fellows, and no such natural understanding or kinship with the practice of organized violence. Strike out when they consider themselves injured they certainly will. But plan and execute a campaign of murder and mayhem? No, that is adult foolishness only. With children, the injuries are forgotten as quickly as the temper is lost.

It was near sunset on our sixth day that a group of men rode up to the house on horseback. They were a ragtag collection, one carrying a tattered Confederate battle flag, their leader dressed in most of a gray Confederate uniform. They made their business clear immediately — they were recruiting to raise a regiment. As physicians, Meigs and I were overlooked for their purposes, it being clear that our services were needed here. I was not to evade their notice for long, however.

While their leader made his way through sick beds, surveying for bodies able enough to accompany him, one of his lieutenants came into the ward, literally dragging young Joseph, the fourteen-year-old, by the scruff of his neck.

"Put me down!" the boy screamed. "I got to stay with my sisters!"

"Women can see to the children," said the fellow carrying him. "Women and those men as aren't fit for manly work," he raked his eyes, burning with hatred, over me.

The man in uniform said, "Little puny, ain't he?"

"Says 'e's fourteen," said the other.

"Well then. Guess you're goin' to war, soldier."

The boy's eyes widened. At this point, his mother charged into the room.

"What do you think you're doing?" she demanded.

"None of your concern, woman," said the officer.

"It certainly is my concern," said she. "The boy is my son."

"Then you should let him be a man," he replied.

"I've had little choice," she said bitterly, "since you drafted my husband. Now he's all I have to help me care for his sisters. You can't take him! Have you no compassion?"

"We're at war," said the man coldly. "There's little room for compassion."

I could keep silent no longer. "See here, friend," I said. "This lad may be of age, in your eyes, but... look at him! He's not fit for battle."

The stranger scowled at me and gestured toward the windows of the room. "Have you seen my men, Doctor? Which of us would you say is fit for combat? But what are we to do, when the Yankee dogs burn our homes to the ground, and leave our children to starve?"

"We are to act as our savior would have us act; to aid our brethren; to have the same compassion that Christ himself had for us. Would He have seen children dragged from their mothers — ?"

He rolled his eyes. "Je-sus Christ! I've had my fill of you Quaker cunts and your love-thy-neighbor preachin'! I loved my neighbor jest fine — until the moment a Northern bayonet went through 'is eye and killed him!"

I swallowed, shaken both by the violence depicted and by his taking of the Lord's name in vain. "God have mercy on you friend, and may His mighty hand heal your wounds. But do not extend your sufferings to this innocent child — "

"It's time for you to shut up," he said. He reached across and took hold of Joseph's arm, pulling hard to draw the boy to his side. Joseph winced in pain as his shoulder was wrenched, but said nothing. His captor drew a knife from his belt and jabbed the tip of it against the soft, white flesh of the child's throat.

"Now," said the officer. "You can come with me, boy, or I can let your mama watch you die here and now. What do you say?"

Joseph's eyes, alive with terror, met mine. I shook my head, not knowing what to say. Were I to tell the officer my opinion of his cowardly behavior, he would surely kill the child for spite.

"Please!" shrieked Joseph's mother. "Don't hurt him!"

The knife remained where it was. "Make your choice, boy."

"I - I'll go," Joseph squeaked out.

The officer, satisfied, shoved him back toward his original captor. "Knife to yer throat kinda puts things in perspective, don't it, Doc?" he sneered.

"For the young," I said. "I wouldn't expect a boy to have the courage to die for his convictions."

"Izzat a fact? So, I s'pose you woulda just let me cut yer fool throat?"

I wondered if my mouth had gotten me in trouble. It often did. "Before I'd agree to kill other children of God, yes, I would."

"Yer lyin'," he spat. "Yer a coward. All ya'll Quakers is."

"Hardly," I said. "It takes true courage to resist violence."

"You callin' me a coward?" he demanded.

"Doctor Autrey, please," the woman begged silently.

"Let him answer!" my opponent barked.

"If the shoe fits," I said.

His face went red. "We'll jest see who's a coward!" He nodded to the other man, who came from behind me and seized my arms in a vise grip.

"Take him out there to that tree by the road," his superior continued. "String him up — "

"No!" called the woman.

The officer ignored her and went on. "But give 'im a chance to beg for his life, 'fore he dies. I wager he'll be ridin' outta here with us."

Meigs came into the room just as they were leading me away. "Shep, what in the world?" he demanded.

The officer pointed at me. "Friend o' yours?"

Philip was silent.

"He is a physician, come to help the needy," I said. "He's done you no harm."

The officer strode over to Philip and looked him in the eye. "You a Quaker too, pansy?"

Philip swallowed. "I - I am. I am here with a writ of safe passage — " he reached into his coat.

The officer knocked his hand away, and drew his gun, leveling it at Philip's head. "Passage is what yer gonna get all right. We're gonna string you up next to your friend."

They led us outside, and to a tree, as promised. When we arrived, ropes had already been cast over the sturdiest of the lower branches, nooses tied on the end.

The strangers crowded around to watch the execution, as did some of the children, herded there by soldiers. At the edge of the circle of faces, I saw Joseph, weeping openly.

"Please," I said to my captors, "I am prepared to die. The Lord will protect me. But may I be allowed to pray with the boy?"

"Good god, Shep, don't make things worse!" cried Philip. I feared he was becoming hysterical.

I ignored him and looked at the officer. "Please," I said. "In the name of Christian charity — "

He drew back and drove his fist into my mouth, loosening the first of my teeth. Then he grabbed my hair, spun me around, and held me out before the assembled mob.

"Anybody care to show him what we think of those what won't fight for their freedom?" he asked. The mob advanced.

And now, here we were, beaten, bloodied, about to be hanged. Three men lifted me bodily and deposited me on the back of a horse. Next to me, Philip, one of his eyes so swollen that, were we to live past this hour, he might surely lose it, was similarly mounted. While the horses were held in place by one man, another, mounted on the shoulders of a third, slipped the nooses around our necks and tightened them.

"Oh god," moaned Philip. "Please..."

"Your friend is about to put on a show for us, I think," said the officer. "You gonna sing, too?"

I shook my head. "I trust in the Lord."

This statement was met with guffaws. "Maybe the Lord'll break the rope for ye!" someone called out.

"Shep, they're going to kill us!" Philip wept.

"Yes," I agreed. "They are." I hoped I sounded calm. I felt sick to my stomach. I was grateful not to be expected to stand, for my knees were weak. I prayed to God to be given the strength to meet death with courage, as Jesus had met His on the cross. "Pray for strength, Philip," I said quietly. "It will be over soon."

But, instead of praying, Philip called out to our attackers, casting his face about, as I think he was blind. "Don't listen to him!" he shrieked. "We aren't ready to die! We'll do whatever you ask!"

"Philip!" I hissed, but someone struck me in the gut with the butt of a rifle.

"Please," Philip went on. "We'll join your army!"

"Will ya?" asked the officer. "Will ya come and kill the yanks with us?"

"Yes," said Philip, trying in vain to nod, despite the rope around his neck. "I'll kill them all! Filthy, Yankee pigs!"

I shut my eyes and began to pray, silently, for my friend's immortal soul.

"Well that's different," said the officer. "If you're willin' t'join us — "

"I am!"

"Then I better put it to a vote!" He turned to the throng about him. "Whaddya say? Should I let 'im live?"

The blood lust was upon them, however. They'd been promised two deaths, and they believed, somehow, that those deaths would ease the pain of their recent losses. It is a foolish belief, but such foolishness is common. As one, they cried out that we should die.

The officer shrugged. "Sorry, friend. It's outta my hands."

"But," Philip protested. "You said — "

"What can I tell ya, friend? War makes animals of us all." Then he threw back his head and laughed, and motioned to the handlers to release the horses and whip them forward.

I closed my eyes again. I heard Philip dissolve into sobs beside me, and smelled ammonia as, in his fear, he lost control of his bladder. I distanced myself from all of this and looked inward, toward the light.

Within me, as within each of us, was that spark of divine fire. I sought it out.

I had a great deal of experience at this kind of inward-looking prayer. In addition to the accepted practice of quiet worship in the Friends' meeting house, I had read works describing the Eastern Buddhist religion, and its practice of meditation. Although Buddhists did not personalize the light, as we did, they did seek it, or a state of being much like communion with it.

Today, this last day of my life, during these final moments, I finally found myself achieving that state of peace, of exclusivity from the outside world, which had so long been my goal. I heard, but did not register the cursing and jeering of the crowd. The smell of the horse on which I sat, the leather of its saddle, did not touch my nose. The coarse fibers of the rope about my neck did not chafe my flesh. I was spirit alone, drifting down, inward, toward a pinnacle of light on the horizon.

The world was balanced. Everything was as it should be. I was at peace. Vaguely I knew I was going to die, but I knew with utter certainty that the author of the universe was pleased with me, and that I was under His care. This death, this little, petty end to my little, petty travels on the corrupt world of my birth, was but a trifle. It was a branch on the pathway, to be noted, stepped over, and forgotten. The true journey lay ahead.

From somewhere far off, I heard a snap, a clatter of hooves, a creak of a branch, as it was weighed down, a sickly, gurgling sound. Someone was being hanged. Was it me? Was it Philip? I thought of Philip, of his fear, his failed dignity, his body, swinging at the end of a rope, his expensive trousers, sodden with his own wastes, even before death had finally relaxed the body's muscles...

I prayed for Philip. I had no concern for myself. It was not that I didn't think of myself — I did — but I had no fear for my own soul. Philip, on the other hand, was frightened, discouraged, a sinner who did not know how to put his sins aside and stand before the Lord. I prayed for him.

Reach out to him, Lord, I called into the light. *Take his hand, gather him to Your bosom. Comfort him, as You have comforted me. He is unworthy of Your love, even as I am. Yet show him compassion.*

I wondered what would happen next. Would God himself appear to me, or Jesus? Was I to be welcomed into the arms of the Savior and the Father? The light brightened. It bathed me. I was sure I felt its heat upon my face. All threat to my physical body, all pain from my wounds, was forgotten. I was traveling home, to the Glory of God.

The light overtook me, and then began to fade...

I landed on my back with a thud. Beside me, I heard groaning. I looked to see Philip, stunned and, like myself, sprawled face up. The mob was gone. The horses were gone. The trees were gone. There were no ropes about our necks, nor was there a stitch of clothing on our bodies. I wriggled and pulled a medium-sized rock from between my shoulder blades. Heaven had a sandy, rocky surface, and the soil was tinged red, like blood. The sky was purplish gray.

To my right, there was a sudden clamor. I turned as quickly as I could, and saw hundreds, no, thousands of men bearing down on us. Some were on foot. Some rode unbelievable contraptions of metal, which moved through the air without support. All were near as naked as we, and all carried weapons of some kind. These they fired or swung, striking the bodies of others similarly clad and armed. Blood spattered the already red sands, and men fell, wounded, even dead, to the ground.

There was war in heaven.

About the Author

Phil Giunta is currently a network administrator and has worked in the IS field for seventeen years at several major corporations. He has a Bachelor's Degree in Information Technology from Saint Joseph's University in Philadelphia, PA. His industry certifications include Microsoft Certified Systems Engineer and Cisco Certified Network Associate. He is an avid freshwater fisherman, science fiction fan, and is deeply interested in the paranormal. Phil lives in Pennsylvania where he is hard at work on his next novel.

Breinigsville, PA USA
01 February 2010
231698BV00001B/1/P